The Way Back Home

~

Finding Rose

The Way Back Home

~

Finding Rose

A Heritage Saga

K. R. BREHMER

Published in the United States of America by K. R. Brehmer.
First Printing, 2015

ISBN 978-0-9864340-0-6 (softcover)
ISBN 978-0-9864340-1-3 (ebook)

Cover and book design by the author.

And the seasons they go round and round
And the painted ponies go up and down
We're captive on the carousel of time
We can't return we can only look
Behind from where we came
And go round and round and round
In the circle game

Joni Mitchell, *The Circle Game*

REMEMBRANCES

When the idea to begin searching for her took place is impossible to say. It had been simmering in a corner of my sub-conscious regions for a long time, since the birth of our daughter at least, even longer, perhaps from the time when I was small child. Looking back, growing up, there was always a sense of something incomplete, something missing, an uneasy feeling—an unframed question lurking in the background, imperceptibly nibbling away for an answer someday. As life wended along its usual busy course and thoughts and efforts were directed towards the daily tasks of dealing with work and family matters, the question that sought an answer remained recessed and undefined—maybe to stay that way forever.

But it didn't.

Over the years there were many conversations with colleagues and friends touching on cultural backgrounds of our respective families and ancestries. At work or in the company of friends at our homes, talk of where parents or grandparents came from, or the percentage of the different ethnicities that made us who we were, often came up as a topic of interest. For most of them a blend of some proportion of several ethnic backgrounds formed the common ancestry denominator. For my own heritage this was also true. But in my case there were only two.

Then there was the black binder given to me one day by

my brother containing the family history of my father's side, my German ancestors and their descendants, starting after their arrival in America. He had received a pair of binders upon a visit to our aunt, my father's sister, one for himself and one to give to me. A group of relatives had collected and arranged genealogical data on our immigrant forefathers and American born family members up until the birth of our daughter. There were pages and pages of detailed information, some even containing copies of old obituary clippings and articles from local newspapers, photographs included. Some of the names were already familiar to me because as a youngster we had traveled by car, with my father at the wheel, from California to the Midwest to visit my grandparents, aunts, uncles and cousins in the state of Iowa where he was born and raised. The last visit we made was on the occasion of my grandparents' fiftieth wedding anniversary, the golden one. There were so many people gathered in the small town it was impossible to meet them all. During our stay at their home my grandfather even took time out to explain to us kids the proper way to dig potatoes in their garden. To this day the musty, earthy smell from the skin of a potato as you peel it or the same but even more intense aroma wafting up upon opening a ten pound bag of brown potatoes reminds me of both of them, the rich, brown earth of Iowa, and the fabulous old two-story wood-frame house that once stood there.

Birthday presents tightly wrapped in brown paper and tied with a piece of twine would arrive regularly during the 1950s, sent in the post from Iowa to California by my grandmother. These packages inevitably contained the perfect book for whatever age I was turning. It was like she had used a crystal ball to see into my mind what I liked best, always a book I couldn't wait to start reading, or put down once I did. Old photographs displayed them both nattily dressed when they paid a visit to California in the mid-1940s to see their children and grandchildren living there. My older brother is captured with them in one of these pictures but not me since I had not yet entered this world when it was snapped. Even with this kind of irregular continuity, infrequent and short in duration as the visits were, it was still sufficient to sustain a clear mental image of them and what they were like. Thus, the distant connection to paternal grandparents, cemented by two or three visits back to America's heartland, stayed alive, engraved in my memory from an early age, and remained so right down to this day.

While I could be somewhat content with my response in semi-knowledgably answering questions from others concerning my father's heritage in America, the same could not be said to be true when asked about my mother and her parents. In fact, it could be safely said my brother and I assumed the only grandparents we had—ever had—were my father's parents; they were our grandpa and grandma and there were no others. Why there was no realization until we were much older that there could be, indeed should be, a second set belonging to my mother, can be laid at the feet of all of us in the family. But even when we were older it was just a fleeting thought without much more than passing interest behind it, soon cast aside and nearly forgotten. Nothing truly registered that there once had been real flesh and blood people—the parents of my mother whom we never knew.

My mother was not one to talk much about her childhood and never in detail, as I recall, about her parents. Perhaps this was a function of surviving the depression era combined with a post-war ethos of looking forward to a future of better times without the burden of dwelling on the past. Or perhaps it was because of her having to look after two obstreperous boys while my father worked long hours, sometimes away for weeks on a job out of town; or perhaps even, it was from living in a semi-isolated, rural area on the fringe of a small city with a mother who was not a strong conversationalist and whose personality gravitated towards being anti-social and reclusive with non-family members. Whatever the reason, the subject of her parents and how life had been spent with them never came up. Discounting the trips we took together as a family to visit my father's parents, this habit of mostly ignoring family background held true for my father as well and it was only on a few occasions, with some prodding, that he mentioned what family life had been like for him as a child.

But one day, without realizing it at the time, the groundwork was laid for a journey to begin, a journey of learning more someday about my mother's family roots—and from that, about myself. This moment came not many months after our daughter was born when my wife and I made a home leave visit back to California, from where we were living and working overseas, to introduce our new addition to my parents. Becoming new parents ourselves had sparked an interest in the importance of knowing at least the very basic rudiments of our family history. Yes, we already knew a little about my father's side and a lot more about my wife's Italian heritage. But for the sake of posterity we now wanted to at least try to add essential names as well to the extremely dim awareness of my mother's side of the equation.

Seizing the rare opportunity of all of us being together, I pulled out the "baby album" from among the bulging bundle of other items we had brought with us while my wife tended to our daughter, and then, with pen at the ready in hand, I turned to my mother, "I know who dad's parents were and have already written them on the family tree page in the baby book, but I have no idea who your parents were."

Thankfully, the very first page of the new album only had fill-in blanks embedded in the branches of a drawing of a tree going back to the generation of our daughter's great-grandparents or else I might never have dared to raise the ancestor question. After all of these years without having posed this seemingly fundamental question, an innocuous query of just who my mother's parents were, a thought suddenly flashed through my mind; maybe there might be reluctance for some reason for her to talk about them even now. It had never been discussed before to the best of my recollection. There had simply been no mention of the subject by either my mother or my father other than that there was an Irish connection of some sort, but even this seemed inconsequential, almost like a vague afterthought. Granted, there was the fact that Saint Patrick's Day was always duly celebrated. Green clothing could always be found in mother's wardrobe for herself as well as something green for us to wear to school on this special day. But Irish identification and celebration on the 17th of March was far from unusual in our community, rather it was commonplace among most of my school chums, no matter what their ethnic makeup and heritage was. So bowing to the wearing of the green could not be taken as a big tipoff to my own background.

However, without hesitation she said, "My father's name was *Patrick Cavanagh*." Even though I knew my mother's maiden name, I had never heard the first name of her father spoken before. I asked her to spell his surname just to be sure I had it right before writing it in the book.

I did.

"And your mother's name?" This was entirely new territory for me. I had neither heard nor seen written the first or maiden names of this mysterious person until this point, nor had I ever given an ounce of conscious thought about it until the page in the baby book demanded it.

Again, without the slightest restraint in her voice, I thought she said, "It was Rose Ann Cameron". Again, before jotting the name in the appropriate blank in the book, wanting to make sure I had heard the first name correctly even though it seemed rather straightforward, I asked her if Rose Ann was one word or two and to spell Ann for me. "Two, and it's spelled A-n-n-a", as she clearly enunciated each letter. As it turned out, I had misheard what she said the first time, for my grandmother's true second name was indeed Anna, not Ann or Anne. Her full name had been *Rose Anna Cameron*. In adding this single letter to the entry, I had no idea at the time how crucial this seemingly most insignificant of details would be in finding Rose.

DREAMS

Donegal, Ireland, June 1889

Summer weather had finally replaced the usual fresh Inishowen mists and scattered clouds of spring. Unaccustomed to the effects of an early season warm spell, Rose found herself in a daydreaming frame of mind, unusual for a person of a character and focus normally steady and sure, as she gazed out the window of the small, one-level, white schoolhouse while seated at her desk. Through the cracked open window she watched a pair of bees whose darting motions of flight gave the appearance of being engaged in an intricate dance. The pair of them zigged and zagged, then turned around one another in ever expanding circles before their spirals took them out of the range of her limited view. A slight breeze reached her chestnut wavy locks, and she turned her head to the right so that it cooled her face and uttered a nearly silent sigh.

Cloverly National School was divided into two parts—one for girls, the other for boys. Pupils at different grade levels of learning and ages were mixed together and taught in common. Presbyterians, Catholics and Protestants sat and were taught side-by-side in a single room but Catholics far outnumbered the other religions at her school. Some of the national schools in Ireland had been around since the late 1830s when the first ones had started. Others came later, spread out over a number of years. However, it was only in recent times that it had become common for the majority of children to actually attend one of them. Rose's parents, Neil and Catherine, made sure the opportunity to educate their children would not be passed by. Rose, after going through infants' school, was in her fourth and final year of formal education for the older children.

Children of farmers often started attending school later, depending on family needs and proximity to the schools, and Rose's own home situation was one of those which had not allowed her to begin until she was older than many of the other girls. But at least by this era she was able to attend school openly. It wasn't so long ago, only prior to the famine years of the 1840's, that the Penal Laws forbade Catholics from going to school at all. Many children circumvented this ban by getting their education at what were known as "hedge schools", hidden places where illegal gatherings of students were sometimes taught outdoors behind actual hedges, as the name suggests, or even occasionally in caves but more often in unsuspected buildings off the beaten path, such as barns or remote houses. They were taught the basics by educated locals or by priests doubling as teachers. No longer secret, these schools still existed in parts of their barony, an administrative land division encompassing many townlands, and operated in parallel with the national schools.

In August she would be turning seventeen. Before the end of the school year it would be time to think about what her next step would be. Already she knew what she would like to do. She was seriously considering that following in her eldest sister's footsteps would be the right choice for her as well, given their family circumstances.

Rose was the fourth child of a tenant farmer family of six girls and one boy. Her only brother, William, second eldest after her sister Mary, had left school four years earlier to join their father working the fields, consisting of some thirty acres of land the family farmed as non-owning occupants. All of the remaining children in Rose's family attended school but the school year was sometimes interrupted by spells of work on the family farm. This was common to many families when more hands were needed to help out during the busiest times of the seasons. So schooling became a broken and irregular affair and progression from the infant's school through the four proceeding class levels was not a rapid and straightforward path, as it would have been if day-to-day learning and attendance had occurred on a steady, unbroken basis throughout the years.

She saw her own prospects for a future life in County Donegal as extremely limited. The traditional and constant practice of land division by the tenant farmer, that is the breaking up of tracts of land large enough at one time to able to sustain an entire family into smaller plots which were parceled out to each of the male offspring, prevalent prior to the Great Famine years of the 1840s, was over. The acreage of the farms had simply dwindled too much in size. Any further sub-division of the land would fragment it into sections unable to support future family generations. Clearly, the time had come in Ireland to adopt the English system of passing the land on to a single family member, usually the eldest son—the tradition known as primogeniture. In her family's case, the only son, William, most often referred to as Willie, would be the benefactor.

Given her place in the birth order, the middle child of

seven siblings, the attention paid to Rose by her parents was not nearly as intense as it had been for Willie, Mary, or even the youngest of the brood, Margaret, or Maggie as she preferred to be called. Having managed to escape much of the close scrutiny they had undergone had, perhaps, incurred additional consequences, though. Rose had not acquired the same degree of typical, traditional attachment to land and family as her brother and sisters had, which had both its positive and negative aspects. On the minus side her father and mother did not seem overly concerned as to what the future held in store for her. A suitable marital partner had been agreeably found for Willie who would bring a small but satisfactory dowry, but little thought had been given to what Rose would do. It was like she had fallen between the cracks in this regard. Could it have been that it was assumed she would remain in the household and tend to her parents as they grew older and infirm? As for her elder sister Mary, she was planning on emigrating, like their father's sister Bridget had done. Bridget had gone from Ireland to Australia with her newly wedded husband back in the 1860s. But Mary's choice of destination was not Queensland where her aunt had eventually settled. Instead, she was determined to leave for America in about a year's time. She had already managed to put away nearly half the fare needed for the passage to New York.

On the plus side, there was young Rose's adventurous, but certainly not carefree character, which, when taken together with the fact she would have very little financially to offer to any prospective husband, made it all the more easy to contemplate uprooting herself from the familiar Inishowen land on the beautiful green slopes overlooking Lough Foyle.

In addition, there was a trend that had emerged over the last decades that found marriage for grown children in Irish families taking place at a much later age in their lives than in the past, often not until their thirties. With the mass exodus of a large part of the Irish population following the Famine, particularly of sons, marriage frequently never occurred at all for those daughters who were left behind to wait.

There was one remaining important issue to be resolved, though, along with securing the blessing of her parents as Mary had done, before she could make a final decision to leave Ireland; his name was John Harte. John was neither a close neighbor nor did he attend the local parish church each Sunday morning, the church where Rose's entire family walked to in fine or inclement weather, a walk of nearly two miles each way done without so much as eating a morsel before they left their house. They lived several miles apart and had met only a handful of times, either at local fairs or on market days. And John's church was one of an altogether different kind. But from the first time they met, they had felt an immediate attraction to each other, becoming more attached following each of the few, relatively brief encounters. Wednesday, market day in Derry City, the only real city in their region some ten miles distant from Rose's home, had been the place where they had made their first acquaintance.

John lived on the other side of Derry City, but still within the borders of County Donegal, in a household adhering to a different religious persuasion—and therein was the central difficulty worrying them both. Thus far, no one, not even her closest sisters, knew of the blossoming relationship between the two, much less that John was Protestant. And, unlike Rose, he was the first born son of a family of two brothers and an older sister. His outlook for inheriting land and having a sustainable future in Ireland was almost guaranteed as opposed to Rose's who would have no land to claim as her own, land which could serve as a launching point when and if she left the confines of her family. Both sets of their respective parents were strongly bound to their faiths and even more staunchly circumscribed by ingrained perceptions of their positions within their respective communities. Interfaith marriages had happened here and there in recent and past generations as they always would, but instances were rare enough when they did occur that they stood out like sore thumbs, often embittering parents and families and occasionally carrying even more harsh consequences, even ostracism, for the married couple who had dared to cross religious lines.

One of the largest markets of the season would be taking place in Derry again in less than a month and the two young people had already pledged to each other to do everything they could to arrange to meet there. Farmers would be buying and selling sheep, cattle, poultry, asses and pigs; there might even be a few horses to boot. The market would be crowded with lots of chaotic activity and deals to negotiate to occupy their parents' attention, giving a suitable diversion for the two of them to slip further away from the town center than they had done in the past. They had already decided on the best place for them to meet—under one of the huge, sheltering willow trees near the bridge.

Daydreaming came to an abrupt end for Rose, not by the teacher's observation of her lack of attentiveness, rather by the fortunate timely announcement of lunch break and the noisy shuffling of chairs and feet. The afternoon came and went without further self-distraction and the finish of the school day meant the usual trek home to help with evening chores before supper.

As Rose approached the house, she saw her father and brother in the distance bringing down freshly cut turf stacks they used for cooking and heating fuel. Her dad, a bewhiskered man of medium height, wearing a fine tweed cap and a grin on his face, shouted out a greeting to her. "There's the lass who knows how to turn a meal fit for kings! She'll soon enough put this turf to good use." She smiled and waved back at them. Their thirty acre holding comprised two offset fields touching only at a single corner point as well as a third completely separate field higher up on the slope, extending to the edge of the peat bogs where the communal open area turf cutting took place. At various times during the year most of the fields were planted in turn with a number of different crops, including in some years a patch of corn. The best crop rotation to accommodate their land conditions followed a prescribed pattern: potatoes first, followed by barley, then flax and oats. Some field areas were left unplanted for the few sheep and a cow or two to graze.

Rose helped with the cooking, swinging to and fro the iron rail of the crane that held the kettle and the pots and pans, which in turn held the meals she had helped to prepare over the flames. When the cooking and washing up were done, the arm was placed in front of the hearth where clean utensils hung awaiting their next use. It pleased her to see the different meals she helped to make with limited ingredients could be fashioned to suit the enjoyment and fulfillment of all of the family members. The remaining hours of evening were mostly spent in sewing garments both for themselves and as paid piecework for the shirt factory in Derry, marked, of course, with chatter about the day's events and what tomorrow's weather may bring. All of the girls were adept seamstresses regardless of their ages; it seemed almost as if they were born with an innate skill. Then it was early to bed in the loft, a snug space nearly pressing her body against the ceiling rafters. On the outside a slate roof kept them dry and cozy in their whitewashed house of modest proportions and close quarters. It was also early to rise during this season of the year, morning chores beginning at five o'clock. As she closed her eyes and wrapped her body into the bedclothes, a smile inched across her face and she slipped once more into thoughts of the upcoming market day and the time she would soon be spending with her John.

BEGINNINGS

Central Coast, California, October 2006

October had brought a period of fine weather not uncommon for this time of year in California coastal areas. There would be several more days, maybe even weeks, before the first rain and cooler daytime autumn temperatures kicked in. But for the moment the warmth of the Indian summer was strong enough so that the blue-belly lizards were out soaking up the sun, making their jerky articulated head movements to keep a sharp eye out in all directions for a tasty morsel to cross their path. It was a good feeling to sit on the backyard bench and to join in their lethargy and relax a bit by watching them. The last major home fix-up project on the drawing board was finally done. To do the entire list had taken the good part of year, a year following early retirement which had been strictly devoted to rectifying a host of deferred house maintenance needs.

The evening before during dinner conversation with friends the discussion had once again touched on ancestry. When my turn came to speak, I reverted to my usual set mantra; the one thing that I knew that seemed certain about my mother's parents was their names. This was the only information I had written down taken from her own words when she was still alive. Besides names, I recollected she had said both her father and mother were from Ireland, and the word *Donegal*, a place in Ireland, was mentioned in regard to one or both of them, wherever this peculiarly sounding place was. That was all there was and no more.

One additional memory floated about in my brain but it was too tenuous to mention at dinner. It was the only instance when I believe my father barely mentioned something about my mother having a stepfather, and that someone was buried in a military cemetery in the San Francisco area. I had spoken about this fuzzy recollection only a few times over the years to a very small number of people, and always with a caveat that it could very well have been just an inaccurate memory. But this time I thought the better of it and held back. It was so long ago it could easily be my mind was playing tricks on me, as they say, so why mention something so dubious and anecdotal at all.

So little to go on, but for some reason something clicked that evening and the stars were in alignment. A silent commitment was made; the time to take action had finally come to try to fill in the blanks and I vowed then and there to put forth my best effort to learn more about my mother's family history. If successful, maybe I would be able to put to rest the vague sense of uneasiness that had quietly persisted since childhood.

But I had no inkling of what lay ahead or how difficult this long, untended path would be to untangle.

Where to start? In principle, starting from the most recent generation and working backwards in time is customary practice in much family history research. But my own mother's personal details were pretty much of a mystery in and of themselves. I didn't even know as much as the exact year of her birth. Her vanity had led her to keep her age well concealed, but from the bits and pieces I had heard over the years, I had the notion she was actually older than my father, whose year of birth was known to me. I also knew she was an only child. What little else I had learned about her life before I existed could be counted on one hand, not that the fault could be attributed entirely to her. My brother and I shared equally in the blame because neither he nor I had been thoughtful or inquisitive enough to ask the right questions during our youth. But told to me in her own words was that she had been born and raised in San Francisco, and had loved to take long walks through that hilly city until reaching one of the shores surrounding it on three of its four sides. Quirkily, her ability to hold her breath for extremely long periods of time also stuck in my memory for some peculiar reason. Was this an ability that could, perhaps, be due to all of the hill walking she did as a child? She proved this feat of lung capacity on several occasions when I timed her with a wristwatch. And the fact that she was an excellent typist—her fingers moving in a blur on the keyboard of the old black Underwood manual typewriter sitting on our desk can still be envisioned—and had a talent for shorthand and stenography as well could not be denied.

A hazy memory also remained of her saying how the nuns she had as teachers at her school in San Francisco were very tough, putting up with no nonsense and liberally meting out punishment with a ruler swat on the hand or wrist of the offending student when it was called for, which seemed to be fairly often at her school. After graduating from a commercially-oriented high school she had worked in the city using secretarial skills she had acquired before meeting my father. He had left his home in the Midwest as young man to try his luck in finding work elsewhere, eventually ending up on the West Coast in San Francisco too. It was the period between the end of the Great Depression and beginning of World War II, during the second half of the 1930s, when they met, eventually marrying in 1939, according to my father. Learning more about her background would obviously be important, indeed, an essential first step to learning about whom her parents—my Irish grandparents—really were.

My parents had both passed away in the 1980s. And my Irish grandparents were gone many years before I was born. I had never had the chance to know them, and only knew of them when I was older. Some small knowledge of basic genealogical resources steered me in the direction of United States censuses as a logical jumping off point. Pouring over the online decennial census surveys for the twentieth century produced only one result showing what appeared to be my mother's name linked to a Rose, her mother's first name. If this listing was a correct one, why wasn't my grandfather also listed with them in this 1920 census? Had he already passed away by this date? A little further research and I had found Grandfather Patrick listed with Rose in the 1910 census but without my mother this time. And going back one decade earlier to 1900, there seemed to be an entry for Rose under her maiden name, Cameron, but no separate entry for Patrick could be found. Earlier censuses were checked but there were no other listings for either of them in San Francisco. But at least from all of the census material reviewed to this point, what my mother had told to me seemed confirmed: Rose had been born in Ireland, my grandfather's name was Patrick Cavanagh, and he too had been born in the old country.

Beyond having written down the names of my

grandparents and a scant number of other half-remembered details there was one more crucial but untapped family source, one silently laying undiscovered and unviewed for many decades. When my mother passed away, my older brother, as executor of her will, was responsible for selling the house and disposing of its contents. Before my wife and I could get there he had taken care of much of the removal; there just wasn't much left to be looked over. But what he wasn't aware of was the existence of a basement storage area hidden behind a well-concealed door, an almost invisible door blending in with the wall paneling. He had moved away from home before my father and I had finished working on the interior of the basement. I had helped put in place this ingenious idea of his. Several years later, before one of our long distance moves, my wife and I had stored some of our things in a nook of another room in the basement and I had shown her the "secret room" at that time, so she knew about it too. To one side in the back of the unlit space were two old steamer trunks, black with brass latches, which I had seen only on rare occasions as a child growing up. My wife decided to give them a shake to see if they were laden with any contents or not. The first trunk, very light, seemed to have no additional weight beyond the trunk container itself and, when opened, was found to be empty. The second rattled when shook. What was found inside turned out to be the first critical piece in a series and of essential building blocks necessary for linking together other discoveries to follow over the next year and a half. At the bottom of the trunk lay a very ancient-looking picture album with a brass clasp and a slightly tattered lavender fabric and leather binding. Upon brief examination, it appeared to contain old style photographs of people I had never seen before. Not seeming of particular value, I granted it only a moment's attention at the time before moving on to something else. However, my wife's good sense in realizing this was something significant enough to be salvaged and taken away with us overrode the lack of interest I showed. This album was to remain unopened for many years afterwards in our own house—stowed away in a cardboard box in a cupboard—only to be recalled and examined again now that I had begun the journey of discovery of my family history.

Of all of the photos in the album, as I thumbed through the pages, only four had any writing on the reverse side. The one that stood out the most was signed "Patrick Kavanaugh and sister". It was dated 1880 and had been taken in San Francisco, determined from the studio name stamp imprinted on it. What was interesting about this picture was that it looked like the surname, Cavanagh, maiden name of my mother as she had related to me, could sound similar in pronunciation to the Kavanaugh spelling version on this photo. Was it possible he had gone by a variant spelling before the turn of the century, possibly before he married my grandmother? That the two different spelling versions of the name were phonetically identical and were, in fact, cognates of the same name was confirmed by more than one Irish surname book as well as by various databases soon afterwards. That he may have actually used the Kavanaugh version for any length of time was only a theory, though. It could have been a single instance recording error. Searching the 1900 census again, this time under Kavanaugh, only one matching entry was located. This Kavanaugh also had a sister listed, which made it a particularly enticing entry, but after following this promising lead for several weeks, it turned out I had been willingly led down a false path and a goodly amount of time had been wasted. It would not be the last time I would let myself be led astray. Still, from the old photo it appeared he actually did have a sister who was also living in San Francisco at the time and, who knows, this extra piece of information could be useful sometime in the future.

From the twentieth century census sheets the ball had at least started to slowly roll. From survey to survey the dates diverged for their year of immigration arrival in the United States. Equally inconsistent were birth dates or ages stated for Patrick, however, occupation data for both Patrick and Rose looked much more reliable. All clues for possible use at a future date. Most of the information corresponded to what I could envision belonging to my grandparents, but censuses are not the kind of primary source that can give absolute proof of a person's identity and family relationship. So, using them only as guideposts, I was ready to move on to the next step of trying to locate the core documents—vital records of birth, marriage and death—for each of them.

A drive to Civic Center in San Francisco was in order to visit the city's Department of Public Health where vital records were accessed. There, applications for a birth certificate for my mother and death certificates for my grandparents were simultaneously made. Unaware of the precise dates for any of these events, a best estimate span of ten years was provided at the counter. The results were depressing. Not a single certificate was found for any of them! Gloom filled the room. Without more precise knowledge of these events, chances of finding any of the documents looked dismal.

With this frustration to bear, but not wanting to write off

the trip as a complete loss and leave empty handed, we walked to the nearby San Francisco Public Library to see if we could at least salvage something by further verifying my grandparents' existence in the city by tracking their residences over time through city directories. Annually published from the 1850s, these directories provided name, address and occupation for each primary household resident listed. For married couples the listings were male-oriented, giving the husband's first and last names with the name of the wife only appearing on occasion in parenthesis in earlier years but more often in later years. There were no separate listings for married women. Using the censuses in conjunction with the listings in the directories yielded a lengthy history of addresses for them, showing Rose and Patrick together for the last time in 1917. Rose's name appeared on its own in 1918 and my mother and she were found paired together at the same address in 1920. Although reassuring, these findings were little compensation for failing to obtain any vital records. Returning home deflated, I wondered where to go next?

ANTICIPATION

Derry City, Ireland, July 1889

Market day had finally arrived. As soon as the first rays of morning light had reached her bedside, Rose softly slipped her petite five foot one frame out of bed. Although they would leave at an early hour for the market, unable to contain her excitement, she was up well in advance of the rest of the family and this would give her the necessary time to take extra care in getting ready. She quietly went downstairs and poured water from the pitcher into a small basin to carefully wash her face, wetting her hair as well to shape it the way she liked best. Then the used water was tossed out the door and the emptied basin replaced for others to soon put to use.

Most of the fairs and markets she had visited in the past were small-sized, held either in her own small village a short half mile down the hill from her house or in a town where relations lived. The Derry market, in comparison, was more like a combination of both fair and market, a true city-size gathering with an importance that drew in participants from a large area of the surrounding countryside. Rose hoped the flattering white blouse with puffed out shoulders, jacket and skirt she would be wearing would be considered fitting the occasion, and would not be remarked upon by her mother as tending towards being excessively well-dressed. To this would be added a black and white scarf to set the outfit off, but only just before reaching the appointed place of encounter with John. For the moment she kept the scarf tucked away, inside her skirt along the underside of its waistband. Only the older children—Rose, her brother Willie and Margaret—would be going this time with their father. The distance being several miles, longer than could be walked in both directions while still being able to spend several hours at the market, meant they would share a horse and cart belonging to an uncle who lived in a different corner of a nearby village. Their arrangement was to walk down their rural lane to where it meets the shoreline road—the main road running north to south—and there rendezvous with her uncle.

They were ready and keen to get started and when the appointed hour arrived their uncle was there to meet them at the designated time despite being up half the night looking after an unwell sheep. The route following the banks of the Foyle estuary to Derry was virtually flat so the trip would be relatively quick and easy. But for Rose it seemed anything but swift even though they were there in less than two hours. After entering the city by crossing the River Foyle on the Craigavon Bridge, her plan was to stay with her family for a short while before her girlfriend, Casey, joined them. She knew she would not be allowed to walk about alone, but with her friend, who was known to and liked by her father, it would likely be permitted. The old walled city, built in the 1600s and located in nearby County Derry, was not only huge and intimidating by County Donegal standards but was also Protestant dominated, making it riskier to be by oneself and recognized as a vulnerable Catholic outsider by those who lived within its walls. By the time they reached the Diamond, the open space in the city center, the ever-changing climate had brought on a mid-morning mist replacing the earlier, mostly clear skies. It was not long before they bumped into another farmer from their area they knew and her father immediately launched into an animated conversation with him about the usual farming subjects: the rotation order of the crop planting, competing methods for putting down potatoes, the kinds of fertilizers working best, and such like.

To keep her rising anxiety in check, Rose tried to concentrate on following their description of different ways of planting potatoes. They mainly talked of kibbing versus the lazy-bed system. The latter, or older method, involved the digging of potato drills, as the rows were referred to, then ridging up the soil, while the new method of kibbing saw the farmer thrusting the spade into the ground a short distance at an angle with his right hand then tilting it a little and filling the gap with a potato set from a bag carried hung around his neck. The tuber was buried as soon as the spade was withdrawn, allowing a row of potatoes to be planted with great rapidity. As intently as she tried to listen to their explanations, her mind kept turning towards when her friend would show up.

Casey, for her part, knew the role she was to play; she also knew the importance that would be given to keeping on schedule in this instance because Rose, usually calm and relaxed in her interactions had been, for her, quite insistent on exact timing. Instructions had been repeated over and over again when they had discussed their plans earlier at school. Before she even reached the family group she made her presence known by emphatically signaling to her with raised arms from a distance. Rose, ever on the lookout, immediately saw her friend and turned to her father. "Da, Casey is here. Is it all right if we go together on our own now for awhile? We won't go far and we'll be back when you tell us to."

He looked up to where she was pointing and saw Casey making her way towards them. "Pay attention to where you are going and be back by the time the church bells ring four. And be mindful of staying together at all times. You know what we've said about talking to strangers in the city?"

"We will and we remember and we know."

Her friend, having joined the group now, upon listening to Rose's father repeat his instructions for her benefit, seconded her understanding of the conditions. "My father wants me back around the same hour as well, so. Don't worry we'll be back on time."

"All right then. Off with you now," reassured that they both understood and promises would be kept.

Arm-in-arm, the girls walked away from the center of town downwards towards the river. The distance was not long for those used to moving on foot at a steady rapid pace to get where they were going. In a short time they found themselves at the second tree of the row of majestic and unmistakable willows lining the banks of the river Foyle to the left of the Shipquay city gate. John was not yet there under the designated tree, the largest one with its long feathery strands overhanging and nearly brushing the water. And he was nowhere to be seen as their eyes scanned in all the directions from where he might be coming.

Waiting even a few more minutes was hard for her. It had been so long in-between seeing each other now and the last time. Indeed, in the scheme of things, they had not known each other for so very long at all and had not met on a great number of occasions. But the difficult circumstances of life during the decades following the famine sometimes had the effect of speeding things up. Bonds of friendship, and of love, were often established in short order, especially if an arranged marriage had not been worked out among parents, which was often the case. And when a solid relationship was made, it usually endured over the longer term since having a partner to share the hardships somehow made it then more tolerable for most. Opportunities were not easy to come by in these days in rural Ireland and when they did present themselves, not readily set aside.

"Do you think something has held him up?" Rose wondered aloud.

"It's only a few moments past when he said so give him a chance Rose. He'll be here before you know it."

"I know, but it's not so easy to wait."

"Just lay back and watch the clouds rush by and I'll keep a keen eye out", Casey said, patting the ground beside her.

While Rose and Casey waited for him to arrive, John's journey to the meeting point had been anything but uneventful. His place as oldest son in the family meant his obligations and responsibilities were greater than his siblings, and his duties took longer than expected this morning on a farm with a good deal more acreage and livestock to tend to than Rose's family had. The younger of his two brothers had felt poorly the day before and John had needed extra time in finishing his brother's work along with his own. The delay was slight in leaving for Derry but enough to make him nervous in getting to their prearranged place on time. With his father, another brother and a sister, the ride was met with several stoppages to greet acquaintances along the way. But the travel distance was shorter for John's family, for while both families lived within the boundaries of the Diocese of

Derry, a large diocese which extended into other Irish counties as well, John's farm was much closer, only a few miles to the west of the city of Derry itself. Each new stop to exchange pleasantries left him with a renewed sinking feeling in his stomach from the worry he would miss their meeting. He prodded the horse to move faster every chance he could until his father asked him to spare the poor beast from keeling over with exhaustion, leaving some of its energy for the trip home later. Descending Creggan Hill and crossing over the same bridge as Rose did earlier, the wagon entered the city and headed in the direction of the Diamond.

Before reaching it, John stopped the cart and with as much of a straight face and normal voice as he could muster, looked over to the side of him. "Would you take over from here, Da? I want to meet some friends and also have a few errands to run." He was not at all confident his strong desire to be on his way elsewhere was not unintentionally being worn on his sleeve for all to see. A sinking stomach had now twisted more into an aching knot.

"That'll be fine, son. Steer clear of any trouble and don't forget we'll need to be looking after some new tools to take home. We'll be near Saint Columb's church in the mid-afternoon."

"Then it's there and then I will be, too, if we don't run into each other beforehand", he said before jumping down to the ground.

And with this, John did his best imitation of nonchalantly sauntering off in the direction of the riverside. As soon as his father was out of sight he broke into a controlled trot believing now for certain he was going to be late. Thoughts that Rose may not be there, that she had come and left because he had not come, or she could not make it for some other reason, ran through his head until he spotted a large willow and what looked from afar like two people sitting beneath it. From a brisk trot he broke into full-out gallop and in a matter of a few long seconds had joined them.

With only a quick greeting and an exchange of knowing nods between them, Casey took her cue from Rose and walked off along the river by herself, leaving Rose and John staring into each other's eyes, eyes full of delight and differing only in shade of brownness. Always, when they met again, there was at first a feeling of tentativeness between them. They had not the luxury of daily or at least more frequent contacts diminishing such inhibitions from forming. Their meetings were, by virtue of distance between their respective homes, spaced out at long intervals. It took a few minutes of searching for those little signs of reassurance that nothing had changed between them—facial expressions, slight body movements, a word or two of familiar kind—but today the looks they exchanged, their eyes, spoke more eloquently than any words could as to where they stood with each other. Then by a shared laugh, a bumping of shoulders or a glancing touch of hands, from these small gestures things were made clearer and seemed right again. Once they were certain their feelings had not changed, were the same as they were when they had left off the last time they saw each other even though it was so long ago, they started to stroll further along the river on the lookout for a spot further from prying eyes. And after a few minutes they turned into a fairly deserted part of the city, well away from the old walls. Stopping at a small plot of green squeezed in between two buildings and moving to the rear part of the grass where there was enough bushy foliage to further conceal their presence from passers-by, they were ready to renew their relationship. "Shall we sit here?" John pointed to a secluded bench. Finally, they felt safe to hold hands and talk at length about everything and anything then talk some more.

Still, they could not let themselves get completely carried away so in time they directed their conversation to what needed to be said before parting once again, the great plans they had for their future together. Quickly reverting to ideas they had mentioned in the past, especially ways of dealing with the dilemma of religious differences of their families without destroying their prospects for a happy life together, they talked over these choices once again.

"What do you think now about what we said before, about leaving these parts and finding a new place to make our home, when we marry?" he was first to bring up. And before Rose could reply he carried on. "I know we would be starting from scratch but the loss of my place in taking over the family farm doesn't bother me a bit. In fact, I would almost consider it a blessing rather than a sacrifice, or even regret it at all, really." Growing up in a farming family he was all too familiar with the kind of work required, he could do it and do it well, but in truth he had never been convinced the tasks of making a living off the land was the right kind of life for him to lead. Instead, for whatever reason, his nature was drawn more towards finding some type of work in a town. And he was well aware his younger brother, whose heart and hands since birth had seemed intended to work the brown earth, would make a much better farmer then he ever would be.

Rose had been mulling this possibility over again in her mind too. However, she had reached a conclusion of a different magnitude, one which had a much more definitive kind of removal to it—emigration. The seed had been planted by her sister's enthusiastic plans to quit Ireland. To follow in Mary's footsteps to the shores of North America had come to consume Rose's thoughts as well. It had the huge advantage of making any handicaps stemming from religious differences seem to evaporate into thin air. America, land of milk and honey, land of liberty and infinite opportunity, freedom to believe and say what you want, where success was the reward for hard work, where tenants could become landowners one day, and land of tolerance where interfaith marriage would not be met with parochial discriminatory treatment and even possible ostracism—a promise of a better life for them both. This was what she wanted to believe and what captivated her imagination.

Reinforcing the inclination to choose emigration from Ireland as the future direction to take was the bitter memory of what happened to her Aunt Agnes not long ago where she lived in Carndonagh, an inland townland in the center of the Inishowen Peninsula, not a great distance from Rose's home itself. Like many other families in the parish of Donagh, in Donegal in general, and throughout Ireland from all accounts, her aunt's landlord had used a flimsy reason to nearly evict her family from their small house. The family had withheld payment of a very small portion of their rent in a token protest to a rent increase based on what they thought was an unrealistically inflated valuation of the land they farmed in comparison to other tenant holdings in the vicinity. Usually, at least as pretence for there were often other underlying reasons, the owing of several months' back rent would be needed and given to justify eviction. But this was not the case here. It was clear her aunt's family were about to be ousted for political reasons because of their association with the Land League, which was playing a leading role in attempting to put an end to exorbitant rent charges. A second reason might well have been the desire of the landlord to consolidate lands and convert them to sheep pasturage, a growing trend in many places in the country. When an eviction notice came in these cases it was final. Rose had seen insubstantial dwellings knocked down in very short order by the very same policemen who had only issued eviction notices a few moments earlier, leaving no possibility of reoccupation.

"Would you be against thinking of moving a bit further away, John? There's my sister Mary already talking of sailing off and settling abroad as you know. And, well, it seems like it's not such a bad way to go in these times. I've been thinking long and hard on it myself, and it would give us a fresh start without any of the home worries that we have here."

He was caught off guard for a moment by this change of course from what had been discussed previously. Leaving Ireland altogether? Regaining his composure, it took only a few moments for his mind to register the advantages of such a far-reaching idea, and after some hesitation he nodded his understanding of its potential.

"You know you may have something there. It would clear up our situation rather neatly, without anyone feeling too badly on either side. But still it seems like a big risk, Rose. Do we really want to leave everything behind?"

"I'd say it's a more of a risk to not do anything in a way."

"I think I see your point. Yes, when you put that way, what is there really to lose?"

Discussing it at more length, her openness to going down a new and completely different road in life started to make more and more sense to him. Some of his other relations had made the leap to leave the homeland. Almost all Irish families had been touched to some extent by the flight of their sons and daughters to distant shores. Why not the two of them starting a new life together across the sea as well? Rose was right about the obvious advantages. Pressures of how to handle local family affairs would all but be removed. The distance would see to that. Strong motivations, the lure of a land where your own drive to do more and do it better meant something, and where the threat of a life surrounded by poverty was removed.

They began to talk more animatedly of how it could be arranged, and the more they talked the more it seemed like something much greater than just another plausible answer to their future happiness. It could be *the* answer. He was sure enough of the qualities of Rose's character to know she was the one person for him. Kind, caring and strong-minded without being hardheaded, perhaps more decisive than him at times, it was not in her nature to bicker or mope. Most of all, she was trustworthy and loyal. He thought her traits fit well with his own self-conception of being straightforward and steadfast with a willingness to see the other side of things when differences of opinion inevitably occurred. He thought they shared a basic sensitivity of soul and resilience to rebound from times when things did not go smoothly, to get on with it. And they certainly didn't waste any time on petty disagreements about small things when they were fortunate enough to be able to see each other.

"Is it America, or to somewhere else you'd be meaning, Rose?"

"Yes, America…to America, to be sure", she said, with glowing eyes meeting his.

Minutes had slipped away like seconds, closing in on the hour of parting before they realized it. As Rose had arranged to meet up with Casey again at the same place by the river while John would take another route, through Bishop's Gate, to rejoin his family at the church, she needed a little more time than he did to get back to her father. They separated with heads buzzing with excitement and with mutual reminders to wait for further communication on when they would try to meet next. Fortunately, both made it back at the agreed time to their respective families, avoiding any need for explanations or repercussions. Asked if her time had passed agreeably by her father, Rose simply and genuinely responded: "It's always a good time when we get together." Of course, she did not let on for a moment the "we" was a totally different pairing in her mind than what was referred to by her father.

"I'm glad to hear that it was. You two looked so grown up when you walked away this morning. I think we're about ready to go now since we're all here." And he wrapped an arm around his daughter's shoulders as they left the church and headed to where the horses were kept.

The wind had risen and the breeze was blowing sharp once more. An off-again-on-again light drizzle dampened their hair and coats as they jostled along the road towards home. With the motion of the wagon and lack of conversation to steal away her thoughts, Rose entered a trance-like state preventing the penetration of any minor distractions from the outside world and allowing her to contentedly dwell on private ruminations of John and when they would next be able to be together again.

ARCHIVES

San Francisco/Peninsula, California, November 2006

With the failure to obtain certificates of death for my grandparents and of birth for my mother in San Francisco, four options presented themselves as possibilities to solve these questions. Thinking the vital records held by the State of California may be more complete then those of San Francisco, a request for the same certificates from the appropriate office at that level was made. The results were the same: nothing, zero, nada. Secondly, the California Death Index covering pre-1940 deaths could be checked for the names of my grandparents. A microprint copy of this index was held at the local Latter-Day Saints family history center (later found available online as well), but searching it resulted in nothing except a case of eyestrain because of the blurry quality of the text images. Again, neither of their names could be clearly identified, although there seemed at least a couple of remote possibilities for Grandfather Patrick. But there was no way to tell for sure unless more details about him were found elsewhere. Next, in lieu of the absence of a civil birth certificate for my mother, there was a chance church baptism information could be found and serve as a substitute source of information for establishing her birth date. And lastly, to try and locate factual data about my grandparents through civil and religious sources in Ireland might prove worthwhile even though it meant breaking with normal family research procedure by skipping over finding more concrete information about my mother at the local level first.

A few months earlier, to try to answer the question about her true age, a request was made to the Social Security Administration to obtain a copy of my mother's original Social Security application, the one she would have initially filled out in order to enroll in the program and to receive her Social Security card. She may never have applied for a card but it was worth the small fee required to find out if she had. In this instance, success was achieved as she had indeed applied to join the program, at the very point in time when Social Security had first gone into effect in San Francisco in 1936. Names of both of her parents, Rose and Patrick, were on the form along with her own unmarried name written in full with a birth date that still seemed a bit suspect. Having this information in hand was important, however, because it was the first primary document collected associating my mother with her parents and it confirmed what she had told me about their names, including their exact spelling. This meant the census records found earlier were likely the correct ones reflecting my family, confirming I was on the right track. Her place of work at the time and a home address in San Francisco were also given on the form, which might come in handy sometime in the future.

After learning that in order to begin receiving Social Security retirement benefits proof of birth, preferably a copy of a birth certificate, must be submitted, it was decided to further pursue this tangential path first before any of the others, and especially before starting what could be a long and tedious process of digging into historical church records. If birth information extracted from a birth certificate or another vital record could be still in her Social Security file, there would be another chance to finally get to the bottom of her actual birth date.

But this door to Social Security records could only be opened if this ever more cautious and privacy concerned agency could be persuaded to cooperate with a request to release information to the son of a long deceased mother. After explaining the situation on the telephone twice in two separate calls to two different staff, receiving the standard bureaucratic replies and getting nowhere each time, an in-person face-to-face visit to the local branch office seemed like it might offer a better approach to receiving a favorable reception. Fortunately, a more willing employee greeted me this time. After listening to my story about the lack of success in obtaining her vital records through normal channels then asking questions and checking documents brought along to verify my relationship, she consented to print out the requested personal data from their database. And then, without additional prompting, promised to contact me later to let me know if a proof of birth document, such as her birth certificate, still existed in their records storage facility located in the eastern part of the country.

No luck again was to be had in finding an actual copy of a birth certificate. Apparently, as it was told to me, these documents were not kept permanently; they were destroyed a certain number of years after the death of the benefits recipient. And the computer printout of her data only added to the confusion. Their database contained three different dates for her birth, varying by as much as five years, from 1909 to 1914. But at least her parents' names were again confirmed, leaving no room for any doubt at this point on that issue. It looked like this was all they had and the end of the road had been reached in researching the Social Security angle.

The challenge presented by the church record avenue of research for my mother was a much more daunting prospect as there are currently over fifty different parishes in San Francisco, about the same number as there were at the time she was thought to be born at the end of the first or beginning of the second decade of the twentieth century. A relative of a friend had mentioned that there existed a filmed archive of older parish baptism and marriage registers at a Catholic seminary a few miles south of San Francisco. However, delving into these church records would require the setting aside of an entire day for a trip to visit the archives situated in the town of Menlo Park. Microfilmed copies of old registers are no picnic to have to physically scan through, but having them consolidated in one place offered a much better alternative than trying to contact staff at a large number of churches individually. To inquire at each one if they still had old registers and then, if they did, ask someone to take the time to leaf through them to find my mother's name without having fairly certain birth date information would pose quite a burden. It would be asking too much, surely, for them to agree to do.

So a day was chosen to drive to the archives, leaving early from home to be at the door and ready to get started as soon as allowed. Permitted to enter the research area before the actual hour of official opening, I met the archivist in charge of the collection already busy at his work. Carrying with me a map of San Francisco, I had highlighted with a marker the street locations where my grandparents had lived according to the addresses previously found in the city directories and censuses. From the colored dots on the map, the knowledgeable archivist was able to suggest the names of the likely churches in which my mother may have been baptized.

Starting with the most likely parish, Saint Peter's, I loaded the film onto the machine and began the process of deciphering handwritten baptism register images, all in Latin, while getting used to the way the film content was organized. Handwriting styles varying in legibility were numerous, as would be expected, in view of the number of years covered. I scanned the entries covering approximately a ten year period surrounding my mother's probable birth date. Unfortunately, nothing close to her name was found in this most likely of all parishes. But the search had just begun.

By the end of the next film covering a different parish close to St. Peter's, I was accustomed to the arrangement of the data and the off-and-on existence of names indexes, and had developed a fairly efficient technique for browsing thoroughly through the films to follow. As I was to be reminded of later, each different microfilm collection requires of the user a breaking in period before the mind interprets and understands the logic of the system and figures out a way to get the most out of time allocation without sacrificing searching thoroughness.

One by one, parish by parish, the old films were pulled from the drawers of the cold steel cabinet holding them. One by one they were threaded on to the machine and rolled through. And one by one I came up empty handed. No time for lunch. Late afternoon and closing time drawing near, I had gone through only half of the parishes of the city. Determined not to leave a stone uncovered, I was already thinking of another trip to check the rest of the churches. It didn't look promising since with each successive film I had geographically moved further away from where it appeared my grandparents had lived.

Somehow, even with the fatigue from intense viewing, a realization surfaced to the forefront of my brain; the very first film I had scanned had not been done as well and as efficiently as the others. I had not yet understood and learned the data layout system at the beginning so it seemed worth taking the last remaining minutes to look at it again now that I had achieved a level of expertise. Call it the educational process or pure blind luck—as you like. This time my heart jumped a beat with a sense of disbelief. The baptism entry for my mother appeared in front of my eyes. And it had been Saint Peter's all along!

Neither of the two microfilm readers had printing capability so all of the details on parish baptism film were taken down by hand as quickly as possible before the archives closed for the day. As soon as the building was exited, a call was placed to Saint Peter's to try to catch someone still there before they shut their doors for the day as well. The hope was the church would have kept the original registers on its premises and someone there would be willing to provide an official baptism certificate using the original source. I also asked if a photocopy of the actual register page could be provided should my mother's entry be located. The very competent sounding woman in charge said they had indeed kept the actual registers, but gave no guarantees, even with the precise date information I had given her from the microfilm, that my mother's specific entry would be found. But good fortune was shining down on me now. A return call let me know the register containing the information I sought was there. And a few days later my mother's baptism certificate arrived in the mail. Finally, the first core vital record about any of my ancestors carrying an official stamp was in my possession.

With solid proof of the names of my grandparents linking them to the parentage of my mother in hand, the much needed encouragement was in place to proceed to the next step. The home address given as part of the register entry on the archive film substantiated the Cavanagh name version with a "C", tracked in the censuses and old San Francisco city directories and presumed to be the one belonging to my grandparents, was the correct one. They had indeed been living in the neighborhood of Noe Valley at the time my mother had been born in 1910.

From their ages as established by the censuses, a rude estimate could now be made to a timeframe when they most likely passed away that would assist in narrowing down the next attempt at finding out what happened to them. Since death certificates were unable to be located earlier, it was decided to try to contact the nearby Catholic cemeteries where they might have been buried.

It was soon learned cemeteries in general no longer existed within the city borders of San Francisco. Running out of room for living and business space, not to mention burial space, in the relatively small confines of the city limits in the late 1800s, a decision had been taken to find open land for burial purposes to the south of the city in San Mateo County where increasing property values and open space were not yet problematic. Not only the recently deceased were to be interred in the newly created group of cemeteries of both religion specific and non-denominational persuasions, but most of the graves in the old cemeteries within the city were to be physically removed and the remains reinterred in them as well. By around 1941 the last remaining ones in the city, Calvary and Laurel Hill, were vacated, but most others had closed well before that time, relocated to the town now known as Colma, or euphemistically as the "City of the Silent". And even more direly—the "City of the Dead".

There were three Catholic cemetery possibilities in Colma as it turned out. The most likely and by far the largest was Holy Cross Cemetery. This was truly a massive cemetery where most of the Irish who had lived and died in San Francisco were buried. The following day telephone calls were placed to all three cemetery offices yielding mixed results. Using their computerized database of burial records, the very helpful assistant at Holy Cross was quickly able to tell me there was no record for my grandmother Rose Cavanagh on the one hand. On the other hand there were too many possibilities for the common name of Patrick Cavanagh under each of the two spellings he appeared to have used in the past to be of any value in discerning if any of them could be my grandfather without having more information on the date he died. And not one of the burial years they had in their files seemed like it fit within the period of his possible death estimated up until that point in time. Some days later the other two cemeteries, having conducted manual searches without the advantage of computerized databases, informed me that no records existed for either of my grandparents in their paper files.

San Francisco/Peninsula, California, December 2006

Bolstered in confidence with the discovery of the baptism of my mother, a second trip to the Catholic archives at the seminary was scheduled a month later. This time the goal would be centered on the marriage of my grandparents in San Francisco. Again, relying on census information as a guidepost for narrowing in on probable dates, it was likely they married sometime between 1900 and 1910. Further narrowing done from their presumed address listed under Patrick's name in a San Francisco city directory brought particular emphasis on the period prior to 1906.

On the previous trip, microfilmed marriage record indexes held at City Hall had been reviewed for a few years following 1906 without success. The earthquake and resulting fire that had devastated much of the heart of the city had likewise destroyed all of the prior civil records, including those of marriages. So if their marriage did take place before 1906, the only chance of finding documentation of its occurrence would be in a parish record. The archivist was quick to forewarn, though, in the case of relatively newly arrived Irish immigrants, one of the most likely churches for their marriage would have been Saint Patrick's, the only church building that had lost all of its registers in the wake of the catastrophe. And no copies had been made of them by that time. Things were starting to look a tad worrisome again, but I had mentally steeled myself to get through as many of the fifty parish films as possible in one day, commencing again with Saint Peter's where my mother's baptism had taken place.

Saint Peter's yielded no results and one after the other

each of the parish films reviewed failed to produce anything positive as well. The hours flew by with the closing hour almost upon me again. As diligent and lucky as I had been once before, there seemed no way it could happen again. But almost as if it was meant to be, like finding the needle in a haystack, twice, it did happen again. It felt like *déjà vu*. For me, this was the holy grail in the search for the origins of grandmother, Rose. At the eleventh hour once again, stunned, there, set out before my eyes on old film but still clear as a bell, was the register entry for the marriage of my grandparents.

In calling over the archivist to share with him my success and to confirm my eyes were not deceiving me, he seemed as surprised as I was to see among all of the films and parishes examined it was in the parish of Saint Celia's, in an unexpected area of the city, Rose Cameron and Patrick Cavanagh were married. The date leapt out: January 1, 1901, **01-01-01**, as did the neatly written phrase *natum in Hibernium*—born in Ireland—written after the name of each of the two newlyweds. And extremely crucial, the Latinized names of their parents, all four of them, were given in full. As suddenly as that, the door to my Irish roots had just flown wide open.

A phone call was made to a helpful staff member at the church on the following morning and within a few days time not only a certified copy of their marriage was received in the mail, but a photocopy of the entry taken from the actual church marriage register as well. Two trips to the archives, two building blocks essential to solving the mystery were now in place. With my grandparent's marriage and my mother's baptism information in hand, the foundation was set to continue searching for more pieces of the puzzle as to precisely where in Ireland my grandparents had come from, and possibly to when and where their lives had ended as well.

CONFIDENCES

Grianán Ailigh, Donegal, Ireland, October 1889

Autumn had fully engaged, the chilly breezes nudging their way through the layers of clothing. Summer crops had been harvested and the year's production could said to be a fair one, neither forcing further tightening of belts nor giving confidence for a table of plenty in the winter months that lay ahead. At least as tenant farmers, Rose's family could, after paying a fixed rent to the middleman who leased the land from the estate owner, keep most of the food that had been grown for their own needs and sell or trade any excess or non-food crops to others. There was never much leftover, though. But the opportunity to be able to take a even few small steps forward during decent years was a big advantage over the situation of some of their "cottier" friends in the neighboring quarterlands making up their townland, many of whose children were classmates of Rose and her sisters at school. Cottiers, among the poorest of the poor, basically traded their labor for a ramshackle dwelling and seed to grow enough food to marginally sustain their families through each year, with a portion of the produce going directly back to the landowner. This minimal hardscrabble existence was a debilitating form of subsistence living still all too prevalent in Donegal in the late 1800s. It put the cottier family in competition with others existing in similar circumstances for very small plots of land, typically of low growing quality, by initiating a bidding war to occupy the land. The result of desperation bidding often caused them to over extend and drift even deeper into poverty.

Rose's birthday had come and gone near the end of August. Although already two months ago now, she liked to think back on how her sisters and brother had made sure her special day was recognized and went well for her, as was customary practice for each of the children's birthdays. Her birthday month had been, as usual, one of the busiest of the summer. But now she smiled to herself as she pictured how the extra quantity of butter had been lavishly spread on her morning barmbrack to start the day off; how Bridget, her youngest sister, quite critical and bossy by nature, had restrained herself, offering to take her dishes from the table to be washed; how her earliest morning chores had been done by William and Mary; and how her parents had presented her with a very elegant, *black and white, polka-dot neck scarf*, which she instantly wrapped around her neck to the oohs and ahhs of her mother and sisters. "You look just like a queen," Mary cried, sharing in her joy. This seemingly small gift was one she would treasure forever.

Turning seventeen caused her again to take pause to reflect on the quandary of the road ahead in her life. The cramped cottage felt a little more crowded each day as she and her siblings grew older. Even the three sections of land laid out in long, rectangular strips of about ten acres each that the family worked partially in a rundale arrangement seemed like they were shrinking in size. Rundale was a popular form of community farming where unfenced fields were shared and tilled with other families, many of whom were related to each other and living in a small cluster of houses. Stone walls enclosed the entire area and penned in the livestock. And the very same rock fences penning in the livestock seemed now to be holding her back as well. Rose was not one to sit and wait for life to come to her. No, she had seen too many others who had done just that and where had it gotten them? For so many it was a hand-to-mouth existence, a life of toil and an early grave. She wondered if John was thinking the same thing at this very moment. He could very well be; they were that much in tune with each other. Had he second thoughts about the idea of leaving Ireland for good? Or would he remain as excited and eager as she was to speak more about coming up with a plan about how it best could be accomplished the next time they met?

It was Sunday, the day of the week reserved for the whole family to attend church at Saint Brendan's, the house of worship closest to their cottage. Whether the climate was mild or they were in the throes of a swirling snowstorm, they rarely missed walking together the two miles to their local parish church early in the morning, always leaving home without having breakfasted first. At this church, in its old graveyard, many of their ancestors were buried. And this chosen site would be the final resting place for many more of the current parish flock that were destined to pass their lives in its vicinity. Father O'Farrell who presided over the pulpit of their small church had a pervasive reach, touching the families of the fervently committed as well as the less devout particularly at times of birth, marriage and death. His awareness of even the mundane daily occurrences could almost be called uncanny for there was little happened of either reverential or civil nature that escaped his eyes and ears. Rose was well aware of his constant presence and penetrating vision.

The return trip home after the morning service, done with some intention to haste, held the reward of a late morning meal to satisfy growling and grumbling stomachs. Rose and her sisters set the table with dishes kept tucked away in an open, recessed wall shelf. Among the unmatched set of plates and cups there were specific pieces to which the children had become particularly attached. A small-sized, mostly plain plate—*creamy white with a thin band of silver a bit below the rim and a silver four-leaf clover in the center*—had caught Rose's fancy and had become her personal favorite, expressly for its simplicity. Most evenings the women of the family, when they were not sewing or patching, were involved with working either lint or wool in one form or another. They grew just enough flax on their farm to fulfill their own household linen needs and sheared wool from their own sheep for fashioning clothes made from yarn. On an evening, one daughter might manage the spinning while another the weaving while two others carded wool, cloved lint or knitted. Rose felt valued playing her role in an interdependent working family but unlike her older sister, Elizabeth, and her younger sisters, Margaret and Catherine, she was beset by an inborn restlessness. The others were all much more inclined to be content with traditional life in their small corner of the world and , worshipping the daily routines binding them together.

In the morning her father and his brother, James, and her brother Willie planned to continue adding fertilizer to one of the fields, a project they had begun the day before. Harvest, normally starting in late August or early September, had finished early this year with the warm weather, permitting an equally early start on preparing the land for the next crops. By October another few acres were ready for their turn to be reinvigorated. Some of the fertilizer they produced themselves from the mutually shared lime kiln built near the top field, in close proximity to the limestone source but well away from their living quarters lower down the slope. They also used seaweed collected from the shores of the Foyle as an additional method for enriching the soil. A combination of lime and seaweed produced a more balanced "feeding" of the land and living not far from the sea as they were, they were fortunate to have access to both.

The morning broke bright and looked as if it was going to stay that way for the whole day. It would make things easier for them if it did. Two of Rose's friends were to join her and her sister Mary for a "Donegal walk", which was a way of saying they were intending to take the day to traipse all the way to Grianán Aileach, the ancient stone ringfort sitting astride a hilltop perch and giving forth spectacular views below of Lough Swilly on one side and of Lough Foyle on the other. Dominantly situated to allow sight in all directions actually, the circular fort had been restored to its former grandeur only ten years before and was reputed to have begun its life as a burial ground sometime around 1700 BC. It was a noted place of pilgrimage for county inhabitants, and even Saint Patrick was said to have visited it during his lifetime in the fifth century A.D. It was also the purported seat of the Kings of Aileach.

On their young and sturdy legs accustomed to wandering the green hills for miles around, they would soon be off. With packed food sufficient for the several hours march of some eleven miles, they knew they wouldn't starve. Two of them had previously been to the mythical, three-tiered ring of stones, but Mary and Sarah had never before found the opportunity to make the trek there. After she was ready, Rose saw her mother busy at the butter churn.

"You know the route we'll be taking, Mam. Casey's been there before and knows the way too. We'll be home by late afternoon. If it comes on wet on the way there then we'll turn around and come back sooner. If it's coming down heavy on the way back we can stop over at uncle's place at Derryvane. But we're planning to be home at the latest by suppertime. After we pass by Tobar Patrick holy well, we'll be meeting up with Casey near Sarah's house and starting together from there."

"That's a distance to go even for your mountain goat legs. Listen to what your sister Mary says about…the lot of you, as she's the eldest. If she tells you to turn back, turn back. Make sure you take covering enough for there's no telling for sure but it looks as if it may be gray and damp later. Have you taken enough to eat?" She spoke without missing a stroke at the churn.

By this time Mary had joined them, looking sure of herself, as an older sister was want to do, knowing that she would be in charge. "Not to worry, I'll take care of them like a mother hen does her brood of chicks. We're all set with all we need, Mam." Her other sisters who were listening in gave sideways looks of disgust to each other without letting their mother see them doing it. With quick brushes of their mother's cheek, they were out the door and on their way.

In very short order they were at Sarah's place. Casey was already waiting there with Sarah. They stopped their chattering as they saw Rose and Mary approaching. Knowing the distance they intended to cover, the four of them wasted no time in carrying on, finding themselves quite able to hold a running conversation while maintaining their lengthy and rapid country strides even when climbing up the steepest hillsides with ease. Inexplicably blessed with more than normal stamina, Rose set a pace that sometimes made the others ask her to stop for a moment to regain their breath when they became too winded to keep up, which usually brought a trace of a whimsical grin to cross her lips. It was a nice feeling to be best in something, even though she kept her head hung low so the others would not see it. They passed close by several other groups of houses, crossed creeks, tramped through shaded areas of heavy overgrowth, all in keeping to the well-worn trails used over the centuries. They also made a point of passing by the huge roundish stone resembling the shape of a mushroom cap cocked to one side, probably having partially collapsed aeons ago so that one end now thrust out and upwards towards the sky. From mystical times, some incarnation of ancient mankind had managed to move the huge stone, known as the Morten God Dolmen, to its present location to mark the entry to a tomb.

They decided against taking a detour to make a stop at the Ardmore Gallan standing stones, another ancient burial place that would normally have been part of a shorter walk roughly in the same direction they were heading. Adorned as they were with timeworn examples of intersecting swirls much akin to linking a number of thumb whorls together and typical of megalithic Celtic spiral art in Ireland, this menhir would be saved for an outing on another day. Nevertheless, two earthen raths, circular mounds where ancient forts once existed, were on their journey's course today as well. In several hours time they had their destination in sight, straight ahead, rising above all of the other surroundings. Along the way they chatted about school, the farms, families and friends, but they waited until arriving at the circle fort before talking about what was uppermost in each of their minds—their plans for the future. Sitting down to eat the food they had brought in a wind-protected section of the middle tier ring with their backs supported by the thick stones, Mary was the first one to broach the subject.

"I know what you're thinking…is she really going to do what she said and leave Ireland for good to go to America…maybe it was just fanciful talk. Or maybe she's even changed her mind about the idea altogether. Well I can tell you nothing's changed, and I'll have put away enough, I think, to be able to leave by next summer." She could expect little help from her parents. It was a given that she had to earn most of the fare to pay her own way; family circumstances simply could not cover the passage cost. Rose herself already knew her sister was holding firm in her intentions but to hear it said with such confidence to their friends sent a shiver rippling from her neck all the way down the length of her spine. She could tell by the expressions on their faces the ever-present idea of emigration was not far from their minds too, as it was with a good many of the young people. So many others had gone before them who had never returned. Thoughts of leaving were commonplace, and not too concerning for that matter—until the decision was final and the passage tickets purchased.

"All of us are going to do whatever we can so she will be able to leave next year. I think it's wonderful to be able for her to be the first in the family to strike out." From her comments of support, but without saying it in so many words, Rose let the others see into the direction of her own leanings as well.

The other two girls were aware that these sisters were cut much from the same mold when it came to adventurous spirits even though there was a difference of six years in their ages. But until this point only Casey knew about the one fact that separated Rose from Mary; Mary had no serious attachment to any of the local lads that would hold her back. But Rose, what would she do about John and their secret courtship, Casey wondered to herself? She did not have long to wait. Rose had decided now was the time to bring her sister and close friends in on her relationship with John. It was hard to hide anything for long in a community as small as theirs so before they learned from another source or guessed, it was time to let them in. Besides, not opening up to someone else was wearing on her mind. In fact, she had heard talk, and already even a few remarks made within her earshot. On more than one occasion others had seen her with an unidentified person, a lad of medium height with dark brown hair. Until now, though, no one had put too much store in these brief glimpses. There was certainly no one who had yet really guessed he was anything more than a mere acquaintance that she knew from somewhere else.

"There's something I've been meaning to tell you all. I've met someone who I've taken a liking to. And what's more he seems to feel the same way about me, for whatever reason I don't know, I'm sure. But before I tell you about him, I want you to swear to keep it amongst ourselves, at least until I let you know differently. Others will learn more about him later, too. But it's better not to bother more than you all with too much now. Do you promise?" Of course they all said they did.

It took a while for her to get the hardest part out but when she finally did the reaction of the girls to John's family being

Protestant was not at all what she expected. They seemed more interested in personal particulars, where he lived and what he looked like, how they managed to get together, and if they could see him up closer sometime, almost ignoring the fact of the religious differences. Relieved, Rose had nearly forgotten how far her generation had moved away from the narrow-minded thinking persistent in her parents' and certainly in her grandparents' times. Already the steadily increasing number of young people in their own townland leaving farm work behind to look for work in Derry was a fact of life. There, in the city away from the family fold, different faiths intermingled in daily life, loosening to some degree the stranglehold of traditional religious prejudices, although it still always paid to be careful.

What did set them back on their heels was when she told them about the idea of emigrating from Ireland together with him. Sarah was the first one to chime in.

"Not you too, Rose? This country won't have enough people to throw stones at if everyone starts thinking of leaving!"

"You know I don't think John or I would be happy staying here with the way things are now. When we talked it over we both decided we wanted to take a new road to somewhere, even if we don't have a clue where it will lead when we get there!"

"Do you know when…where would you aim for"? Casey asked.

"Not yet, really. Nothing like that yet is completely settled for certain."

There was no question to be sure, Rose emphasized, that they were both too young now to marry soon, not to mention the question of money that always stood in the way. Mary was not surprised for she understood Rose's temperament well but she was somewhat taken back that Rose had not spoken about it first with her, before announcing it to their little group of friends. Losing some of her talkativeness, she decided not to mention her disappointment to her now rather she would save it for a time when they were alone together at home.

Typical, strong, gusty winds were whirling around the fort by early afternoon. But the walk back saw them diminish and the fine weather held as they made their descent from the high point. There was no pressure to hurry, giving them plenty of time to ruminate over the possible disappearance of not one but two of the four of them from their homeland. It was same old tune played on the fiddle—the Irish affliction of lost friendships and broken-hearted parents.

HOLY CROSS CEMETERY

San Francisco/Peninsula, California, January 2007

Rethinking the information gathered together on my Irish grandparents to this stage, the fact that my grandfather Patrick Cavanagh was not found in the 1920 census and no record of his death had yet been located either in San Francisco or among California State vital records stood out once more as being bizarrely significant. What was needed was an official document of some sort linking my grandparents as living together other than the church baptismal record of my mother and the information obtained from the Social Security office. And what was needed was something other than a census reference, while looking like it belonged to them, remained unproven. The same could be said of the city directory listings. If only something official existed that spelled out plainly that they were both Irish born, removing any lingering doubts and validating what my mother had told me so long ago. Something beyond even the Latin phrase inscribed in the 1901 church marriage register inscribed with the Kavanaugh version of the name spelling.

When I had talked by phone a month earlier to the assistant at Holy Cross Cemetery she had asked for an approximate death date for Patrick. Not having one to give her, I had made a hasty assumption he had probably died prior to the 1920 census since he was not included along with Rose and my mother who were both listed. But just to be cautious, I had asked her to look for anyone with the correct name, under both variants of spelling, who had been buried in the range 1915 to 1925. A divorce had never been mentioned and seemed almost out of the question for Catholics during that time period.

There were a number of Patrick Cavanaghs in the 1930 census but none of the listings associated any of them with Rose or my mother. And neither Patrick nor Rose could be found separately listed in the San Francisco enumeration of that year. Their absence could be interpreted in at least two ways: it could be seen to support the belief Patrick may have died much earlier on the one hand; it could also be taken as putting a cloud over the constant assumption Rose and her daughter had never left the city. Maybe the family had temporarily left San Francisco? But searching further afield in California and beyond revealed no sign of them living elsewhere. Perhaps, then, they had slipped through the census takers net altogether? What other explanations could there be?

The more I thought about it and the more I read about its history, especially the Catholic exclusiveness of Holy Cross Cemetery, the more it seemed like it would be worthwhile to take the time to make a visit there in person to ask a few more questions. So, another trip to the San Francisco area was planned and made in late January.

Similar to speaking to cemetery staff over the phone but even more so in person, the first line attendants were genuinely pleased to be as helpful as they could be in checking all of the name possibilities in their database. They searched for all of the spelling variations for my grandparents, even under Rose's maiden name as a precaution, as well as for a possible sister of my grandfather whose apparent existence had been noted on the old photograph. What's more, they kindly offered to pull all of the physical cards matching his first name and surname variants, about ten in number, to let me look through them to see if I might be able to identify some bit of information that would signal which one might be his. About midway in going through the stack, one of them struck me hard—it had to be the right one.

Believing it was likely he had changed the spelling of his name from Kavanaugh to Cavanagh sometime between his marriage to Rose in 1901 and my mother's baptism in 1910, the card I held in my hand did nothing to undo that belief. Just the opposite. Amazingly, at the top of the card was the name of the decedent, *Patrick Cavanagh*, while at the bottom left corner the name *Patrick Kavanaugh* was typed in as owner of the burial plot purchased, oddly enough, long before in the year of 1888! So the assumption the surname Kavanaugh had morphed into Cavanagh now looked irrefutable; they had to be one and the same person. And the icing on the cake was that place of birth was clearly denoted as Ireland.

But there was more to this story. Two more cards were associated with the first. The first one was for Helen Kavanaugh, buried in 1888—whose relationship to Patrick was duly noted as *wife*—and the other card was for an infant, buried in 1901, after having lived only one day. It was now crystal clear—all three of them were buried in the same plot, purchased by Grandfather Patrick at the time of an earlier wife's death.

It took awhile for all of this to sink in and then move on to trying to find his actual gravesite, the site which enclosed his first wife as well as of a short-lived son, a son evidently of

Patrick and Rose. The cemetery was massive, sprawling over some three hundred acres of beautifully maintained sloping greenery. Even the cemetery staff was not absolutely certain of the total numbers buried in it, but their ball park figure was upwards of four hundred thousand. Making it even harder to pinpoint the location of their gravesite was because it was unmarked. So many graves without headstones, a telling reminder of the conditions of the struggling working class members of society who failed to achieve sufficient economic success to attain the American dream of plenty to which they so dreamed and aspired. Giving up on finding the site without assistance, a cemetery attendant eventually guided us to the exact location. Even without a headstone, gazing at the empty grassy spot between two marked graves on either side was a revelation. A giant step towards an increasing sense of completeness was taken. Grandfather Patrick's final resting place had been found at last.

But as often happens one answer often leads to another question. The question begging to be answered was why Rose was not buried with him or, possibly, anywhere in the cemetery? The card for Patrick had been made at the time of the plot purchase, at the death of his first wife, so naturally Rose's name would not appear on it, but there was no additional card for her that was associated with Patrick's plot or even in relation to his name. In fact, it appeared she might not be buried in Holy Cross at all. But if she were, and it was not in the same plot with my grandfather and their son, then her place of repose must still be out there somewhere in the green silent vastness.

It was now evident that estimate of his death range based on interpretation of census data had been wrong. He had not only been alive in 1920 but was living, although unwell, even during the taking of the next decennial census in April of 1930, only to pass on afterwards during the same year. His death date was several years later than estimated so this could explain why the health department in San Francisco had been unable to pull up his record before. And upon further examination of the photocopies of the cemetery cards that I had been given, a detail that was overlooked in the initial throes of excitement now leaped out—his place of death was stated as the Laguna Honda Home in San Francisco.

Not having time enough to pursue both a death certificate and the actual place of death in a single afternoon, a decision was taken to try again to obtain a death certificate downtown at the health department before closing time, leaving Laguna Honda, a name with a familiar sounding ring to it, to be further looked into when we got back home. With presentation to the health department of the exact death date as well as place of death, it was hoped the chances of finding a certificate would be greatly increased. However, I remained anything but confident in the service, having had not one iota of success in previous attempts in person or by mail.

A long line of people applying for birth and death certificates awaited me. Finally reaching the window and passing through my request, I was told it would take a couple of hours to research as this record was not in the computerized database and would have to be researched on film. This was much too long to sit and wait in the gloomy hallway twiddling my fingers. Joining my wife who was again at the San Francisco Public Library doing more city directory lookups seemed like a much better option. A long two hours passed much like a dental appointment, excruciatingly slow, but the hour of reckoning eventually approached. Back at the health department it was another wait before someone deigned to come to the document pick-up window. Worried I would, like before, receive a blank certificate form save for brief words to the effect that no certificate existed for him, my skepticism and fears proved to be unfounded this time around. I could see at first glance enough scattered, smudgy letters to indicate a document of some kind from a bygone printing era.

First thing was to make sure the "Patrick Cavanagh" named on the certificate was the same person as the one on the Holy Cross burial record; date of death and place of death matched perfectly. Next was to look at his exact year of birth. Marked down was the year 1862: a difference of three years from the 1865 birth date which was noted in the 1900 census, a census listing which had earlier been assumed to be his. Holding my breath, my eyes then hunted for the all-telling piece of information meaning he was the husband of my grandmother. Was there a wife's name listed and was it Rose? It was there—in black and white—legibly written so there could be no mistake. A big sigh of relief was slowly exhaled across the city.

Then, a shock with respect to place of birth—*Roscommon, Ireland* was listed, not Donegal as had been previously suspected! Unfortunately, nothing with regard to an Irish town had been given by the informant, which was to be expected.

So was my mother wrong, or did I only imagine she gave the name Donegal when referring to where her parents came from? Maybe she had been just referring to her mother? Everything else I recalled her saying had been right to this moment —now this belief began to show signs of a crack.

IRELAND RESEARCH

Central Coast, California, January-February 2007

During the first two months of the year, before having gathered any credible information with regard to Irish locations, especially Patrick's death certificate giving Roscommon as his birth place, the process was begun of extending the search for my grandparents' exact places of birth to Ireland itself. Since so many obstacles had been encountered in trying to uncover this information from records in California, it was time to let go of the time-tested approach. With the essential names of Rose's and Patrick's parents in hand, it was now possible, and probably worth the time and expense, to contact genealogy centers situated in each of the two Irish counties in which they were thought to have lived before emigrating from Ireland. By far the fastest and most comprehensive way to delve into both parish records and civil records, these centers had transcribed most vital records into computerized databases only just a few years before.

In parallel with the genealogy centers, the General Register Office also needed to be contacted. The GRO, for a charge, would search for civil birth records limited to a five-year birth span for each person requested. Mandatory civil birth registration was established by law in 1864 in Ireland. U.S. census birth dates that I had found for both of my grandparents were mostly after that date, especially for the more recent survey decades. However, these dates were often inaccurate. The census taker could have misheard or simply made an error in jotting down an incorrect number. Or the information provider could have intentionally given a fictitious date or even one poorly recalled. Penmanship itself could cause a misreading. The quality of the extant survey sheet itself, or the filming of it, could have been an extremely poor rendering, making the handwritten data difficult to read. The keeping of Irish parish records varied from place to place but most churches started earlier than collection of civil records did.

Using the local family history center of the Latter-Day Saints, a third channel for researching Irish birth information, had proven to be a congenial if tedious experience. Even if I had better information and was able to identify the exact microfilm needed on the first go, the time between ordering and receiving the film was often agonizingly long. With what turned out to be inexact information, the repetitive exercise became one of frustration. It would have taken more years than I had left in waiting as each submission of a request for a reel of microfilm to the LDS mother library in Salt Lake City took anywhere from two weeks to two months before the film arrived in the local building for viewing.

Overall, though, there was a kind of redemption in attempting this research strategy because the helpful staff and good general collection of traditional paper genealogical resources for Ireland at the local center enhanced the research process itself. Through the sources at the center as well as a basic guide on doing Irish research that I had picked up at a book sale, the types and scope of documents available were learned, use of genealogical software was introduced, name origins unraveled and much more was deposited in my personal data bank. And discussing research methods as well as actual successes and failures with fellow researchers served as mutually reinforcing camaraderie that had the effect of making the effort seem doable and worthwhile no matter how many misfires one encountered. However, the one drawback was that none of the staff appeared to know much about doing Irish research since they were engaged in unearthing ancestor roots from other countries.

About the same time as the undertaking of LDS-based research, a most intriguing document was stumbled upon on the Web. Using experience gained from a career of analytical research, names and other important biographical data pertaining to my Irish ancestors were combined in different ways by exploiting the advance features of a Web search engine. One evening in searching for traces of my grandmother a new interplay of terms resulted in producing a page from a website that contained a comprehensive listing of baptisms that someone had diligently transcribed from a single church register in County Donegal.

What was remarkable about this particular listing of parish baptisms, and the reason it turned up in the first place, was that in comparing the known details of my grandmother's profile from the previous information collected in California to those on the web pages, seven of the eight biographical elements were identical! Her Christian names; year of birth; month of birth; her mother's first name; her mother's maiden name; father's first name; and Donegal (from my mother) were all identical to the facts I had gleaned from other sources. Even the day of baptism was only off by a single digit.

But the eighth element was the glaring stumbling block,

bringing the train to an abrupt halt: the family name on the baptism sheet listed was *McMartin*, totally different from *Cameron*, the maiden name of my grandmother that had been both orally related to me by my mother and, by this point, confirmed in several written documents as well. What could be more critical in doing family research than having surnames that match? Because of this all-important surname incongruity, the other elements seemed as if they would have to be reduced to coincidence. Regrettably, the near match on the website list of baptisms was set aside, but not altogether dismissed or forgotten.

Naturally, the first genealogy center in Ireland contacted to conduct a paid search of their database of vital records for both Rose and Patrick was the one in County Donegal. Delays were experienced in getting a response from them so a second center, situated in adjoining County Derry, was contacted afterwards. The Derry Genealogy Centre overlapped with the Donegal center, covering both County Derry and the part of Donegal that falls within the boundaries of the Diocese of Derry. This coverage particularly included the Inishowen Peninsula. In addition to the names and birth dates of my grandparents, the surname from the website baptism list was also given to them just in case there was a chance that it could somehow be useful in determining some type of linkage. Their search came up empty for Patrick Cavanagh and Rose Cameron, but they did find the record for a *Rose McMartin*. However, given the radical difference in last names, their expert conclusion, confirming my own feeling, was that it was a series of coincidental facts and there was no meaningful connection between them. Rose McMartin and Rose Cameron seemed to be two distinct, unrelated individuals from two distinct, unrelated families precluding any need to look into the McMartin name any further.

After Derry, a number of genealogy centers in neighboring northern Irish counties were contacted one after the other, including the counties of Armagh, Down, Tyrone, Antrim, Leitrim, and Fermanagh, with each database search coming up negative, unable to locate even remotely close records for either of my grandparents. Each step of the way it had been a battle in digging out information about these elusive people and now this endless futility on the Ireland side had to be endured as well. It was almost as if my ancestors had intentionally tried to hide information about themselves to make tracing them by future generations as difficult as possible. Despondency was beginning to prevail and best options looked to be about exhausted as far as Ireland was concerned.

POTEEN

Donegal, Ireland, July-August 1890

Reality had finally sunk in. A state of anxiety among the Camerons had been fueled by months of built-up anticipation: Mary's time for departure was drawing near. She would soon be the first of their close-knit family to take passage for America. As hard as they tried to put on brave faces and go about their daily activities in a normal way there was no stopping the expanding somber mood that seemed to invade all the nooks and crannies of their small dwelling. What would they do without her? It would be one thing if she were leaving the family fold to join a husband. Her daily presence would be sorely missed for a while but hopefully she would be living in a place that was not so far away as to prevent occasional, if not frequent, visiting between them. And marriage—at least some marriages—could often work to enlarge family gatherings and create prospects for other forms of interaction as well. Then again, she may never have married, like so many others, and stayed on to help her parents with the farm and raising the other children. Either of these scenarios would have been so much more preferable than boarding a ship and sailing away to a foreign land, even if it was to the promised land of America. There was that reality again: those that left rarely returned and goodbyes were usually forever.

As much as everyone's resignation to her forthcoming

departure unhappily permeated the household, a strong will and a decisive personality engrained in Mary since she had entered the world would not be deterred by any of the long faces surrounding her. There was no stopping her once she had made her mind up—she was bound for new shores whether they liked it or not. The fare had been raised by hard work, and her family had also contributed a small amount of cash to tide her over. Two small empty suitcases to hold her worldly belongings sat ready to be filled in a corner. And a ticket had already been purchased for a ship leaving on the third day of August, just three short weeks away.

Rose admired her sister's boldness and tenacity. And there was little doubt that she and Mary were the closest of the Camerons in terms of personality. Sure of themselves in whatever they chose to take on, they both were of the type to keep sentimentality at arm's length. That is not to say that their tougher practical side was not complemented by a strong sense of caring and empathy, but neither of them showed these characteristics much in public, leaving such displays to their more overtly emotional sisters. And it was Maggie, the youngest of them, who at this moment barged through the front door with a brow full of wrinkles.

"They've come, a lot of them. Will they take him? The dogs won't shut-up. Oh, they're already smashing everything, and maybe coming here next, so…what'll we do?" she spat out in a flurry of words.

"Hold on, my dear. Take a breath and then tell us slowly what you are on about now." Her mother, accustomed to her daughter's dramatic effusions, knew that they would not be able to make heads or tails out of what she was saying unless she could get her to calm down a bit and start over.

Gathering herself together, she began again. "It's the revenue police. There must be six of them at least. They've found the still near Cousin Michael's land and they are smashing it to bits. Will they take away his family do you think? What about the rest of us who know about it too, will they be after us?"

Now they understood the reason for her outburst. Poteen stills were widespread and secreted in hideaways all over Ireland. Donegal had more than its fair share being one of the largest counties in terms of physical size as well as being more remotely situated in the northwest corner of the country. Also known as moonshine or mountain dew, the production of poteen, an illegal fermented mash whiskey, had been part of the Irish landscape for as long as one could remember. And for almost just as long homegrown distilled spirits had been the target of the revenue men in one guise or another. Sometimes it was made from malted barley or potatoes, more often from sugar and treacle these days, but whatever it had for ingredients, it was always potent, it could supplement a farmer's income, distillation was illicit, and the revenue police were out to catch those who flaunted the law. When the police did manage to catch someone, and it didn't happen that often for poteen brewers were masters at lightning speed dismantlement and concealment, it could happen that they would choose to make examples of these so-called "criminals". The fines accessed could be onerous for the marginal way of life of most farming families. What's more the penalty could be extended to all of those living around the family of concern if they too were considered to be involved in some capacity in the activity, sometimes assumed to be the case based on living proximity alone.

Although these Protestant enforcers were often right in assuming that close neighbors shared in poteen making in one way or another, the thinking that by punishing not just the caught-in-the-act offenders but a number of others in a small community considered to be associates would somehow serve to create a divisiveness and animosity among local families, leading to a halt in the practice was quite misguided. In fact the opposite was true. What actually occurred was greater interdependence among those families involved, a stronger unity in which the families pulled together even more closely than before in developing new schemes for better concealment of their activities, often higher yet in the Inishowen hills.

By this time all of the girls had joined their mother and were waiting to see what she would do. "We'll get what others we can then go together to see what these men are about. Mary, Margaret, Rose…as quick as rabbits, go to the others and bring them to the crossing. Then we're…" They were out the door before the last words left her mouth.

Altogether there were eleven of them that met and rushed up the slope to become part of an already large crowd of spectators gathered there. And it didn't take long for a swarm of other field workers to find their way to the site for a word with the ring of urgency to it had a way of spreading quickly in times of crisis in their small community. There was no way the presence of a group of lawmen could escape notice when there were alert eyes and ears trained to be attuned to their movements.

Before they got there, the still had already been completely smashed to smithereens and the few kegs of confiscated spirit placed in the cart the police had brought with them. They would drive it back to the station in Derry

City and once there, pour the brew out—at least that's what was purportedly done. Tales of very lively times in certain parts of the city were not unknown after snagging a substantial load of poteen. But in this instance the raid could be considered only of marginal success. What had been seized was only a drop in the bucket, so to speak, of the whiskey that was made, distributed and stored throughout their village. Fines would be levied and the still would be rebuilt at another location. And money handed over would soon be forgotten while poteen making would continue as it always had. As much as a form of a traditional resistance and expression of empowerment as it was a way for supplementing income, it was part and parcel of existence.

Numbers of inhabitants present substantial as they were, many still carrying their farm implements, the revenue men showed wisdom in their restraint this time around, fearing incitement of the crowd any more than necessary. They did their work and left promptly well aware that there had been incidences in the past where violence had broken out with injuries, even fatal ones, when a crowd such as was assembled became agitated enough to take physical action. However in this instance the scene of conflict having quieted down now, the crowd dispersed, neighbors speaking briefly to one another as they made their way back down the hillside to their homes and fields. At least for the Camerons the incident had one positive outcome to it, serving as it did as a distraction to the family focus on Mary. It was bound to become the topic of conversation for the next few days and all were silently relieved not to have the thought of her voyage on the tips of their tongues for a short while even if it meant dealing with other problems. There would be another distraction before she embarked, though; it was traditional at harvest time for the local households to hold a dance to celebrate the coming end of the summer season. This year, however, the festivities would be bittersweet for both Mary and Rose.

Mary did not want to see the celebration turn into a morose good-bye party for herself. She wholeheartedly wished, especially after the drama of the poteen raid, that the gathering would be one of merriment, as it always had been in the past, not one with overtones of gloom dripping from the rafters. She spoke with her mother first.

"Mam, I don't want others feeling sad over my leaving at a time when folks are supposed to laughing and having fun. Anything you and Da can do to take the attention off me would be for the best for everyone, I think."

"I understand what's going through your mind. And I'll do my best, but things have a way of taking their own course, so don't be too flustered if there's a bit of bother. It's normal. People expect it."

"Well, I know I want to have the best time I can. Those are the kind of memories I want to take with me…to forever keep by me."

Her father said basically the same thing. They both readily agreed to try to abide by her wishes to the best of their abilities. In doing so, they made it known that their influence only went so far as their own extended family and they could not forcibly prevail on any of the others in attendance to act similarly, to just ignore that she was leaving soon. But to further convince her all would be fine, her father, showing his usual insight in such matters, said that once the younger ones got past their first reservations feet would be flying as usual and laughter and good times would outshine any needless worries of a pall being cast over the dance because of her forthcoming departure. He thought the musicians would be playing for all get out, and then the older people would soon be taking a turn on the floor because everyone was looking to put their cares behind them for an evening—with just a little help from the remaining stash of undiscovered brew.

Her father had a knack of being able to wipe away what could be called unnecessary anxiety, feelings that were allowed to dwell too much on life's larger or even smaller concerns. It was commonplace for him and his role in a household where six daughters and a son were raised to be able to find just a few well-chosen words delivered at the right time to restore a sense of equilibrium to runaway thoughts that may have swung too far astray in one direction or the other from the reasonable. His soft spoken words to Mary at this moment worked like a charm and she felt herself grow calmer and relax as doubts about the evening ahead receded.

Even though she would also have to hold back her emotions during the evening, Rose's sense of abandonment was steadily growing. Already beginning to feel the loss of her steadfast sister and best friend, she knew she would dearly miss this person of many similar traits more than she could say. Along with her unflappable personality, Mary, whose shorter stature and more rounded features contrasted with her own angular structure, allowed nothing to faze her that could be shown to be of little consequence in the long run, just like her father.

But the occasion of the dance would also be marked by the absence of John. In her wildest fancies, she wished that he would just show up uninvited and their relationship brought out into the wide open so that the ordeal of secretiveness would no longer have to be borne by either of them. But was it worth the risk of bringing down the wrath of the community on herself and John, not to mention reactions of their immediate families and friends? No. It would only be folly that would stir up hard feelings needlessly for so many. They would have to bide their time for a private celebration between just the two of them to acknowledge the passing of the summer season, bringing them another step closer to the time when they could be together permanently. So she felt herself doubly afflicted, but like her sister Mary she would never let on to others that this was the case. She was not one to wear her emotions on her sleeve either.

And subsequently, at the dance, Rose easily found the resolve to join in when asked to take the floor first by Thomas then Joseph then James, in turn, without letting on at all she was any less sharing in the enjoyment of the moment than they seemed to be. It wasn't that hard because she just pretended in her mind that each of them was John then let the rhythmic sounds of fiddles, pipes and pounding drums carry her away. Rose could never be accused of being short on imagination!

LAGUNA HONDA

San Francisco/Peninsula, California, February 2007

Another "brick wall" had risen up on trying to ferret out the exact birthplaces of my Irish grandparents through American documents and by requesting database searches at Irish genealogy centers in the most likely counties in Ireland as well. A new strategy was called for. There were a few more leads that could be tackled in the San Francisco area, but before making yet another trip there, it might be useful to try to explore more fully historical information from Ireland freely available online instead. These would be different sources than the vital records databases the genealogy centers had searched for a fee.

Until the discovery from his San Francisco death certificate was made showing my grandfather Patrick had hailed from Roscommon, not Donegal as originally thought, the focus of research had been on County Donegal for both grandparents. As far as my grandmother's heritage was concerned, it remained that way since no facts contradicting my mother's statements had been uncovered to this point. So continuing to concentrate on that county as well as Roscommon still seemed like a reasonable approach and a more thorough investigation of sources on the Web could well be the ticket for gaining further ground. Basic research guidebooks identified two essential Irish genealogy sources that could be accessed on the internet in abridged forms—*Griffith's Primary Valuation of Ireland* and the *Tithe Applotment Books.*

Both of these surveys were conducted in the 1800s in order to gather data for tax assessment purposes on those farming land, either as owners or as tenant occupants. Revenues collected from rate payers, based on the of amount land and buildings held, either went to the Church of Ireland, that is to say the Protestant church, to support the poor as in the instance of the *Tithe*, or served to support the Poor Law Union, as in the case of *Griffith's.*

Created by the 1838 Poor Law Act, the Poor Law Unions were geographical areas intended to financially aid paupers within their jurisdiction by taxing the inhabitants. Each of the initial one hundred and thirty, later expanded to one hundred and sixty-three, Poor Law Unions had a workhouse in which the poorest of the poor sometimes ended up and these workhouses were infamous for often having worse conditions than what they had left behind them. Perhaps the hardest thing to bear was the tearing apart of families under the workhouse model. The PLUs served the purpose as districts for civil registration to which administration of housing, health and sanitation were added as functions within its boundaries as it evolved over time. In conducting Irish research, the introduction of the PLU was one more layer of administrative division further complicating matters. Counties, baronies, district electoral divisions, dioceses, civil and religious parishes, Poor Law Unions, and townlands all with different boundaries, coexisted and overlapped in Ireland of that era in what at times must have been a bureaucratic nightmare.

The importance of the *Tithe* and *Griffith's* surveys cannot be overstated in associating specific surnames of individuals with small places. Both of them form part of what is termed in genealogy jargon as "census substitutes". In other words, they help to fill the void left by the destruction of many of the original nineteenth century paper censuses in Ireland for which no other copies existed. Akin to the loss of the earlier civil birth, marriage and death records in San Francisco resulting from the 1906 earthquake and fire, the disastrous loss of Irish decennial census records covering the huge span of years between 1821 and 1851 places a high, but not always insurmountable, barrier to finding links to ancestors during the period. The first organized census in Ireland was the one surveyed in 1821 so nearly nothing exists before that date that is equivalent in terms of comprehensive description of names of individuals of all economic strata and the places they lived. Making the matters worse is that the censuses from 1861 to 1891 are gone as well.

What happened to these censuses? Sifting through the various analyses of their destruction there does seem to be some degree of consensus. There is no argument these later four survey returns of 1861, 1871, 1881 and 1891 were intentionally destroyed during the First World War, probably in the year of 1918, by order of the Irish government. Where there is disagreement it is over whether or not these records were pulped to create new paper to support the war effort. The earlier census returns, those of 1821 through 1851, were destroyed during the Irish Civil War in 1922. They were burned during the fighting that took place at the Public Records Office in Dublin. The disagreement here, though, is over which side was more responsible for their destruction, those supporting the treaty with England or those opposed to it. Regardless, the net result for researchers hoping to find their Irish ancestors through meticulous examination of historic censuses is at best—very limited. Of the older censuses only the 1901 and 1911 remain intact and available to the researcher. These two remaining surveys are very useful despite a robust taint of doubt as to the accuracy of some of the data collected, especially ages of the household members.

Both of the census substitutes, the *Tithe*, conducted between 1823 and 1838, and *Griffith's*, surveyed over the years 1848 to1864, collected data from occupants of dwellings with respect to name of occupier (occupant), exact townland location, acres of land and buildings held. Map coordinates for the land corresponding to maps drawn at the time are also provided in *Griffith's*. The main value of these records is the association of the occupant with a county, parish, townland and specific plot of land with or without buildings. And while family members are not listed, having resources which establish a connection between the single name provided and a geographical area helps to hone in on the trail of possible ancestors. Using the online *Griffith's* websites to search for the surnames of both my grandmother's parents produced results that did seem to indicate their names were well represented in the Inishowen area of County Donegal. Where the Diocese of Derry extended its boundaries beyond those of County Derry itself and into County Donegal appeared to hold a particularly strong likelihood as being a possible place of origin for my grandmother, Rose. No cast iron conclusions could be drawn, however, for there could be many other regions of the county, or the country as a whole, where a surname/geographical area association could be found in concentrated abundance as well. But at the minimum, this area was definitely ruled in rather than out.

It was now time to temporarily put online research aside and get back into the car to see if the missing all-important place of birth in Ireland could yet be found somewhere in the musty record vaults of San Francisco. That my grandfather, Patrick Cavanagh, was from Roscommon had been determined by his death certificate obtained in the city. But the town of birth had been left blank, without which it would be very difficult to ultimately secure concrete proof of his birth through an official Irish birth certificate record. In mentally reaching out, a kind of lateral thinking, for anything else that could have recorded his presence that might still have a chance of remaining in existence somewhere, two details from the Holy Cross Cemetery card sprang to mind. The first was the notation of the undertaker's company name and the second was the place of death—the Laguna Honda Home.

The name Laguna Honda in connection with San Francisco sounded vaguely familiar to me but no actual contextual meaning could be generated from my memory bank other than a feeling. A funeral home going by the name of Joseph Fogerty and Sons looked like the easier task to pursue, even though some seventy-five years had elapsed in the meantime. So it was back to the computer and the internet to see if by some far out chance a funeral director still existed under the same name. Online telephone directories for San Francisco turned out to be wanting and the search was soon opened to the wider Web. After some trial and error using different search terms, a snippet of history was found that linked the old Fogarty's with a funeral firm currently in business called Duffy's. Over the course of several weeks several phone calls were placed that eventually resulted in establishing that long ago Duffy's had indeed replaced Fogarty's, inheriting a portion of the latter's files of which some were believed to have been kept but were not located at the current business premises. The old-timer who provided the information was the institutional memory, having worked for both firms in his day. He promised to get back to me soon. But since he didn't, I called him again. He said that he had checked the files and the older record dates that applied to my grandfather's era were no longer among them. They had probably been destroyed long ago. So another long wait with fairly high expectations had come to naught and one more door slammed shut.

Sights were shifted and set on the second alternative—the Laguna Honda Home. Some background information had already been gathered during the weeks waiting for a response from the funeral home. Holy Cross Cemetery information had confirmed the fact of the early use of the spelling variant Kavanaugh instead of Cavanagh by my grandfather. Another look at the 1900 and 1880 censuses for the Kavanaugh spelling seemed worthwhile, especially since the address of his residence in 1888 was among the details given on the cemetery card, but neither census year included a listing for him. Next, the list of all Cavanagh and Kavanaugh directory entries for San Francisco that had been transcribed earlier was reviewed for any address congruity. Low and behold there was a Patrick Kavanaugh that matched addresses with the cemetery card! What differed from census surveys taking place in more recent decades when he was older was his occupation: he was listed as a coach driver.

The faint sensation of coming across the Laguna Honda name sometime in the past was borne out after looking again at the paper map of San Francisco. It must have been during the earlier plotting of the Catholic parishes on the city map that I had noticed a large yellow shaded area in the Twin Peaks neighborhood, up over the hill and not too distant from Noe Valley, labeled Laguna Honda. And now reexamining the map brought about another recollection of seeing the words Laguna Honda somewhere else. A 1930 census entry for a Patrick Cavanagh that had I found and rejected as not belonging to my grandfather because it neither listed Rose's nor my mother's name in conjunction with his own now appeared worthy of another look. It also had been dismissed for a second reason: the word *inmate* had been entered into the "Relation" column and the address given was the Laguna Honda Home, which appeared as if it could be some sort of correctional facility.

But now this census entry took on renewed significance as it matched my grandfather's cemetery and death certificate address details. And upon closer scrutiny of the top area of the census page, a note in parenthesis next to Laguna Honda Home shed further light on the kind of place that it actually was. In small tight handwriting it read "Relief Home for the Aged and Infirm". So it was not a kind of prison after all. And the term "inmate" instead of denoting a prisoner now appeared to be an antiquated synonym for someone who today would be called a patient. Rejected before for the same reasons, a 1920 census entry for an inmate by the name of Patrick Cavanagh residing at a "Relief Home" was restored to its rightful place of relevance as well.

What was termed by the census taker as Relief Home or Laguna Honda Home turned out to be an iconic landmark in the history of San Francisco, iconic for its prominent location, for its imposing size, and for the long-term role it in played in caring for those without means. Founded in 1866, Laguna Honda first opened its doors in 1867 as the City and County Alms House or the Alms House for the Poor. Later the name was changed to the Relief Home of the Aged and Infirm, and again changed to the Laguna Honda Home in 1926 and eventually to the Laguna Honda Hospital. Throughout its operation of over 140 years, this public care facility—currently known as the Laguna Honda Hospital and Rehabilitation Center—has gone through many incarnations but has basically served as a kind of nursing home of last resort for the indigent and elderly poor, the disabled and the chronically ill during each of them.

So why did my grandfather end his days in this public nursing home? What circumstances had brought him to its doorstep in the first place? To try to get to the bottom of these and other questions, a side stopover to San Francisco was squeezed into a previously planned trip to Contra Costa County on the other side of the Bay. As my wife and I drove up to the site, the size and placement of the buildings, done in Mediterranean revival style, took us totally by surprise. The institution was massive and dominantly situated on a hill. It must have been one of the largest buildings in the city at the time it was constructed. Evidently built to last for the long term, it could bed as many as twelve to thirteen hundred residents at one time in a pinch. Working our way up the floors, the office responsible for all patient files was reached. To say the least, an inquiry about a patient from so long ago raised eyebrows—and maybe a little suspicion too.

As could be expected of a huge, bureaucratic, public entity, several forms had to be filled out. But once this initial obstacle had been willingly surmounted, the institutional resistance increased and additional terms of engagement were laid down. First we were told that there would be a fee charged because an old file such as his would need to be searched and retrieved from an offsite storage facility in an unspecified location in the city. It would take a week or more to complete this process. If that wasn't enough dissuasion, and you could see by the look in their eyes that it was meant to be just that, the next requirement halted the whole business even before it had hardly been started. In view of their record confidentially policy, indisputable documentary proof was necessary that showed I was a direct descendant of my grandfather. I would need a certificate of my birth showing my mother's name, proof of my mother's birth with her father's name clearly present and marriage documents for my mother and her father before any patient information could be released. This was their policy even though it had been over seventy-five years since my grandfather had passed away. It was essential that the documents irrefutably made clear the generational connections. Empty handed for the moment but not willing to let them deter me, I vowed without a flinch to return with the needed documents and a check to cover the search amount within a couple of weeks' time.

It took a little longer than hoped for to get back to Laguna Honda, but the ladies' expressions reflected instant recognition as we approached their counter once again. We must have impressed them during our first visit by a resolute attitude indicating that we would not be denied. As soon as we presented the necessary documents and wrote out a check for payment, they instantly produced a brown envelope handily stowed away in a nearby location. They had gone ahead and ordered my grandfather's file to be retrieved from the storage facility in advance, before having evidence of the fulfillment of their regulations, and had it ready for our return. Thus, we were spared another week or two of waiting, and probably another drive to San Francisco, by their understanding of the mission we were on and by their forethought. In handing over the information, a caveat, almost an apology, was spoken before we opened it: his file was one of those that had held a minimum of data. Their eyes searched our faces for any sign of disappointment when we pulled out of the envelope what essentially amounted to two brief pages. Maybe even a worry that we might insist on a refund was in their minds but they needn't have been concerned because no such request would be forthcoming from us since anything that came into our possession from such a long time past could be chalked up as a victory.

While his record was limited in size, what it accomplished wasn't. It consisted of the actual application for admission to the Relief Home for the Aged and Infirm, Department of Public Health, and was dated 1918. My grandfather's name, age, and name and address of last employer were all clearly spelled out. These details conformed to both the Holy Cross Cemetery and census details already in hand but now I knew the exact date he had made the transition from home life to hospital care. As a bonus, the name of his last employer, the Board of Public Works in San Francisco, was entered on the form too. This information gave credence to a tentative assumption that had been made based on the type of occupation listed for him in one of the census records that gave the appearance he could have been a public employee. Now there was no doubt it.

Another piece of data on the admission application had a twofold impact. In the blank entitled "Children's names" was a single name: "Mary". It was followed by the notation "8 yrs", and the address was shown as "with wife". It was now absolutely one hundred percent certain that the "inmate" in Laguna Honda was indeed my grandfather and, by concurrence with her baptismal record, a certainty that my mother had been born in the year of 1910.

The reason why he became a resident at the home was now also demystified: under the heading "physical condition" on the application, "chronic rheumatism" was stated. And in the only known sample of his handwriting, the shaky signature, "P Cavanaugh", which chattered and jerked across the bottom of the form, gave vivid testimony to the suffering he was experiencing as he wrote it, which, by then, had become his permanent state of health. So he had not been one of aged or infirm homeless residents, rather someone who had become chronically ill and handicapped who had obviously been forced by poor health circumstances to give up his job— and apparently his family as well. It appeared from the 1920 census—the first one that listed only my grandmother and my mother together at the same address without my grandfather— that he had spent the last years of his life in this institution, for him a sanatorium, leaving Rose by herself to raise my mother from the age of eight onwards. How did she manage to be mother, homemaker and breadwinner from the end of World War I through those difficult years ahead that were a prelude to the Great Depression?

As valuable as this nursing home admission record was in learning more about him and Rose, it still had not answered the burning question of my grandfather's specific place of origin. If there had been just two more blanks on the form, one for country of nativity and another for town of birth, I would have been well on my way to finding his family roots in Ireland. Why hadn't someone considered these integral pieces of information to be of importance?

ROOKS

Donegal, Ireland, March 1892

John Harte was tired and hot. Very hot. It had been bizarre weather for the past two days. It was only late March when the temperatures should have been still cool and typically drizzly but the sun had shone itself like it was the middle of a dreamed of, but seldom seen, Irish summer. Each day the temperature had inched its way up another couple of notches causing the sweat to poor off the brows of the unaccustomed native laborers. Even the rooks that for generations had inhabited the estate trees seemed to be acting strangely, almost if they were driven aggressively half mad by the sweltering sun, or perhaps by being threatened by the unusual presence of intruders into their lofty territory.

Three of them, John and two other local lads, were doing roof repair on the main house of the nearby McClellan estate. A terrific gale that had preceded the current hot spell by only a week had blown off slates in several spots and damaged portions of the eves as well. It was not the kind of weather that one would pick on purpose to be directly exposed to for any length of time, but when a decent paying opportunity calling for immediate attention came along once in a blue moon there was no thought of turning it down. For John, it was like a gift horse to be jumped on and rode without hesitation and there was no question for him of not seizing the reigns and doing so.

The owner's representative wanted the roof work done now, before the weather took a turn back to the more normal spring downpours. And the extra hard cash that he would be bringing in could make things just that much easier for Rose and himself when the time came to start their new life. Their moment was almost upon them; this was the month during which they would take their leave. They did not consider it running away—they simply thought they had waited long enough to be together and eagerly looked forward to the challenges and surprises that lay before them. For nearly two years they had bided their time, seeing each other only sporadically but with no less commitment each time, rather just the opposite, with ever the same united devotion to their goal of striking out for America.

Two months previously they had separately booked passage on the same ship now leaving in just four days time, a ship named the Norwegian. It would be departing from Glasgow then calling at Moville to pick up Irish emigrants before traversing the Atlantic. Only a few of their closest friends were privy to their plans to sail aboard the same ship together. Preparations for departure had been done within their respective family households, independently, and without the slightest knowledge that the two of them would soon be uniting as a couple when they reached new shores. In the end they had thought it best to let feathers stay unruffled at home and let distance serve as the peacemaker in a land far enough away where traditional religious differences were said to be no longer a thorn in the side.

But every last effort of labor they made figured into the amount they could accumulate and put towards settlement in America. Every bead of sweat that fell from their brows now could be counted and converted into a stake that would make the future life they envisioned attainable much sooner. John could wash his dark black hair and scrub the dirt off his angular face and lean body at the end of the day while knowing he had done his best before leaving. Once they set foot in their new land Rose reasoned she would take up domestic work at first, while he would engage in manual labor of some sort to get started. He was clever with his hands and should not have much trouble in finding employment quickly from what they had learned about the kind of work opportunities needed there. After getting established, perhaps even a small business that they could run together would be in their future. They had not been reluctant to roll up their sleeves in Ireland and they held no fear of hard work in securing their livelihoods and the kind of life they wanted and dreamed of in America.

John and Rose agreed they would not meet again until after boarding the ship. They would be just two among the some four hundred steerage, or third class, passengers who were set to make a steamship journey of about ten days to two weeks before reaching their New York destination if all went according to normal crossing expectations. Once on board they would be free to be together openly for the first time and would be able to share each other's company without looking over their shoulders during the passage. It would be an immense relief in putting behind them all of the past pressures and anxieties they had experienced. John intended to take a liner-tender paddle steamer from the quay at the Port of Derry onto Moville, where the Norwegian, moored in deeper waters offshore, would lay by to board more passengers. For Rose, members of her family would take her by road directly to

Moville itself, a coastal town much closer to her home than to John's, and see her off from there.

It was strange. As each day passed, drawing ever closer to the sailing date, the hours of a day seemed to stretch out absurdly long from rising to bedtime while at the same time it felt as if there were not enough minutes and seconds to allow her to meaningfully share in the usual daily activities with her family before parting. Outdoors, near the turf stacks, Rose was thinking again on just this—how it could be both of these sensations coexisted at the same time within her—when her mother, speaking through an open window, interrupted these thoughts.

"Margaret's been to the post office and had a card from Mary. Did she show it to you yet?"

Dashing into the house, Rose nearly knocked into her mother who was starting to prepare the evening meal. "Is everything all right? She's still there, isn't she? Has something happened? Will she still be at the dock in New York waiting for…looking out for me?" Just in the nick of time she had bitten her tongue. She had almost let slip the word "us" instead of the singular "me".

"Well, my dear, there it rests on the table and you can read it for yourself. Of course your sister will be there to meet you. Why wouldn't she be?" Little more was said on the postcard as the writing space was cramped and words squeezed in sparingly as was the habit of the times. But it was enough to satisfy her, and it had arrived just at the right time to tame some of her mounting jitters before the impending departure.

Mary, sticking to her plans, had left Ireland for America a little less than two years before, striking shore in late August of 1890. She had passed through New York City's Castle Garden immigration facilities with little trouble, young and healthy at the age of twenty-four. As optimistic and directed as she always was, even Mary was shaken by the sheer number of immigrants passing through immigration controls. As days and weeks passed by following her arrival, the multitudes of newcomers beating the pavement for work and the overcrowded living conditions she encountered in "Little Ireland" on the lower east side, her first place of residence, had added to her disenchantment. She counted herself among the lucky ones, make no mistake, for in only a few weeks after her arrival she found herself employed as servant help for a wealthy family living on Fifth Avenue.

But her disillusionment with the atmosphere of the city that had developed early would not be easily shed. And she had vowed to herself that New York would only be a temporary stop on her way towards Boston, a place that carried with it a reputation of being more welcoming and hospitable and one, she believed, holding a greater chance for a single Irish woman to make her way. She would not allow herself to budge, however, until the second wayward Cameron, her sister Rose, arrived and had had a chance to become familiar with her new American surroundings. So, she had found a boarding house in Brooklyn, much less expensive and crowded than Little Ireland, and the commute to her job was not a difficult one. Her last postcard sent home, the one that had just arrived in Donegal, had been sent precisely to reassure her sister that she would be there to meet her at the port of entry. She would never let her sister down by leaving her stranded even if she would be with someone else. Of course she was wise enough not to mention John in it even though Rose had made her well-aware of their plans to voyage together.

Her two suitcases packed and tucked away in a corner of the cottage, Rose could do no more than try to occupy the remaining hours by continuing with the routine of her daily chores. Like her sister Mary's leaving two years before, she preferred a low-key farewell without any additional fanfare. Her father's and mother's offers to take her to Derry one last time or to leave off their farming and home activities for a day or two to stay by her were firmly rebuffed as unnecessary. Indeed, she wanted to take with her memories of their normal comings and goings, just as they had been each day as she passed through childhood into the young woman she had now become. But it proved impossible to act the same way with friends and other relations living close by as she could with her own family so she could not altogether avoid their wishes to spend extra time with her before she left. Her uncles, aunts and cousins either stopped by or she felt obligated to go to their houses to pay a last visit with them there. She would dearly miss them all but would place her trust in the mail to stay in touch by writing to the younger generation who, unlike a good many of their parents, could both read and write. Of course she set aside time to spend with her best friend, Casey, on each of the remaining days, especially to talk about John while strolling privately around their village. They, too, remarked constantly on the abnormally, almost unheard of, hot weather, seeking out shaded wooded areas where they could stay a bit cooler during their walking and talking sojourns. Casey brought with her news of John when she had it. She did her best to extract and collect any snippet from a branch of her family who lived not far from the Harte farm and could now pass on what she had learned.

"John's family wants him put his tools aside and to give it up to get ready to leave. But he says they're almost finished with the house repair and he's not about to stop until it's done. He's working so hard in this heat…I don't know. It will be a miracle if he does manage to finish up without exhausting himself," were the first words out of her mouth as soon as they parted company from the others and were free to speak alone.

"There'll no be stopping him if he's set his mind to it. Besides, if he's like me, and I've no doubt that he is, he wants to fill the time and give over to counting hours until we leave. He'll be thinking that there'll be enough time to rest up later on the crossing."

"You're right there. Sure, he's one for keeping his nose to the grind. You're fortunate, Rose, he's…the two of you will do well together there's no question. One day I may be able to make the trip too." But this was said only half-heartedly. Casey's situation was different. Her mother was often unwell and Casey was needed to fill her role in caring for her, sharing out the duties with other family members. She knew that for the time being her place was at home.

"It would be a dream to have you there too, if you do come."

"Wouldn't we have a grand time together", she sighed.

"A grand old time, indeed", Rose echoed

Today's promenade took them on a path that led up the brae, through the heather and peat fields around and down the other side of the steep hill. At times they had glimpses of Crockadaddy, Crockglass and other local mountains framing their landscape to the west. As they rambled and talked, Rose's let her senses take in the countless shades of green, soft tans and freshly plowed dark brown fields, drawn in patchworks by the boundaries of the farms, which meandered in undulating tiers descending to the Foyle seaside on one side of them and rising to the edge of the barren heights of the distant hilltops on the other. Consciously, she let her gaze linger longer at each view, committing the images to a different region of her brain, one where picture memories would stay locked away and be everlasting. The scenes, scents, the springy feel of earth to her feet would not be lost once she had left this place of her birth and childhood. They would stay tattooed on her soul no matter where she and John would eventually put down new roots. And they would always be there within her, to compare and to measure all other surroundings against.

Her thoughts, too, drifted to the times when family togetherness was especially intense—the celebration of Halloweve with its superstitions, the other special nights at St. Brendan's and Christmas Eves, the stories of Irish folk legends on magical evenings, or the family gatherings on Easter Sunday. These memories, too, would remain magically imprinted on her soul. But as they reached the outskirts of her home, her focus of attention returned to John. In her mind, she felt she could almost reach out and touch him then the urgency to actually convert thoughts into a reality sent a tingling sensation that crept through her body from her toes to her fingertips while filling her heart to the brim.

The last three days took their drawn-out course, winding down way too gradually in some ways for the likes of the both of them, but finally the dawn broke of the day before their departure. There was one more thing Rose had waited to the last moment to do, one more image that she wanted to hold fast in her host of stored memories before taking her leave. The old cemetery of the parish church, the resting place of ancestors who had paved the road ahead for generations in the past, must be visited one last time. With its assortment of maintained and unlooked after graves, some with flat markers others with standing headstones, often listing in one direction or another, high crosses and basic rectangular slabs, individual and group plots mixed together with those having no markers at all, indicating poorer families, the small cemetery was the embodiment of the legacy of her family and their small community in a nutshell. Rose, rising early, wanted to make this personal pilgrimage alone and had told her family she would not be long but would be back in time to sit with them for the morning meal. When she returned to join them, she no longer felt anxious. The few minutes at the cemetery had had the effect of bringing on calmness, a certain peace of mind unwinding the tensions accumulated over the past few days.

She knew she was more than ready to take the next step.

As for John, he was equally as ready as she was. Incredibly, the heat had continued to build to even greater intensity during the last few days and the three workmen could not wait to be done with the roof repair. Starting as early in the morning after sunrise as light permitted to beat the heat and to be able to complete everything on John's last day of work, they toiled relentlessly until taking a late break to sit in the shade to slake their thirst and to eat a bite. There was only one last tricky area to get to in the afternoon: under the front eve a hole had been left after a piece of siding had torn loose. They wondered how they could get close enough to have a go at patching over the cumbersome area properly. Hugh, turning to John and Peter was the first to suggest an idea.

"Even though it's so high and awkwardly located, do you think we could get at it by first attaching some short lengths of wood to the upper rungs of both of the ladders to make a brace at the same height for each of them? The braces should be just long enough to butt against the wall. We'll nail a cleat into the wall under each one to make sure it won't slide down the wall. Then we'll lay a plank across so a man could free both hands to make the repair."

John looked at Peter and shook his head. "We don't have much in the way of proper timber.

Don't know if what we do have would be strong enough to hold a man's weight, Hugh." But neither of them could think of another idea so they grew quiet for a moment.

"You know, lads, we could give it a try on lower rungs first to see if the support works and is steady enough, too," Peter finally suggested. "We don't want it wobbling about on us, so."

"I'd go along with that. Would that do for you?" Hugh asked John.

And so they decided to give it a try. Each one took turns walking across to test it, and while it gave a bit in the middle, it seemed to hold fine under each of their weights. The sag was the least when, John, the lightest of them, nimbly stepped to the center of the board. Convinced now that it would hold and was safe, they fixed it into position on attached braces off the upper level rungs, moved the plank up then took turns using their makeshift scaffolding. Only one man could be working at a time while the other two steadied the ladders to prevent any shaking or shifting.

With the last of the work in sight and their platform holding stable, even though the sizzling heat of the late afternoon had worn them down to a frazzle, John took the final turn to complete the job before they allowed themselves any rest. Earlier in the day they had all remarked on how this kind of extreme weather had made the cows jumpy. They had seen them on more than one occasion acting as if something had spooked them into behaving jittery. For whatever reason they would run together as a group in one direction only to suddenly turn and head off in another direction the next instant. And their loud anxious lowing to one another was extraordinary for the time of day when they normally would be resting under trees or lazily grazing. It was like they were calling out that it was time to be milked when milking was still hours away.

John, standing on the perch, peered over his right shoulder and downwards to see more than one whirlwind of dry leaves swirling and dancing only inches above the gravel walkways when one bunch soared upwards like a small cyclone, for now strong, gusty breezes had joined with the anomaly of overwhelming heat. As he turned back towards the eve to continue working, out of nowhere and without warning, a small army of swooping, squawking, madly flapping black projectiles set upon him.

The rooks were in full assault!

His arms and hands shot to his head and face to protect himself in an involuntary reaction. But in his reaction his balance was lost. He tried to regain his footing but his left foot found nothing but air, missing the plank altogether. A cry bellowed from his mouth so strong it might have been heard from miles away.

What caused the birds to behave the way they did will never be known but perhaps it was like with the cows, a kind of madness that had addled their brains brought on by the dire weather conditions, or perhaps it was defensive reaction to a territorial or nesting disturbance that had stirred them into a frenzy, or perhaps something else completely unfathomable had startled them, taking them away from their usual behavior. Whatever the reason, John, unable to regain his balance, had just enough presence of mind to recall in a flash that directly under the scaffolding were sizeable, unforgiving stones. So in the split second he had to try and guide his fall, he pushed off the wall with one hand and sprung out and away from the side of the house with the remaining foot, an instinctive maneuver which might just as well have saved his life.

It happened so fast that Peter and Hugh, hesitated for just a moment, stunned and frozen in their tracks in disbelief, before scrambling to John's side: the fall had not rendered him unconscious. With pain spread across his contorted face, a few words could be understood through the groans.

"It's my leg…it's…there was a…a snap."

Their eyes immediately went to both his legs. It was clear at once by the angle of the lower right leg that it was broken, and when they saw the sharp point of the bone protruding from the skin they knew it for sure.

"It's broken, John. We can see where. Don't try to move. There's nothing else we can see yet." Peter continued to talk to him as calmly as he could while Hugh carefully checked his body for other injuries.

"I can't find any other wounds. Are you hurting badly anywhere else? Tell us if you can John?"

Since he complained of no other injury, and as soon as the initial shock had slightly subsided, they began to ponder on what to do next. Hugh's home was the closest so it was decided to take him there. Then from there Peter would leave to fetch a doctor. Supporting his arms and body weight on their shoulders, placing their inner hands under his thighs to make sure his legs were never close enough to the ground to risk dragging them, and moving as carefully as possible to avoid any jarring, the procession of the trio moved slowly but steadily, stopping many times for breathers before reaching their destination as late afternoon was turning to dusk. By then it was already too late for Peter to travel to Derry for the doctor and return that night so it was decided he would start before sunrise next morning instead. John lay the night between stabs of sharp pain and unrelenting aches throughout his body, half conscious, with only the dreams of Rose racing through his head to give him peace.

The fates had rudely spoken.

His departure for America was more than in jeopardy, it was now beyond possible with a badly fractured leg, and there was nothing he could do about it. Given the height from which he had fallen, he was lucky to still be alive.

SCHOOLS

San Francisco/Peninsula, California, February-March 2007

Could there be any other way to determine where my grandmother, Rose Cameron, was actually born in Ireland? There must be. The uncovering of her husband's—my grandfather Patrick's—nursing home admission record as well as his death certificate, both within the confines of San Francisco, were strategic in tracing their history as a couple. Much more could now be established about the course of his life and his county of origin in Ireland but nothing really had been gained, nothing revealed, towards pinpointing Rose's precise place of birth. What else could possibly provide this information that had been overlooked so far?

As for the end of her life, an equally gaping information hole existed. All of the health department and cemetery efforts to locate death information had resulted in absolutely nothing. By virtue of their very absence, a nagging question persisted over the possibility that she may have left San Francisco, even California, to live elsewhere before she died. This scenario did not seem to fit the known facts, however, since my grandfather had died in San Francisco and my mother, although older and independent, had continued to live in the city until she married my father, years after her father's death. The timing of her separation from her mother could be clearly documented through the trail of addresses and occupations listed in the San Francisco city directories during the late 1920's and first half of the 1930s. No, something was amiss. And even though the last mention of Rose under her married surname of Cavanagh occurred in the 1922 directory, the fuzzy recollection my grandmother may have remarried and my mother may have had a step-father made its return. This could be the explanation. My grandmother and her second husband living still in San Francisco, but under a surname different from my grandfather's, seemed like a theory that could hold water and definitely worth pursuing.

Since it was nearing the time of year when income tax returns were due, the idea that the information contained in old tax records could be of value and might still be stored somewhere by the federal government came to mind. As thorny of a proposition this could pose, it just might be worth trying to deal with the Internal Revenue Service to see if it was possible for a grandson to obtain old tax returns, or at least portions thereof, long ago submitted by his grandparents for family history purposes. One thing was almost certain— they must have filed returns during their lifetimes.

Getting past the recorded instructions on the phone to reach an actual human being was the first hurdle to be cleared. Round and round I went trying to figure out which phone button when pressed might do the trick of getting me past the automatic system and into a queue for talking to a representative. When I finally did manage to reach a real human, the nature of my request was so uncommon and peculiar that I was passed onto a series of other IRS staff all of whom were unable to answer my question and unsure of where to transfer me next. It was trial by error for them, a guessing game.

On and off again over several days I repeated my phone explanations until someone finally seemed to understand why I was seeking tax records of relatives from the early 1900s. By this person, said to be of some authority on the matter on older tax records, I was told in short order that records were only retained about seven or so years; the prior ones were destroyed. Having little faith that this was actually true and still believing that there was good chance old records were held somewhere, either without the knowledge of most IRS employees, or with instructions not to divulge that they were, I was not ready to throw in the towel just yet. So sure was I that a second employee was ultimately contacted on a different day who basically gave the same response. Without the wherewithal to spend any more time going further down this road, I decided I had to accept this as a dead end and let it drop.

In light of the lack of positive results from requests placed earlier with most of the genealogy information centers in the province of Ulster, a more extensive, in-depth search by a local Donegal expert seemed like a good idea to try next. The centers had only been given the most meager details—my grandmother's name, a range of possible birth years, and names of her parents—because these were all I possessed. The sources they searched were limited to comprehensive databases of church baptisms. There was no computerized data base of civil birth, marriage or death records at that time; a search of these records was done manually through the paper book indexes or their microform equivalents leading to the full paper or microfilmed records themselves, a time consuming activity to say the least.

So with a growing sense of frustration bordering on

desperation, the Web was used once again to search for businesses, preferably located in Ulster, which could perform more extensive research using a greater range of family history research tools at their disposal. Without much trouble one was found that appeared to offer the kind of thoroughgoing research desired at a reasonable cost. To assist the researcher in narrowing the investigation to the most likely geographical area of interest, a list of the townlands in Donegal, Derry and other nearby counties found earlier in *Griffith's,* which corresponded to my great-grandfather's name of Denis Cameron, was provided, along with two possible dates of birth of my grandmother, Rose, noted in the U.S. federal censuses covering San Francisco. A recently found passenger listing fitting what I knew at this stage, without any certainty attached to it, was also sent to him. It wasn't much, but the researcher agreed to take the project on with the caveat of needing a minimum of a couple of months to carry out the investigation.

Meanwhile, my attention returned to San Francisco and trying to brainstorm on what other traces of my mother and her parents could still be out there which remained unexplored. Recalling that she had mentioned that nuns were involved in her schooling, and especially their use of physical discipline when they found it necessary to make a point , I wondered if there was a chance that her school records still existed in a church archives somewhere in the city. Using the same process as I had for the parishes, I plotted out on a map the closest Catholic schools that had existed during her school days based on listings in old San Francisco city directories in relation to the various addresses I had identified for her family. Most of the lower schools were attached to parish churches, including the most obvious one—the one where she was baptized—Saint Peters. Unlike parish baptismal records for Catholic churches in San Francisco that were housed as a microfilm collection in the Roman Catholic Archives, there was no single place that kept all of the old Catholic school records. They had not been put on microfilm and the parishes at some point must have decided, in case of a disaster or for other reasons, it was better for each one of them to retain their own original paper records, as they had with the original bound baptism registers. Decentralization had its security advantages in this respect but doesn't make things any easier for the information seeker.

Ever helpful and organized, the staff at the church of St. Peter wasted no time in checking through the school's files but in the end were unsuccessful in finding my mother's name among them. This was particularly disheartening because the high school of St. Peter's offered a program that concentrated on commercial skills, the same skills that my mother had somewhere acquired before starting work immediately after high school graduation. So it was on to the next closest high school to where she had lived and so on for the next few weeks, moving further afield with each new attempt, until even the remotest ones had been contacted unsuccessfully. Downcast somewhat by how difficult it was to lay hands on records of my mother's past and calling my own faulty memory into question once again, an approach that widened the circle of school records beyond Catholic schools was embarked upon. Once again, old San Francisco city directories corresponding to my mother's school years between 1914 and 1927 were plowed through to identify which public high schools existed in proximity to where she lived at the time:

Lowell, Polytechnic, Mission, Galileo, High School of Commerce, and Girl's High School were the ones that emerged as viable candidates.

Next, on the internet, each high school was researched individually to see if it still existed today and could be contacted. Surprisingly, all of them, with the exception of High School of Commerce and Girl's High School, continued to be in operation. During this process it was noted that all of these currently functioning public high schools, along with many other primary and secondary schools, were now under the umbrella of the San Francisco Unified School District. With a bit more searching of the Web, the office responsible for transcripts for the SFUSD was found. A phone call was immediately placed to the office to see if they, perchance, still retained student records from bygone times. A positive reply that they did was contravened by the fact that they were short staffed with only two people currently in the office. With the daily demands placed upon their time for assistance to the schools there was little chance they would have time in the foreseeable future to look through a microform collection of old school records for my mother's.

In the ensuing weeks several more follow-up attempts were made to vocally demonstrate my unwavering interest in having the files searched. Return calls were promised each time I phoned but never made. I even offered to make a trip to San Francisco to look through the microfiche myself but was told that policy did not allow non-staff to peruse school records even if a direct relationship to the former student could be proven. Finally, after several months of waiting, I phoned again and this time someone was reached who had the authority and was agreeable to making the effort to carry out a search if I faxed to her all of the details I had about my mother as well as a list of the high schools with the strongest likelihood of her attendance. First on the list was the High School of Commerce, mainly because of its strengths similar to its Catholic counterpart of St. Peter's in teaching secretarial skills such as stenography, short hand and typing. Two days later I received a call back with the great news that my mother's record had been found and her transcript could be mailed to me, if I wanted. Boy, did I ever!

It looked like my memory of my mother speaking once about the nuns she had at Catholic school for teachers must have been purely imaginative. I had wasted a good deal of time in going down the wrong track—again. As promised, the envelope duly arrived in a couple of days time and although there was a degree of initial disappointment because the document copies it contained did not mention birthplace of either my grandmother or my grandfather, the rest of the information was very interesting. Three documents had been found. The first entitled *Registration of Minors Under 18 Years of Age* showed the names of both Patrick and Rose Cavanagh, their address, my mother's name and birth date, the school she was attending and grade she was in. The second was a copy of her *Permanent Record Report* from the *San Francisco High School of Commerce*, the very same school which was at the top of my list and the first one searched by the staff member! She was pleased her work had been made much easier than anticipated. I had made the right deduction and, ironically, the high school building was located only two short blocks away, on Van Ness and Grove, from the new San Francisco Public Library and the Department of Health where much of my previous research had taken place.

This official transcript had her grades in each of the subjects she had taken and at the bottom of the sheet it was noted she had graduated in December of 1929. Along with the usual subjects, she had taken typewriting, shorthand, bookkeeping and penmanship, as surmised. No wonder my mother's handwriting was so fine and elegant! The third sheet proved to be an unexpected bonus for it testified to the fact that she had spent her first years of high school at St. Vincent's, a Catholic school, before transferring to High School of Commerce for her last two years. It also contained all of the grades and credits for the various subjects she had undertaken while at St Vincent's.

Vindicated that my efforts in searching for Catholic schools had not been misguided, I wondered if a San Francisco genealogy website I had often consulted before might include the yearbook for the year when she graduated from the public high school and her name might appear among the transcribed list of students. Regrettably, other years around her own were covered but not hers. It had been noted in previous visits to the San Francisco Public Library that they also had a historical collection of San Francisco high school yearbooks and this time, by telephone, luck was with me; they did have the year I was looking for. Even though they could not lend this particular type of item, they were willing to pull it from the shelves and thumb through it. And after having done so, they assured me that both my mother's name and photo were in it. Appetite now totally whetted, I turned back to the internet, to one of the major buying and selling websites, and found a copy of this 1929 yearbook available for sale. Amazingly, within a few days I had the copy in my hands. Within its tattered binding, sure enough, there was a page perfectly preserved with my mother's photo, looking very Roaring Twenties in sporting a typically short flapper hairstyle common to young women of the era as evidenced by how many other photographs of girls in the yearbook showed them wearing their hair in the same fashion.

With a sense of relief I knew now that my memory had not failed me across the years—at least in this instance! Catholic education had indeed been part of the equation. This time when I turned to the Web to learn more about the history and current status of St. Vincent's, surprisingly, little of relevance was found. Then it occurred to me that there just might be something about the school at the San Francisco Public Library since their collections were so deep in local history. Their online library catalog was searched and a single reference to this high school was listed. But when it is the right one, a single one is enough. The entry note provided the needed answer for solving the school's history, albeit a bit complicated. Sometime in the past St. Vincent High School had changed names to become Cathedral High School. And later Cathedral High School joined together with another school first named Sacred Heart College High School then shortened to become Sacred Heart High School. This merger in 1987 formed the presently active Sacred Heart Cathedral Preparatory school. St. Vincent as part of the name had been completely lost along the way.

Of course not wanting to leave any stones unturned—an obvious pattern of self-behavior by now—SHCP school was the next place of interest to go after. Another phone call was placed to a very willing-to-be-of-assistance school staff member who acknowledged that she thought the old records for St. Vincent's High were kept at her school and she would send me what she found, if anything. A few days later a single sheet copied from an old student record book came in the post. Mainly containing the courses she took in 1925 and 1926, it also reiterated her parents' names, address, the date she entered and the date she transferred to the High School of Commerce, and that she had been baptized at St. Peter's. If I had only managed to find this document earlier, it would have saved me a whole lot of effort in the early days of searching through reels and reels of microfilm for the church in which my mother had been baptized! But again, similar to the record of the high school from where she eventually graduated, this record was of no help in determining the place of birth for either of my Irish grandparents. And the continuity of documenting the transition between schools ceased with this record for it failed to designate the primary schools that my mother had attended. As her primary school education had very probably been in Catholic schools and she had moved about several times during her youth, there would be a number of likely schools to check and a string of addresses to contact, if they still existed. But the chance that lower school records had survived and that they would give more detailed information about her parents than those of the high schools seemed small so further research in along the same vein was set aside for another time.

DEPARTURE

Donegal, Ireland, March 26, 1892

Trembling on the outside with pent-up excitement, and even more agitated internally, Rose rifled through her two bags yet one more time to make sure all of things that she needed were still there and packed as she remembered, and that nothing else that she should be taking had been overlooked. In her mind she knew there was no need to look again but she couldn't stop herself. The one item meaning most to her, the *polka-dot scarf*, the same one given to her by her family on the occasion of her last birthday, she saw tucked safely in the corner of one of the pieces of luggage. She was not an overly superstitious person but as long as this particular scarf was near her wherever she went she felt in some way more secure; just knowing it was there gave her a greater sense of well-being.

Once she was certain and relieved once again that all was as it should be with her packing she went outdoors to take in deep breaths of the fresh Irish air she would soon be leaving behind. She was fortunate to have awakened early before the uncommonly hot weather seized the day once again. What a day to be sailing from Ireland's shores. It was so unlike the chilly and blustery days so customary in the spring. She took it as a special omen of good tidings. She envisioned John already stirring early too, having a morsel to eat then loading the cart for the trip to Derry City. He would board the small paddle steamer at the debarkation quay there, which would ferry him to the larger transatlantic ship moored in Moville. In less than a half a day's time their lives would begin a transformation that could not be reversed. When the ship left its berth it would be the launching of their new life together as well.

The voices of her father and brother, who had risen even earlier than Rose, could be heard along with the clomping footfalls of the horses down the road. Two carts had been borrowed to carry family members to her sendoff at the port in Moville. They would set out at an early hour to leave plenty of time to cover the eight and a half mile distance of the journey, knowing there were sure to be well-wishers to bid farewell which could cause delays at various points along the way.

Her father caught sight of her first. "You'd be up before the rest them, lass, like us. With this heat rising again as it is, we're best be starting off even sooner than we thought last evening. In this heat we'll need more time so the horses can go at a slower pace so as not to weary. This is the last day of it, though, by the looks of it. By tomorrow, with the wind shifting the way it is and the clouds forming up in the sky over to the west, this spell will soon be coming to an end, I'd say."

Her father seemed to intuitively understand talking about the weather or other usual subjects was a good way to keep Rose from dwelling overly much on her leaving. This was part of his plan. The night before he had intentionally made up his mind to try to deflect any undue stress the situation was likely to cause. To his credit, it seemed to be working.

"Not just these horses will be feeling it soon—we'll all be suffering if we allow the sun to take over the day before we're well on our way, won't we now?"

Rose nodded her agreement then ran a hand across her forehead where she could already feel small beads of sweat forming. She wasn't sure if they came from the heat or from nervousness.

An hour passed and now the whole family should be awake. But to be sure everyone was up and getting ready to go, Rose went back into the cottage to check on their progress. Her mother was sitting rather than standing for once, with a kind of bewildered look on her face. If Rose could have burrowed into her thoughts, she would have seen the divided state of mind her mother was experiencing at the moment. Practically, she believed that the greatest opportunity for one in Rose's position lay ahead in America, but emotionally she could only feel the repeated loss of a second daughter to a family that loved her and counted on her so much. With mixed emotions slipping in and out, the very same grief from when Mary had left home welled up to the surface again. But she refused to let it out with words and her lips stayed tightly sealed even if her face was an open book.

"Everything's ready for the trip, Mam. Are you feeling alright? I can help with anything that still needs doing." She still got no verbal response, only an inclination of the head.

"It will be all right, you'll see," she whispered as she leaned over and wrapped her arms around her mother's shoulders, resting her head against her mother's cheek.

Now the last hours passed swiftly and before Rose knew it they had arranged themselves in the cart and were on their way down the track from their cottage heading for the coastal road. Lingering was not her family's intention. No one wanted to overly extend this part of the leaving. There would be no melodrama. It was already hard enough to countenance without adding any further unnecessary pangs of conscience. At her own leisure over the past weeks, Rose had filled herself with all of the precious home impressions she would take with her so there would be no regrets bothering her from that standpoint. And now there was no need to take a last look back so she kept her eyes fixed straight ahead down the road.

As expected, relatives and friends met her along the road to wish her safe journey until their descent reached the Foyle shore road. Despite the mounting heat of the morning, they made good time passing through Whitecastle, Drung, Redcastle and Glebe and other places dotting the route north. Before long the shops on the main street of Moville were in sight. The distinctive houses clothed in so many different colors of paint—so unusual in contrast to the typical white cottages of the countryside—were a novelty to behold, brightening this coastal town and their spirits as they made their way down to the harbor. At the quay the changing wind direction was easily felt. Although it was still morning, already the temperature was starting to subside rather than increase as it had done in the previous days. A return to cool weather and rain seemed to be well on its way, as her father had foretold. In the minds of many of the emigrants at the dock the same thought struck them—the shift in weather was a manifestation, a kind of token, of the changes that lay ahead.

Rose's eyes flitted around the tightly packed crowd and the commotion it was making, searching for others she might know but finding only families of strangers, all seeming to try to remain cheerful amidst the sorrow of separation. A crewman told them the tender would be transporting the first group of emigrants to the ship in less than an hour's time.

Then, before she knew it, the last minutes had ticked down and the call on shore was made to board. Family members enwrapped each other in final embraces. The sadness she herself had tried to keep at bay in parting from her own family up until now had been partially lessened by the thrill of anticipation of being on the ship with John in only a few more moments. But now, visibly expressing more distress than her family was accustomed to ever seeing from her, they were unsure of how to react at first. Then, shrugging it off, they put it down to finality of the moment sinking in even for their normally unemotional daughter. She hugged each of them in turn before letting go and falling into the queue moving towards the edge of the water then up the gangway. Twisting her head to look back every few seconds she easily kept the faces of her family in view. Then someone shouted that the next group, including latecomers, would catch a second excursion of the tender when it returned.

The short distance took only a quarter of an hour before they were on board. Before she could make her way to the deck railings to look back towards the quay and wave goodbye, she and all of the rest of the new passengers were required to present their tickets and have their name, age, occupation and country of origin verified on the ship's manifest. As soon as this was done, and before finding her berth as the passengers in front of her had already started to do, she scoured the deck with her eyes in every direction for John. He must have watched her tender come from the shore and be waiting somewhere nearby. But she could not spot him yet so began to walk the deck herself. Not finding him there, she went below to see if he might be looking for his room. She peered in every direction, down every hallway and into every nook and cranny, but there was no sign of him anywhere. Where on earth could he be? She began asking other passengers and members of the crew hoping that someone had seen someone who looked like him but no one had.

Then the man with the passenger manifest came to mind. She flew back to his station.

"Pardon me, sir. I'm looking for a friend, a fellow passenger by the name of John Harte, could you check to see if he's on your list?" interrupting his concentration. He raised eyes from the ledger and noted the worry plainly evident in the tone of her voice and by the look on her face.

"Yes, his name is here, but he seems not to have come aboard yet, miss. He's down for boarding in Derry, but maybe something happened and he'll be joining the next loading of the tender. It wouldn't be the first time."

Feeling an immediate shortage of breath, she could barely talk.

"Thank you, sir", she squeezed out. And with this news Rose hurriedly stepped to the railings again, but the tender had not yet left and the distance to shore was too great to be able to pick individuals out of the remaining number of people clustered together on the dock. All she could do now was to keep her eyes glued to the shore for it to begin its second and final shuttle crossing to the ship and pray that John was on it.

***

He slept only fitfully, awakening many times during the night both because of the constant leg pain and from the chill of being soaked in cold sweat, and as much again because of the confused, hallucinatory-like thoughts pulsating through his

116

brain. John awoke for good in the early morning with dizziness and aching head. His wandering mind could not reconcile his driving desire to be meeting Rose in a short few hours on board the ship with the fact that he was now totally immobile, flat on his back in bed. He had never felt so helpless before in his life. What could he possibly do now about their intentions to seal their life together with marriage as soon as they reached New York? Over and over he calculated the distance and time it would take to send a messenger to tell Rose of his accident and the answer always was the same. While the fastest rider could probably make it to her house in the nick of time, given there was willing rider and fresh spare horse, there would be no way to make up the added distance from there onto Moville, where she would soon be, to get word to her before the ship was due to sail.

By the time his family had visited him where he lay bedridden and had persuaded him to eat a bit of breakfast in spite of his protests of lack of hunger, Peter, who had left before dawn to ride to Derry, entered the house with the doctor in tow.

"I'm Dr. Brady, lad. How're you feeling?

"There've been better mornings I've seen, doc…but I think…I hope it's only the one leg that took the brunt of it."

"Let's have a look at the damage that's been done. Peter's told me about the nasty fall so I've brought along everything needed for putting a broken leg back to right. But let's check the rest of you as well just to make sure there's nothing else besides that needs attending to."

The doctor could find nothing else wrong except for bruises and aches aplenty. That the leg had only one large fracture as well as an enormous contusion above the break was a kind of blessing considering the height of the fall. All the while he was being examined John kept his eyes riveted on the face of the doctor, attempting to read in his expressions the severity of the situation. Finally, he could wait no longer.

"How bad is it, doc? How long before it mends and can…will it get back to working the way it did as before, do you think?"

"It's a bad break, lad, there's no denying it. The likes of a bit of bone poking through the skin makes it more difficult. It will take a goodly while, several months at least, before it heals and you'll have a considerable limp afterwards, I should say. At least for a while. But it should eventually disappear for the most part at your age. When it does then you'll know you're right again. You don't want to get in a hurry to start running across any fields, do you now? Give it time. Pay attention to any other problems that might show up, especially during the next week or two. With a fall like yours there could also be internal injuries we can't tell about immediately. You're young and tough, though. So you should be as good as new in the end."

And then the doctor remembered what Peter had said John would have most on his mind. "If you're still looking to sail off soon, as I heard, you should be ready to withstand a sea journey within two or three months time…so long as you're mindful of what I say, of taking care to make it no worse."

It was like a stab in the heart—words were at a loss to him. All he could manage was to shake his head from side to side, indicating to the doctor that he would not be for worsening the situation. The doctor understood the silent gesture while seeing the look of bitter disappointment for which there was no attempt to conceal.

"Good lad. Now get yourself ready. In a wee moment or two we'll be setting the leg back to where it belongs. Peter and Hugh will help steady you."

With this prognosis only halfway digested, thoughts began to spin through his mind about rebooking passage on another vessel. There should be no problem, he speculated, in using the paid ticket he had on another ship as long as it was on the same ship line, the Allan Line it was. He knew where Rose would be going at first, to her sister Mary's, and maybe, before his time came to embark, he would get word from her about her address in New York should she have moved to her own place by the time he was ready to join her. No matter what the circumstances, he would find where she was at.

But before long he stopped dwelling on himself and turned to thinking of Rose—neither seeing him on board ship nor hearing from him or anyone else about his accident before the ship steamed away from Moville. What must it be like to be in her shoes when she realized that he would not be joining her on board without so much as a word of explanation? What would she be thinking? What would she do—leave the ship, perhaps? But what reason could she give to her family? They would not take kindly to having their secret explained out of necessity. Or would she think at the eleventh hour he had cold feet about their forthcoming married life together and had jilted her? He couldn't let himself believe that she would entertain an idea like that for more than a moment knowing each other as they did—what they shared was unquestionable and unbreakable.

The searing pain came as the doctor began his work with the assistance of the others holding him as still as possible, reducing all of these reflections, comingled with images of Rose and spinning around in opposite directions on a collision course, into detached groans of agony; then suddenly there was nothing at all.

***

From her vantage point, Rose could see that the crowd on shore was no longer one in constant motion. It looked quite settled now, you could say subdued in comparison to the shuffling activity of a few minutes before. The tender was back near the dock but it was stationary now after having made its second round trip without delivering John. The opposite was true on the ship itself. Crew members were scattering quickly in all directions and the rumble of engines could be distinctly heard between the elevated voices of the sailors and the excited and nervous chattering of the passengers. Then she heard the grinding noise of metal on metal as it spread down the length of the ship, which could only mean one thing—they were weighing anchor and the ship would soon be underway. With the hubbub on board, the finality of her predicament took hold—she was about to set sail off on her own and all of their plans had been shattered.

At first her mind went blank and body numb. She could not move as she leaned against a wall of the ship as if to keep her upright instead of keeling over. But then after a few minutes, as the initial shock began to taper off, she vigorously shook her head back and forth to further clear out the cobwebs and began to mentally run down the same path of reasoning and doubt John, in his semi-delirium, had done but a short time before. Was there some side to him that she didn't know?

She had been as sure of him as the standing stones that had lain in the fields in Ireland for time immemorial. His steadfast character was not capable of last minute change of heart. And he could no more turn her into a spurned woman than give up breathing. Their loyalty to each other was their source of strength, their enduring bond. Then another scenario slipped into her head. Maybe his family had found out about their arrangement and prevented him from coming by force? That was more likely to have happened. It was not at all unheard of that a family that felt religiously threatened might take the measure of restraining or even locking up a son or daughter who they considered disobedient and detrimental to the welfare of the family as a whole. But lastly, a third and equally viable possibility was that something untoward had happened to him—he might have been injured and become incapacitated, or the almost unthinkable, he may even have died. Without any way of knowing it, and almost uncannily, she had come around to striking at the truth.

Whatever the reason, she was now on her own. Again, she moved back to a spot on the deck where she could wave a more distant farewell to the amorphous group on shore, sure that her family was still among them and waving back at her as well even though she was unable to pick them out of the crowd. For a brief moment her gaze shifted downward from the rail, to where the churning of the ships propellers had turned the water into swirling ringlets of waves. The shuttering sound of the engines changed pitch as the ship began to ply forward faster, steaming on its way up the estuary and out into the open sea.

WORK

San Francisco/Peninsula, California, March 2007

Having exhausted the high school line of investigation, helpful as it was, it still shed no light on learning anything more about exact birthplaces of my grandparents. I struggled to think once more of any other documents that could still exist that might produce that kind of precise information; what other records had been deemed worthy enough to be retained and could be dug out after all the years gone by?

In going back over the censuses again the first thing that caught my attention as something not fully explored was the column entitled "Year of Naturalization". Naturalization was the path to becoming a citizen of the United States for foreign born residents. And retained court records were sometimes useful resources for noting place of birth, address and other facts. Based on remarks in other documents, it appeared fairly consistent that both of my Irish grandparents had immigrated to New York as opposed to the other popular but less frequent destinations of Boston or Philadelphia. For my grandfather Patrick, who crossed the sea many years before Rose did—he seemed he have moved to San Francisco by 1880—the possibility he had spent several years in the East before heading out West seemed very likely. Grandmother Rose's first positive address in San Francisco twenty years later was documented in the 1900 census. As pre-1906 naturalization documents had not been centralized nor computerized comprehensively, records held at both the San Francisco and at the New York National Archives regional offices would need to be manually searched either in person or by the much slower method of snail mail.

The NARA Pacific Region facility for Northern California was situated just a few miles south of San Francisco so on the next trip north a stop was made there. At this branch of the National Archives and Records Administration naturalization records were accessed through a paper card file index similar to the now outmoded traditional library catalog cards. A careful look through them divulged neither a Patrick Kavanaugh/Cavanagh nor a Rose Cameron matching the particulars of either of my grandparents in terms of dates and origins. This was not a surprise for Rose. Women often did not gain citizenship through the naturalization process, rather they became citizens through marriage their husbands having been born on American soil, or having successfully completed naturalization at some earlier point themselves.

Naturalization records can be a difficult proposition. The San Francisco NARA collection consists only of United States Circuit and District Court records, that is, applications the applicant opted to submit at a Federal court level. Even if one or both of my grandparents had gone to a Federal court, not all of these records had been transferred to NARA; they could still reside at the court itself. Also, applicants could have selected a state, municipal or county court instead, so my expectations were low for the outcome of this visit. And in the case of San Francisco, our old friend interfered again. The 1906 disaster saw the destruction of the courthouses, State Circuit and the San Francisco Superior Courts, and the records they maintained, effectively eliminating any chance of discovering court documents at the non-Federal levels prior to that date.

New York, the other state where they could have undergone naturalization, since it appeared to be their port of entry, became the secondary location for investigation. In the case of New York City itself as well as Brooklyn—also known as King's County—the process of searching through a naturalization index, fortunately, did not require an on site visit as it did with the town close to San Francisco. The index for the boroughs could be accessed online through a provider of a major conglomeration of genealogical databases. This time there were several possibilities that roughly fit the parameters of data for my grandfather and too many for my grandmother, whose name was even more common than his. Thus, the index information was used to retrieve the actual online scanned card images, similar in appearance to the hardcopy ones in San Francisco, for him only. To be certain that these records were not abridged versions of records held in paper format in New York, written requests were made to the boroughs as well requesting photocopies of the complete original records. The net result from both efforts was that none of them could be positively identified as belonging to my grandfather since the information contained in them was too scanty to be of much value. It was time to move on and try a different approach.

It was recalled that 1936 Social Security application details for my mother obtained much earlier had given the names of her parents along with her place of work and its exact address in San Francisco. Normally, attempting to research a business for which someone had once worked over seventy years ago would be of little use because it would have long ago disappeared. Other employers with whom she had held jobs that had been found listed in the San Francisco city directories had fallen into the category of the disappeared. But the company she was working for at the time of her application was no slouch—its address being the prominent, heart-of-the-city location of 225 Bush Street. And the name of the corporation was the Standard Oil Company of California. Who could forget the omnipresent Standard service stations of my childhood and on into the 1980s when Standard Oil of California eventually morphed into the Chevron Corporation. It seemed like it happened overnight; suddenly one day there were no more Standard red, white and blue signs to be seen anywhere. They had been replaced by the same patriotic-like insignia but with Chevron as the single word at the top. And they have remained the same to this day. There was a possibility a company of such stature and longevity could have established an archive of old records. And in such an archive could repose old personnel files, files surviving the test of time and the urge to discard, files containing information about my mother, and maybe even her parents. It was well worth a try at least, especially should there have been a pension involved.

Their website indicated the headquarters for Chevron in California was in the town of San Ramon. A phone call to the all-purpose number listed led to a series of other numbers over a period of several days and to contacts with various personnel at this office and elsewhere, including the records storage service, ultimately resulting in a negative response. Their payroll operations and reporting teams had conducted an extensive search, according to the contact. Although they had said that historical employment records going as far back as her time had been kept, my mother's was not among them for some unknown reason. It was quite a long time in the past and her position had been a modest one of secretary. Her work history as a means of a discovery could now be scratched off the list.

But what about my grandfather Patrick—hadn't there been mention of his work place somewhere, too? My thoughts recurred to a piece of information on a document not given much of my attention when it was attained. I recalled it had been noted on the admission sheet to Laguna Honda Home that his employer at the time was the Board of Public Works of the City of San Francisco. When I first saw this document my concentration had been so intent on looking for an exact place of birth other details had been glossed over. A city public works had the ring of permanency to it. Didn't all cities have a public works department to maintain basic infrastructure? The word "Board" threw me, though. Possibly this meant that somehow he was employed by a group of people who oversaw a department of public works but this image did not fit the occupations listed in city directories and censuses where the earliest noted him working as a coachman. All of the succeeding entries following the 1906 catastrophe listed him as some form of laborer including those of sewerman and side sewerman, an important and necessary job at a time when there had been so much need for the rebuilding of the city's infrastructure.

Before being able to go any further it would be important to see if something could be learned about the history of the Board of Public Works itself. Did it still exist as such or had the tides of time seen it disappear or be reincarnated under some new banner? With a little patience, the Web revealed that the Board in my grandfather's era was indeed a group of appointees, three commissioners to be exact, appointed by the mayor of San Francisco. It was established in 1900 under the auspices of a new city and county charter replacing the elective Superintendent of Streets. According to the charter, there was technically a Department of Public Works that selected unit heads under the supervision of the Board. But for whatever reason, the term Department was not commonly used during the early 1900s in referring to Public Works rather both the Board and Department segments were lumped together under one rubric denoted as the Board. This cleared up the confusion, and obviously was the case in the designation of my grandfather's employer on the Laguna Honda admission form.

Nowadays, there no longer exists a board component to the Department of Public Works. The department is headed by a director who reports directly to the mayor and any past confusion among board and department has melted away. On the first phone call to them, the receptionist admitted that she did not know much about older personnel files—my grandfather worked for the city from 1910 to 1917—and no one else currently in the department would know either, especially since they no longer had an archivist position. Undeterred, I was insistent that someone in the department or among city employees must know where the old employee records were kept, if they still existed at all. Noting my growing concern by the tone in my voice, she relented and gave me the name and phone number of another departmental staff member who might be of help. I called her many times over several days. She neither answered the phone nor returned my calls after I left detailed messages describing exactly the kind of information I sought. Maybe she was just a phantom after all. Bypassing her for the time being, the Human Resources Department of the City of San Francisco was contacted next. They surely must have a handle on the whereabouts of historic employee records for the city. In talking to the staff person there, it looked like I had reached someone who gave the impression of at least wanting to help, but there too, after promising to get back to me on the same day on more than one occasion, never did. A final attempt was made and after a brief conversation it was clear she had not pursued the matter and would be of no further assistance in determining where old personnel records were kept. However, she did promise to contact the phantom employee in Public Works for whom I had left repeated messages, but I had little faith she actually would.

Weeks had passed in what for all intents and purposes looked every bit like a stereotypical bureaucratic approach of putting me off until I grew weary and called uncle—or perhaps could it have been plain and pure simple ineptitude? Whatever the reason, my patience was gone and only frustration remained. Then light dawned. In a final effort to break through, a letter to the mayor was written, without naming names, detailing the nature of all of the communications I had with the city and emphasizing their attitude of unhelpfulness and the feeling of being stonewalled I had experienced. It was noted in the letter that the lack of service was so consistent that it seemed like it could be an endemic function of the leadership philosophy, an ingrained corporate culture of the city. And in an effort to bolster my complaint, to make sure it wasn't overlooked, and to elicit some empathy, it was spelled out clearly that three generations of my family had lived and worked in San Francisco, two of which worked as public employees and the third, my mother, having worked there in the private sector. Shoddy treatment was poor recompense for past contributions made by city citizens.

Perhaps the final paragraph of my letter gave the most important impetus to move things forward: "… in all frankness and with the sense of my frustration that you can gather from this letter, if no response is received within the next two weeks, the Board of Supervisors shall be contacted as well as the media. They may be very interested in real life examples occurring in three departments of the current workings of the City, especially when it concerns three generations of individuals who gave part of their lives to making things work right."

Three days after sending the letter the phone rang and on the other end was a lady from the Department of Public Works. Was it coincidence or had my letter worked? In actuality—surprise, surprise—they did keep personnel archives for Public Works employees and they were located right in the department itself! They had not been merged with other city records kept by human resources. Someone with the requisite knowledge of the collection had searched them for my grandfather, and his record had been found! What they had was very brief, according to the staff person, but she was quick to offer to mail or fax a copy of it to me. Naturally, not having immense faith by this time that it would ever be put in the mail, I asked for it to be faxed. Within five minutes there was immediate gratification with long sought after and fought for information in my hands. She was right, only a paltry amount of data was contained on the record but what was there both verified the fact that he had indeed been a public works employee and his occupation and address were given. The congruity between census, cemetery, nursing home and city directory addresses was cemented by the fact that his work terminated with the department in 1917 due to illness. It also indicated the wage he was earning—$4.50 a day. Not a bad salary for the year preceding the onset of World War I. What it failed to do again was give his birth date or birthplace. Not even a country was noted in this instance. Aside from that, with the successful conclusion in ultimately obtaining his employee record, there seemed to be no further leads along this line of inquiry to be taken up.

PASSAGES

Donegal, Ireland, April 1892

As the ship steamed up the Foyle estuary, gusts of wind greater than those created by the ship itself, began to whip through the deck and were followed shortly by the fall of the first raindrops. It seemed to be the beginning of her voyage was destined to be a rough and stormy one, consistent with a mind in the midst of conflict and turmoil. The houses and hills receded in the distance, the people on shore becoming mere specks. The die had been cast and there was no turning back now.

The notion that John must still be somewhere on board and would suddenly spring out in surprise haunted her for a few more minutes—until, from her place on deck, she spotted plumes of smoke and flashes of light coming from the local hillsides above the channel. The tradition that Mary had experienced when she had left was still alive and well. Bonfires, like a series of beacons, were lit along the hills as a final salute to mark the loss of another loved one to emigration, to provide a lasting memory of where home was and to signify a fond farewell. With a tiny bit of imagination Rose thought she could pick out the very glow of the fire that blazed near her family's house and the warmth of the gesture helped to diminish the chill of John's absence running through her. When the last of Ireland's green shores and the mouth of the Foyle had been left behind she wasted no time in finding her berth then collapsing on the bed, devastated and overcome by mental fatigue from the strain of worry.

Like so many other ships, the Norwegian had departed from Glasgow with a sampling of all sorts of nationalities who had made their way to Scotland from Scandinavia and from other countries further to the east. Stopping in Moville to pick up Irish citizens to fill the remaining places, steamships then plied their way to New York in about a week to ten days time. Before steamships began replacing sailing ships in the 1860s the crossing of the Atlantic was a much more daunting affair. The risk of undergoing shipboard misery, or even death, in a passage that endured for three to four weeks at best, and sometimes as much as thirty-five days, was so much greater than it was now in her day.

In the past, the dormitory-style rooms of the sailing ships consisted of bunks against the two longer walls with tables down the middle. Breathing, especially on warm nights, often became difficult from overcrowding the rooms and inadequate ventilation, and seasickness was the order of the day in stormy weather, and even when it was calm for the most susceptible. Diseases borne by contaminated water or food, such as cholera, or those carried by lice and fleas, like typhus, could spread infection rapidly in the close quarters on the accommodation decks. With the advent of steamships, the crossing was reduced to a bit more than a week on average and living conditions had been vastly upgraded for the majority of passengers who travelled in steerage, the cheapest fare, such as the cabin in which Rose found herself now seated. The increasing number of immigrants stimulated competition between the steamship companies, which helped to some extent the establishment of new standards improving greatly upon those set previously in the mid 1850s. Limiting the number of passengers per cabin, better food and improved sanitation, while still not guaranteeing a high degree of comfort, generally allowed for a more satisfactory journey and a greater expectation of survival than in the preceding decades.

Rose's attempt to rest a little and regain her composure did not last for long. As the ship headed into the open sea, the rain and wind intensified, and for those unaccustomed to sailing in inclement weather, caused enough agitation to force many to seek the open deck. Both Rose and a cabin-mate, a tall red-haired girl of about the same age, were among those whose queasiness compelled them to seek fresh air topside. In-between moments of unsteadiness from the pitching and rolling of the craft, trying to exercise enough self-control to not let seasickness win the battle to overwhelm them, the young woman struck up a conversation with Rose.

"I know what they mean when they talk about having sea legs now. Why couldn't the hot weather have lasted just a wee bit longer? I'm traveling on my own…would yourself be doing the same?"

Stunned that the very first words spoken to her by a fellow passenger should go straight to the core of her predicament, her impulse was to answer no—and that her John was waiting nearby in another cabin. That's the way it should have been. But she gathered herself back together just in time.

"I know no one else on board. You're the first one with whom I've had a decent word, other than the manifest gentleman. My name is Rose Cameron—from Inishowen."

"That makes two of us. My home is near Culdaff.

Siobhán Duffy I'm called…very pleased to meet you, Rose. I take it you've never been on a ship like this before and it's your first time, like myself?""You're so right there, Siobhán. Is it the lack of color in my face that gives it away?"

A kind face looking back at her, equally pallid from the motion of the rolling sea, and a few friendly words were already helping her to regain better spirits. "Was it from your home you came this morning or did you stay overnight somewhere along the way?"

"We did it in one fell swoop…started before dawn this morning. My brother did the driving. My father passed nigh on a year ago so it was only my mother and sister who came along to see me off. Do you…" her voice trailing off for a moment as she fought again to settle her churning stomach down "… have family in New York you'll be going to?"

"Aye, my sister's there. Mary left home two years ago and has stayed in the city ever since, though I think she wants to move on from there soon. Others I know of are sprinkled here and there in different states, but it's New York where I'm expecting to stay for a while at first. And yourself?"

"I'm staying in New York just till I get my two feet on the ground. There are a couple of cousins living far to the other side—in San Francisco—and that's where I want to go as soon as I can. It's not like New York, not so crowded, although things have gotten better there too, I hear, now that the Irish are not all squeezed into Little Ireland on Manhattan's Lower East Side like they used to be. But opportunities in San Francisco, they say, are really much better for us. And there's the fair climate. That must be something to behold. Plenty of California sunshine just waiting to be soaked up by the likes of myself. But just to make us feel at home, I've heard that they even get some of our Irish mists to cool down the summer months, too!"

"What's Little Ireland?" Was it somehow a miniature version of home, Rose wondered?

"It's the old neighborhood that most of the Irish lived at first. More like they were confined to, especially when folks of our parents' age emigrated, from what's been told. Somewhere we wouldn't want to be because of the conditions, and no longer need to worry about nowadays."

The two young women, having restored themselves with a sufficient quantity of sea air by now, felt stable enough to be able to return indoors where it was dry. There they introduced themselves to several other passengers in their cabin and began to learn about onboard amenities. In addition to the lavatories for their class, there was a narrow dining room with benches, and a saloon and smoking-room. While glimpses of the ocean through the portholes could be had from inside, there was also plenty of space on deck to take promenades should they have a mind to when the weather was better. In fact, it was nothing like the appalling conditions passengers had suffered through during earlier times. Everything was clean and functional but still the overall atmosphere, to which accumulating shipboard odors continued to contribute over the course of the voyage, was one in which you would be happy to leave behind when the time finally came.

Over the course of the voyage Rose and Siobhán continued to spend their days together talking, eating, walking the deck, playing at games, and even partaking in a dance with music provided by a small band. Bit by bit they had struck up what would turn out to be a lasting friendship almost without realizing it. Of course they bemoaned the lack of sufficient water for washing properly, the cramped shared quarters and the plainness of the food in comparison to what they heard the second-cabin or saloon passengers were offered, and speculated on what they wanted to do first after docking in New York. But it was only in the last days of the crossing that Rose finally opened up to Siobhán, sharing her sorrowful story of details of plans that had failed to materialize with John.

"Sure, I don't know how you kept it to yourself all this time. You really are something else, Rose, to be able to not let on so as no one would suspect while being brokenhearted all the time as now I can only too plainly see. Here I've been going on about myself so much and you with a load of bother weighing you down having to listen to my prattling. What's there to do? How will you be able to work it out?"

"There's nothing I can see to be done straight away, is there now? I can only guess at why he didn't come. Maybe he just decided it was not the right thing for him to do after all, after he thought it over one more time. Or maybe something else happened that could explain it. I'll just have to get on with it until I have some news from home. At first I wanted to scream out "stop the engines" then jump off the boat before it left Moville harbor. But I've had to go back now to looking to whatever lies ahead. With or without John, doesn't it look like America will be the right place for me?" Her words came out much more self-assured on the surface than the hollow feeling she had inside as they left her lips.

A perfunctory medical examination to meet entry requirements was given on board, including verification of vaccination, or administration of an injection if it hadn't been done prior to boarding. The collection of any personal information lacking to passenger list details, reminders of customs limitations, and other inconveniences such as bouts of turbulent seas when combined with the positive parts, such as socializing with other passengers, made the days pass swiftly, the morning of their much anticipated arrival brilliantly breaking above the horizon before they knew it. Now the anxiety of facing immigration procedures, with the possibility of being rejected from admittance, loomed only minutes before them. That is not to say any of the passengers wanted to stay on board any longer than they had to. They were well-informed about the closure of Castle Garden, the old port of emigration in Battery Park, and the Barge Office that had served as a temporary immigration facility for a brief two years afterwards. Now a brand new screening station had been built on Ellis Island. It was so recently opened they had not heard any news from the relatively few others who had passed through its gates as to what it was really like.

When their ship's engines finally came to a standstill in New York harbor the passengers were asked to stay put until American authorities had given clearance to the immigrant transport barge to begin ferrying them to the island, a brief sojourn that took them past the Statue of Liberty overlooking their arrival nearby. She stared at it as if no one else around her was caught up in doing exactly the same thing, as if she were the first one to ever see it. Its impressive size and significance made her feel that it had been placed there just for her, standing tall in the water to personally welcome her to America—to her new home.

Once safely ashore, on unsteady legs that were now more accustomed to the motion of the sea than that of terra firma, they were directed to walk in single file to present their papers. They would be asked to show they had the required minimum amount of money in hand, and to demonstrate their health was good in order to avoid being placed among those who had been quarantined for cholera or other infectious or contagious diseases. Rose and Siobhán stuck together like glue hoping the strength of two would make it easier to deal with mounting anxiety as they went through each of the different steps of the entry process. Waiting her turn, Rose thought of the story she had heard of the initial immigrant to pass through the new immigration buildings on Ellis Island only just a few months before her own arrival. An Irish girl it was like herself, only fifteen years of age, by the name of Annie Moore from County Cork. She had been the very first to register on January 1, 1892—who could forget that date—and now just four months later, on April 6th of the same year, she was nipping on Annie's heels in reaching the same distant land she had so recently set foot upon.

They saw several immigrants from their ship, as well as passengers from other vessels, pulled aside for additional inspection procedures, but both Rose and Siobhán managed to proceed through the stages without a hitch, save for one document Siobhán had accidentally let slip out of her hand to the floor. She soon realized it was missing and recovered it quickly, but even this minor mishap had caused her temperature to sore in a flash, moistening her forehead and setting her heart fluttering at a tempo that she thought all of those around her would be able to observe. But if fears of the unknown caused her nerves to be jangled they were compensated by the shared courage to go forward to meet each hurdle as it arose, which Rose and all of the rest of the newcomers demonstrated as a group. None of them had come this far to let rattled nerves get the best of them at this final stage. But for the two girls from Donegal it was a far cry from the peaceful mountains and green glens of their homeland so recently called their own to the somber regimented lines of humanity ready to swallow up their individuality.

Later in the day—after reuniting themselves with their luggage that had been checked during the inspection then riding the ferry from the island to the Battery waterfront—they made their way out of the building. Finding themselves on the bustling, formidable streets at the southern tip of Manhattan, with suitcases and overstuffed bags in their hands and looking across at a row of most uninviting boarding houses, they turned towards each other and smiled.

"I shouldn't like staying in one of those much. Thank goodness I've got Mary and you've got people coming for yourself too."

"Wouldn't we be looking over our shoulders every minute if we tried to lay our heads down in this part of town? I wouldn't feel safe for a minute." Siobhán automatically moved closer to Mary, hooking arms, to make them feel less alone and vulnerable.

These tawdry looking buildings were meant only for very temporary residence, either for those who had come a day or two before and were waiting to meet arriving family or friends once they had successfully passed the Ellis Island inspections, or for those new immigrants whose relatives were still on their way to the port to meet and take them to their homes. Siobhán's New York relations, Brian and Cathleen Murphy, had spotted her almost immediately after they had gone out the doors of the building and they rushed to greet each other with warm embraces all around.

Meanwhile, Rose perused gatherings of people scattered

in every direction, searching for her sister Mary. After eleven days at sea, beginning so disastrously without John, fears were already rising that she may be left alone on this side of the world as well. It couldn't be happening a second time, could it? Siobhán stole Rose's attention away for a moment, halting all of the twisting and turning efforts she was making to try to catch a glimpse of her sister somewhere in the crowd, to introduce her to the relations with whom she would be staying for a short time in New York. The young companions had already exchanged local addresses before leaving the ship and now again they promised to get together before Siobhán made the trip out to San Francisco. But when she saw the furrowed brow and crestfallen look on Rose's face she was about to suggest she too could come to stay with them if they had space. With an imploring glance towards the Murphys and their answering nod of understanding, Siobhan knew she could go ahead, when a frantic voice rang out like music to all of their ears.

"It's Mary. There she is", she shouted at the top of her lungs.

And in the instant just before it was their turn to fly into each other's arms, Rose's depressed state somersaulted into one of joy and relief.

"Rose, I'm so sorry. I thought I was in plenty of time. I went to the wrong building at first. Aren't I the fool? You'll not be forgiving me soon for my tardiness, so."

Mary, breathless from her haste to reach them, had been nearly as dejected as Rose for fear that somehow they had missed each other before she realized another possibility existed.

"Don't be too hard on yourself, dear sister. Can't you see

I'm so thankful to see you I don't know which one will give out first my voice or my legs? My whole body is shaking."

But where was John? Mary quickly decided that now was not the time to bring it up; there must be some logical explanation her sister would tell her about later.

Their mutual worries having now subsided, they exchanged introductions with others in the small group, and blessings were uttered all around giving thanks that the two young women had safely arrived and were now under the wings of those who would look after them. And with that they parted ways, Rose off to her sister's small living quarters in Brooklyn, and Siobhán to Queens. Life in America in this strange but strikingly entrancing city beckoned down every long block and around every corner as they made their way through it. She couldn't wait to join in and start being part of it!

BREAKTHROUGH

Central Coast, California, March-April 2007

With the negative results from the centers in Donegal, as well as the rest of Ulster, the most likely of the counties checked previously, conducting separate searches at the centers in the next group of counties to the south would seem to hold little prospect for striking gold. It even bordered on looking like a desperate measure. Nevertheless, even if the chances were becoming slimmer and slimmer as the radius expanded, due diligence in following almost every possibility to its conclusion demanded that requests be made at least to the centers that were nearest in proximity, those of Monaghan, Sligo, Galway and Mayo. Within days replies came back— none of them of the positive kind.

The databases of baptismal records in Ireland had become so comprehensive by this point, claiming to contain over ninety-nine percent of all the extant church records, it seemed that my grandmother's record should be found in one of them, given the data I had collected and submitted to the centers was accurate. And now doubts started to creep in on what the outcome would likely be from the efforts of the researcher I had earlier engaged in County Donegal. It was still too soon to expect that he had already sifted through all of the sources available to him to see if any of the information I had provided in February would concur with his findings. He had said that it could take up to twelve weeks to complete the work. But now the growing body of evidence was beginning to indicate that something crucial was missing. And if this were true, it could make his job at best difficult or at worst impossible. I began to prepare myself for yet another let down. Something in the information that had been collected on my grandmother must be out of kilter—it just wasn't adding up.

In parallel with having databases searched in Ireland, I had ordered two microfilm reels from the local LDS family history center library. They were the General Register Office of Ireland Index to Births for the presumed year of Grandmother Rose's birth, plus the year afterwards just in case there was a lag in registration. These indexes, the first step in a two step process, listed five births with the name of Rose Cameron, giving the volume and page number for locating the full details on copies of the actual birth registers on different reels of microfilm. These entries also named the Poor Law Union, PLU for short as mentioned earlier, in which the births took place. While the PLUs for the five different entries for Rose Cameron I had found in the indexes were geographically widely scattered, it was worthwhile to order all five of the corresponding birth microfilms. Normally, several weeks elapsed, sometimes turning into months, between ordering and receiving a film; a method not recommended for those concerned with making rapid headway or dealing with time constraints. In this instance, the films finally arrived after a three week wait. As before, disappointment resulted, for none of the entries had correct date information with regard to birth month and even more significantly, names of my grandmother's parents.

After months of painstaking research on my part in

California and by others in Ireland, all I had achieved was an assortment of bits of information that matched a maximum of two characteristics relating to my grandmother Rose: the last name, a year of birth, a first or last name of a parent—but never more than two together in any particular record. All of the other data in the records was negligible. By now I had reached a conclusion that even with all of the common and repetitive Irish names among millions of individuals searched in these enormous databases, the odds of more than two elements being identical were very small, indeed so small that if ever this happened it should immediately set off a red flag. And with this realization drawn through hard fought experience, there came back to me, after floating about for what seemed like an eternity somewhere in the nether regions of my brain, the discovery that I had made in scouring the Web some months before of the website listing of transcribed baptism register entries from a single parish in Donegal.

How could I have been so cavalier at the time to have discarded so quickly a baptism listing in this register that had not one or even two, but seven out of eight vital characteristics in common with my grandmother's traits? Granted, what had stopped me before was that the all-important surname was totally different—McMartin did not even come close to resembling my grandmother's maiden name of Cameron. But in the meantime it had also been learned that the coupling of Anna—not the Ann or Anne spelling variants of the name my mother had told me were incorrect so long ago—with the first name of Rose was not all that common. And when factoring in both the right year and month of birth, as had been noted in the 1900 census, plus the exact first and last names for her mother, first name of her father, and that all of these elements applied to an individual baptized at a church in Donegal, there should have been no question in hindsight: this lead should have been followed to its end wherever it led.

Where to begin? First of all, there was the question as to whether or not information on the website was entirely accurate. Not knowing about the authoritativeness of the site meant an assumption it was totally factual could not be made without double checking. One way for verifying if it were true or not would be to re-contact the Derry genealogy center which had earlier been provided with all of the known data—except the focus for a surname this time around would be on *McMartin* instead of Cameron—to see if the research staff there could provide copies of the civil birth or church baptismal records in their database corresponding to the parish record web pages. Within the request, I explained my belief that there was a distinct possibility that the surname might have changed to Cameron from McMartin at some point after the birth/baptism of Rose even though they had rejected this possibility earlier. Since they had already been paid to conduct the search under the name Cameron and had mentioned that a record for a Rose McMartin existed in our previous correspondence, they graciously ran the search again for no charge. This time they were able to determine that they held both baptism and civil record birth extracts for a *Rose Anna McMartin*. And upon receipt of these records, it was evident that these records mostly corroborated the information provided in the website parish listing.

However, an opinion was again proffered by a member of the staff at the center. In her view these two records were unlikely to be the ones for my grandmother due solely to the surname discrepancy. She firmly believed this baptismal record must be for another family in spite of everything else matching almost perfectly. In this record, along with the surname, only the day of the month of the birth date differed by a single digit from the previously noted date in the census record for Rose Cameron. But for the second record, the civil birth record, there remained an unexplained difference in month—September instead of August—and worse still, the civil birth date was after the date on the church baptism record. How could this discrepancy be accounted for and explained away? Not willing to let her conclusion discourage me in following up as it had done in the past when it had been my own tentative conclusion as well, it was kept in mind the researcher was not aware of the rest of the information I had collected. She would not have calculated the odds against having so many identical facts in view of what I had come to know about Rose.

Left without much other apparent recourse, why not fall back on the internet once again to see if anything else could be uncovered to prove or disprove the theory of a changed family name? In this instance it would mean taking the surname McMartin in conjunction with different combinations of the same biographical details that had been tried before to see what would emerge. What elements could be found to be in common by both the bona fide baptism and civil birth records recently documented in Ireland and by the information from the 1900 census and church records for my grandmother under the name of Cameron in San Francisco?

Several evenings of searching passed before a posting on a genealogy message board surfaced in response to the mix of biographical data that I had entered into the search engine on that day. It was a brief message but there was enough in it to peak my curiosity instantly. There was little doubt that the person who had posted it was trying to find the same *Rose Anna McMartin* that I was now seeking more information about—the same person that was in the online parish baptism listing as well as in the baptism and birth database records from Ireland. In the message Daniel wrote: *I am seeking to learn what happened to Mary and Rose Anna McMartin, two of their daughters.* That he had clearly written **Anna** instead of Ann or Anne was crucial. The second person mentioned, Mary—the sister of Rose Anna—for whom he was searching for as well, could also be significant going forth. Both were daughters of his great- grandparents.

The one drawback was the posting was over a year and a half old and there had not been a single follow-up to his message in all of the intervening time. After mulling it around for a few days, I decided to try to reply to the posting in such a way that highlighted the near exactness in the facts that were included in the body of his message to those of my grandmother while at the same time also clearly emphasizing awareness that the McMartin surname of his ancestors was not the same as the Cameron of mine, for which an answer would be necessary in order to go forward.

My reply posting concluded like this:

I know it is a long shot, but I am wondering if, perhaps, a first marriage was to a McMartin, they had children, and then the wife remarried to a Cameron at which time Rose Anna took the name Cameron. Can anyone shed any light on this possibility? My mother said that her mother was born in Donegal and so far, in all my searching for her birthplace there, this is the closest I have come to finding it.

Two days later my email account alerted me of a follow-up posting in response to mine that could be found by going to the message board. It was from the same person who had written before. What was said in the second sentence of the lengthy response instantly grabbed my total attention. It noted that he had been aware of some of the McMartin families changing their surname to Cameron when they immigrated to Scotland. To check further into this recollection, he had phoned his older brother who could possibly be of some help. Like myself, my correspondent thought the similar characteristics were too close to have been ignored.

Continuing on, he wrote that he thought Rose Anna had gone to America sometime close to the turn of the century, perhaps to New York, according to his brother. But what his brother did know for certain was that their McMartins of Donegal used the name Cameron for an unknown reason. And his brother had proof of this in the form of postcards sent to members of the McMartin family addressed under the name of Cameron. As a next step, the postcards and any other relevant material would be scanned and sent to him from his brother— and on to me afterwards. He concluded in expressing his optimism over the possibility of this being a true connection. And it was certainly by now beginning to bear the earmarks of one to me as well.

One last reply to his was posted to the message board the next day containing my details for personal communication through email. In this message, a little more background on the surname dilemma was given:

In searching for new clues via genealogy centers in Ireland and here in California, I kept reverting to the possibility that the McMartin name somehow was changed to Cameron. The coincidence just seemed too strong to be dismissed. Like you, I had even seen mentioned that the Scottish name of Cameron might have a relationship to McMartin.

In the same message it was mentioned that I was in possession of an old photo album. After taking the time to scrutinize each picture much more closely than I did when the album was discovered ages ago in my mother's steamer trunk, it looked like it could contain a assortment of photos of both Rose's and her husband Patrick's Irish relatives by virtue of the fashions worn, hairstyles and age appearance of the pictures. Two of the photos had tiny studio embossed printing on the front side, indicating they were taken in Londonderry. They were the only ones that could be positively said to be Irish in origin instead of American at this point.

AMERICA

New York, December 1892

Mary's room in a smallish building in Brooklyn was by New York standards much more commodious than what many of the new immigrants to New York normally had to settle for. It wasn't a large, rundown rooming house in a depressed neighborhood which was in itself rather unusual. She knew this for a fact for during her first few months following her arrival in the city she had lived in exactly that kind of accommodation. Single people with no economic advantages working in the kind of menial jobs that were available to them were often relegated to living in conditions worse than they had left behind in their home country.

That was why Mary, on the tip from an acquaintance, had moved out as soon as she was able, sacrificing the greater convenience of having an address in Manhattan where she worked at the time in order to have decent quarters in a less hectic and less expensive locale. After all, water transportation no longer was the only way of reaching Manhattan. In 1883 the Brooklyn Bridge had been completed, the leading step, much to the chagrin of many who deplored the loss of their city's independent status, in paving the way for Brooklyn to become one of the five boroughs of New York City in 1898. But now that she had changed jobs, working closer to home in the Stuyvesant Heights neighborhood of Brooklyn, the walk to the large house where she was employed in service was easily done from her building on the fringe of Bushwick.

There was even just enough space in which to squeeze Rose and her two pieces of luggage until she got on her feet and was able to afford her own room. They both were aware it wouldn't be suitable for long but for the time being they were happy to have each other's company no matter how tight the living arrangement was. After all, hadn't seven of them shared living quarters in their almost as small cottage in Ireland? During the two years since Mary had left home Rose could see her sister had adapted well, becoming a young urban woman while leaving the most obvious traces of her country roots far behind. Her dress and even some of her mannerisms had changed, and she seemed to be almost oblivious to the commotion caused by the constant ebb and flow of city life. Mary, for her part, found her sister no longer the young school girl she remembered, but a self-possessed twenty year old who had changed a good deal herself. Rose's late spurt of growth in height, now taller than she was, had only added to her natural beauty and self-confidence.

The two sisters spent hours talking at length about their family back in Ireland, the changes to the farmstead and the effects of the Land Purchase Acts on the growing movement away from estates leasing to tenants and towards actual land ownership by the common man. This change would be a long time coming to the remotest parts of Ireland, such as the Inishowen Peninsula in Donegal, but locals would be ready to welcome it with open arms when it finally did. They discussed Irish politics, especially recent events in the nationalist movement for Irish Home Rule following the death of its leader Charles Stewart Parnell in 1891, only a year after Mary had emigrated from the country. The seemingly minor happenings in the lives of friends and neighbors known to them both were gone over in detail, including all of the very latest gossip Rose had brought with her. The same minute level of dissection of Mary's experience with local living and daily existence in Manhattan was shared with Rose. Her description of the different types of working situations, including the dealing with a variety of employer temperaments—many of them not so pleasant—was foremost among topics of interest to her sister.

But it would be several days before Mary dared to broach the subject of the circumstances of John.

Mail correspondence between Mary and family members and friends in Ireland had been sparse, limited to a few words on postcards and a letter or two of longer length, and nothing from what she read had led her to believe the plans of Rose and John had altered in any way. Obviously, he had not immigrated to New York on the same ship as Rose, and the fact she had not yet mentioned him did not bode well. She waited patiently for the moment when she sensed her sister was ready, to when she sensed she almost wanted to tell her about him.

"Have you had time to make acquaintance with any of the local lads…anyone special?" was the provocative question posed by Rose that gave an opening for Mary to respond in kind.

"Aye, only a couple that I've taken a stroll with—but nothings come of it so far, no one I particularly fancy. There was one that I met at a small café…don't you know I may see him again. But Rose what about you? You haven't said anything about John. How goes it with you and him? Has anything changed between yourselves?"

She knew that she would have to talk about him sooner or later, but the emotional sound in her own voice was surprising, almost unrecognizable to herself, as she began. "As far as I know everything was fine before we were about to leave. As for me, nothing has changed, so. We were still supposed to be sailing together but…" for a moment her lips trembled and the words failed to come out "…but he wasn't there." It was an admission difficult to make to one's own sister.

Before her sister could ask anything more, she continued: "I've gone over and over all the possible reasons why, Mary. All I can say is that I honestly just don't know what happened. I can only wait and hope to hear about the reasons why from home someday. Perhaps Casey will be able to find out something and let me know. I've sent her a card already."

Mary, hesitantly and carefully, asked one more question. "There wasn't…a kind of difference of opinion…a small disagreement on something, before you left or…"

But Rose's interruption was so swift and sharp it immediately laid that line of thought to rest. "No, never to any account did we argue—tease, yes, but not really argue. Just to the contrary, we couldn't wait to be off together. Ah, it's no use speculating too much more, I can only wait to hear—and hope maybe he's on his way and will be here soon. Meanwhile, I just need to get on with my life here until then. But one thing you can be sure, there'll be no going back for me no matter what."

"What a pity everything's gotten so muddled. Thanks for telling me, Rose. But enough said." Mary could see the pain her sister was suffering when many others could not. She knew Rose would do her best to conceal her emotions—this was Rose and several other of their family members summed up—but she could read from her gestures and small changes in tone of voice the level of her distress. She wanted to ask more questions, however, she could see that it would only provoke her sister to do so at this point. There would be other occasions to inquire further, but for now it seemed best to hold off in the expectation that Rose would hear back from Casey or someone else with news to clear the murky waters.

It didn't take long before Rose was able to find a place as a cook conveniently situated in a house in Brooklyn as well, thanks to connections from her sister and her sister's employer. Rose's solid foundation in basic cooking skills could be attributed to her eagerness to help her mother do something that captured her youthful interest, and to a nearly infallible ability to choose and mix ingredients in such proportions as to please the palate of most everyone within and without the household who tasted her dishes. And only once in a rare while in her new job did something not come out right. When this happened, she was wise enough not to jeopardize her reputation by serving it, to the benefit of some lucky dog or cat in a nearby alley way.

Yet, as unsullied as her cooking expertise was, she could not escape feeling this family who provided her with room and board in their house looked down on her as inferior, as someone who was quite beneath them in class. There was no doubt they were wealthy and she was only living there to work for what to them was a pittance—this disparity was crystal clear and not a problem. Rather it was the demeaning comments she had overheard that bothered her, along the lines that she probably was one of those who never wore shoes until coming to America and had spent her youth running around barefoot in the northwestern wilds of an uncivilized community. Or others harkening back to earlier years of immigration, when Irish were derogatorily referred to as potato eaters. When she heard such remarks or similar ones, she bit her tongue—weren't these people she served Irish as well? For Rose each person had their work to do in society and they should be judged and respected only on how well the job was done, particularly if you lived in America. But she was prudent enough not to jeopardize her position at this juncture. She just took a deep breath while seething inside, realizing afterwards that believing competency as a basic criterion for respect had been naïve. In truth, the fairness and equality issues so proudly embodied in the policies of the labor unions that were springing up seemed to have no real impact on the right to be protected from ill-treatment. And the growing signs that things were tightening up in the economy were testified to by the frequent news headlines citing the increasing loss of jobs and number of business failures. But she neither forgot nor forgave them these remarks.

When they did manage to have a common day off—as seldom as it was—Mary, Rose and her shipboard friend Siobhán made a point of meeting together. As they had pledged to one another in parting after arrival at Ellis Island, the two had continued their friendship. Siobhán had found employment in Manhattan so they did not work near enough to each other for frequent contact. Yet with their youthful energy, the distance between the two places did not prevent them from taking the time to get together whenever they could. It was on one of these outings several weeks later that the subject of John came up again. This time it was Siobhán who gently prodded Rose for any news about him.

"Have you had a word yet from Ireland, Rose?" She need not be more specific than that for it was evident to all what she was referring to.

She looked down and away for a brief moment before replying, "From my sister Bridget, aye, but nothing yet from Casey—or from John."

The few seconds of dead silence following did nothing to diminish the questioning thoughts behind the looks in their eyes and their sympathetic expressions. There was no use for Mary or Siobhán to try to gloss over the situation with hypothetical explanatory platitudes in an effort to try to comfort her. They knew that Rose would have none of that anyhow. And they had not detected in her demeanor any sense of betrayal or anger. But neither could Mary just let the topic drop cold again this time. "I wonder what's happened. There must be something that's got in the way…an interference of some sort. It's just not like him…so out of character." To which Rose just shrugged her shoulders in response.

***

If only they could have had the powers to be able to peer across the wide ocean, they would have found the answers they sought, and their doubts would have withered away in knowing the truth.

John's broken leg had given all appearances of being a straightforward case. The bone had not been fragmented and had been put back in place and properly splinted until a plaster cast was made, with no further complications. The doctor had said he would come by again in a few days to check on him. Before he could return, though, John broke out in heavy sweats and chills—a fever had set in. The doctor was summoned again to come immediately, and after a reexamination found that a swollen area above the fracture he had put down to a deep bruise upon initial examination, was in fact a second, smaller, closed break which left untreated had become mildly infected, perhaps because of its proximity to the first exposed break. Concerned with the seriousness of the infection and kind of treatment that would be required, the doctor had John removed to the clinic in Derry. The skin would have to be opened, the area thoroughly cleaned and, among other remedies, a poultice of heated bread and milk applied to end the infection. It would turn into a long stay there with many additional weeks needed before both fractures were sufficiently healed for him to be released to go back home.

Of course, Casey had eventually heard a good deal later an accident had occurred of such severity John could not have possibly gone on the same ship with Rose after all. It had taken days, however, for the news to spread between the parishes. But as soon as it had reached her, she had made plans to visit him at his home before being told that he was no longer there but in hospital in Derry instead. So she would have to wait until she could get to the city before hearing the whole story from him, not a frequent circumstance nowadays since her mother's illness needed more and more attention from her,.

When she finally made it to the Derry clinic she was appalled by the change in his appearance. Drawn and pale, without a trace of his normal glow of Irish ruddiness or even a hint of brownish tinge leftover from that spate of abnormally warm days they had worked through while fixing the estate house, he appeared to have lost at least two stone. There was also a downtrodden air, a dullness about him that went beyond the haggard physical change. In place of the usual sparkle in his eyes was a look of emptiness. But ever so slowly as he became more accustomed to conversing again, he began to let his story trickle out to someone who had played an important role in guarding the secrecy of his relationship with Rose. Bit by bit, she could see his mood making a visible swing the longer they spent together, a transformation was taking place. His eyes began to make contact with hers again. From dull to now semi-animated he spoke of his greatest pain—much greater than the physical pain he suffered—of having Rose think that he was not a man of his word, of having her think he had completely left her forsaken. Casey did her best to remind him: everything had happened was not by intention and he could not hold himself at fault. An accident could not be the end of everything. When healed, he would again be ready to pick up where they left off. By the time they she had left, she believed she had broken through and restored him somewhat to his former self or, lacking that much, at least to a better frame of mind. She had given him back a little of his hope and showed him that an open path still lay ahead that could see a life together with Rose.

Meanwhile, as each week passed, she expected to have news from Rose—at least a card with an address so she could write her back—but nary a word had yet arrived in the post. As far as she could tell, no one had been able to inform Rose before she had left Ireland of the tide of events that had transpired. Casey wondered if Rose might have received word from some other source by now. She didn't want to dwell long on what her state of mind would be if she hadn't heard anything. A promise of becoming husband and wife would not be thrown off lightly from someone with her strong commitment towards a future life together. If she would only jot down a quick note to say where she was living—just pick up a pen, Rose!

***

Kept in the dark as they were, no powers of sight could reveal the plight of John's circumstances to them so far away in America. And Rose had indeed already written. So she could only do her best with earning a living to making ends meet while waiting for an answer to fall into her hands someday.

PHOTOGRAPHS

Central Coast, California, April 2007

In the next set of email exchanges with my newly found correspondent, Daniel said the family he came from was a large one. His home was in Glasgow, Scotland and he had brothers and sisters living in the United States, Canada, Ireland and Scotland. On both sides the excitement of sealing a true connection between us was palpable. We were practically living in each other's shoes in waiting for his brother in Ireland to lay his hands on the postcards that would positively establish the use of both the Cameron and McMartin surnames within the same family, his ancestors and perhaps mine as well. And in the very next message, he attached a photograph of his great-grandparents, Denis and Mary, as well as a second one of Mary with one of her daughters and her only son William—Daniel's grandfather. Although I was almost certain that these people did not appear among those depicted in the old photo album of my mother's, I immediately and carefully compared the faces to all of those contained within it. Not a single one could be found among them.

Looking again through the old album gave me the idea to scan and send to Daniel the two photos that were definitely taken in Londonderry, the two which would be most likely to be of a person who could resemble someone in the pictures in the collection accessible to him. And now, seeing how close the potential home of my grandmother was to the city of Derry, the center of many shirt factories among other employment opportunities, it could be easily speculated that many local area people from Inishowen had sought work there. One of the Londonderry photos was actually a portrait postcard, with a studio photo on one side and a blank place for message and address on the reverse. Also sent was a third photo of a woman taken in San Francisco who bore some resemblance to the women in the photos he had sent.

In my email I wrote:

Also sending a scan of a photo postcard of either a relative or friend taken in Londonderry. This postcard was never mailed I think, since it does not have any postage stamp on it. It may have been given to Rose Anna before she left Ireland or maybe brought to her in San Francisco by another immigrant. On the reverse side it says "From Brigid to Rose". Ever hear of any mention of a Brigid? A third scan of two women is of a picture also taken in Londonderry, at The Ulster Photographic Co., 20 Carlisle Road. Again, I don't know who these people are. Rose Anna died well before I was born and my mother never pointed her out in a picture as far as I can remember. In looking through the old album, I am probably seeing her picture but just don't know who I am looking at. If only people wrote on the back of the pictures who these people were, but I guess this is human nature as I'm guilty of the same negligence as well. Is there any chance among things that your brother or another relative may have, that a picture of her may exist?

In rapid succession, two messages were sent back by Daniel:

Open the attachment only after reading the following

The old photo with the inscription you named "From Brigid to Rose" was one that felt as if I had seen before. It could have been a picture on a website I had looked at recently (deep down I was hoping not to find it there), and while after checking I found several other photos, yours was not among them. Then I searched a bunch of old photos I brought from my mother's house after she passed away. No luck here either. When I was in Ireland recently looking for more information about my father's ancestors I scanned some old photos and have them on my computer. Now in looking through these photos I came across one that seems a bit similar to your "Brigid to Rose" picture above. Please read next email.

Attached to the first message was a photograph that looked identical in appearance to the one I had sent. The first thought that entered my mind was that it must be an effort to lessen the tension that we were both experiencing in trying to come up with some answers. But the second message explained what we were both hoping for:

This was my way of trying to be a bit humorous after having returned from a crazy day at work. Sorry.

Of course, as you can tell, the two photos are exactly the same. Chills ran through me after this picture was found and compared with yours and the realization of what it meant. And there is another picture you sent I am certain I have seen before. There are two women in it, one who is standing and the other sitting.

There is no doubt for me that you have provided the

answer to the mystery of my two great aunts while you have gained the knowledge of the family you were searching for. Great research has been done in finding our connection and we now can start to exchange more information.

The chills rippling up and down, in and around, throughout every inch of my body were no less than his excitement, I'm sure, especially after a careful examination of the scans of both photographs showed that the name of the studio embossed on the lower right side of each picture was in a slightly different place, leaving no doubts that they were exact replicas of each other in every respect except for this single distinguishing feature, obviously added after the print run had concluded. Judging from the style of fashion worn by the woman and the appearance of the postcard itself, it seemed that it was likely taken during the first decade of the 1900s.

A hasty review of Daniel's original posting confirmed what I recollected—he had mentioned that the parents of Rose Anna and her sister Mary were his great-grandparents. This relationship was reiterated in greater detail, including exact places and years of birth for a number of siblings of the pair. Could it be that the painstaking, inch-by-inch hunt for my grandmother's origins I had embarked upon over six months before had truly reached a successful conclusion? The postcards proving the use of the two different surnames by family members had not yet materialized. But his message ended on the optimistic note:

Material still hasn't come from my brother but it will likely just confirm what we now know.

Daniel

The kind of impact it had can be drawn from my reply:

When I saw your copy of the photo I sent to you I thought it must be a joke. It really is incredible you should actually have the same one. Big thanks to the internet and other family seekers allowing me to first find the McMartin baptismal record, then to find you by virtue of your research methods using genealogy message boards. A few years back none of this could have happened.

For me, I am convinced, at this point, I have indeed found my grandmother's family. If your brother's postcards also bear proof of the surnames connection, this, for me at least, would be beyond circumstantial evidence. As I mentioned before, having seven out of eight biographical elements the same, with only the McMartin surname differing, was the big tip off. With photos and, maybe, postcards arriving soon to further substantiate all of this, any doubt on my part would be erased. And as you can tell, I am beyond happy about it and don't have the right words to describe my feelings.

All of these revelations happened as the special March holiday approached—it seemed only fitting. The ending of his next message said it all. *P.S. Have a great St Patrick's Day and law of the mountain dew.*

With the swift unfolding of events such as it was with Daniel, it occurred to me now the data I had provided to the researcher in Ireland could very well be leading him in the wrong direction. Without wasting another moment, I wrote him of the new developments:

Before contacting you I had come across a baptismal

record that had all facts correct that I know about my grandmother except for the surname of her father and herself. All of the elements were the same for year of birth, month of birth, grandmother's first name Rose Anna, great-grandmother's last name, great-grandmother's first name, great-grandfather's first name, birthplace County Donegal. The seemingly critical sole difference was the surname, listed on the record as being McMartin instead of Cameron. I hesitated to mention this coincidence before because of this surname discrepancy. **Now, what I consider extraordinary new information has been collected that confirms that Rose Anna McMartin and Rose Anna Cameron are the same person and the one I am searching for**.

With the new information that had been obtained, including the date and parish of marriage of my great-grandparents, he was directed to reorient his research to finding the McMartin family. Even without this information until now, he had already honed in on the same parish in Donegal as a likely contender based on the Cameron surname version of my grandmother in conjunction with the other data provided.

The non-materialization of the postcards to add to the evidence of the photographs spurred a personal desire to find if there was some sort of written recognition of an affinity between the two surnames either on the Web or in the traditional reference literature. A thoroughgoing search of the internet gave me what I was hoping for on two different websites. According to the first, the McMartin name was considered to be another name for Cameron, in fact, during the 1700s and 1800s the two names seemed to have been used interchangeably from generation to generation. Adding to the legitimacy of the first, the writer on the second website said the origins of his McMartin family was indeed a Gallowglass tribe scion of the Camerons of Scotland. The name connection thus borne out lessened to some degree my impatience to view images of the cards, but my fingers were still crossed they would soon be found.

Not having given Daniel all of the information on my grandfather Patrick, Rose's husband, he began using his resources to see if he could help me find this particular Kavanaugh's origins in Donegal as well. But before he spent much time, I told him that I had recently learned from his death certificate his place of birth was County Roscommon, not Donegal, as previously thought. However, some doubts still lingered over Roscommon, both because of whom the informant was on the certificate, and because my mother never mentioned Roscommon when she spoke of her parents. Further credence was given to these reservations by the fact that the authoritative and comprehensive genealogy center in Roscommon, Ireland was neither able to locate his baptism in their parish record database, nor could recordings of his parents be identified for certain among the civil death records given the number of decedents with the same names. If he had been born in Roscommon, he had left no clearly discernible tracings behind.

The next message exchange between us revealed that Daniel's impatience and passion in pursuing a body of evidence that further supported and developed what we had gathered and learned equaled or surpassed my own. Instead of waiting any longer for his brother in Ireland to go through his collection of documents and send them on to him, his excitement over our joint discoveries got the better of him, and he decided to quickly put together a trip from Glasgow to Donegal by car ferry across the North Channel of the Irish Sea. Once there he would be able to delve more deeply into both the collections and childhood recollections his older brother had of the McMartin family, and would also be able to visit with a second brother in the same Inishowen neighborhood as well as with a sister now living in County Galway. He would also be stopping in Letterkenny, the largest town in County Donegal, at one of its hospitals that serves as the local county registry office where vital records for birth, marriage and death are kept for the region. Taking his portable scanner with him, he promised to scan everything in sight, keeping me apprised of what turned up by stopping at internet cafes scattered along the route.

WESTWARD

New York and San Francisco, California, June-September 1893

Months slid by. Seasons changed and the cold and snowy New York winter slowly melted away into the tentative promise of spring. But the same two threads of discontent continued to tug at the sisters. For Rose, despite making small efforts to let her employers understand that she was not comfortable with their off-hand remarks, spoken just loudly enough for her to overhear when she was leaving the room, the affronts continued in the same proportion as her feeling of being ill at ease grew.

Both when she was alone and when she was with her sister or friends, the work situation was often hovering in the background of her thoughts. In talking with Mary, it sometimes moved to the vocal forefront and they both realized her normal personality was beginning to show signs of strain associated with the kind of psychological abuse she was undergoing. She could not go as far as to say that it took the shape of outright scorn, but still, it was like an insidious assault on her self-worth. They both also separately realized that it would only be a matter of time before the cracks showing in her mental toughness would inevitably lead to a regrettable outburst that would be too late to retract to save her job. It would be better to end it sooner rather than later, before that kind of eventuality came to pass.

It was now nearly three years since Mary had come to New York. Her employment situation, unlike Rose's, was satisfactory if not entirely satisfying. Even so, she felt she had waited long enough to carry out her long-held plans of making the move to Massachusetts; she was more than ready to test the waters in Boston. Another large city it was, she was well aware of that fact, but one with a decided Irishness about it, much more than she had felt in New York. She had put aside enough cash for the train trip there with something left over to keep her afloat for a month or two while she sought out a placement, which, wishfully, would be more interesting than her current one.

So the sisters, at an age still young enough to be able to set aside heavy hearts of parting from one another, began to make plans for the next stage of their lives. For Rose, this meant taking time to look for new work in New York, especially enlisting the aid of her friends in keeping their ears open for something suitable. She and Mary would be seeing Siobhán in three days and they would both tell her of what their intentions were then. As a very outgoing, gregarious person, Siobhán always had plenty of news from various segments of the Irish community to relate so she would be one of the best ones of their companions from whom to learn about new job prospects.

When they did meet—before the sisters had barely a chance to make the merest mention of what they had decided—Siobhán overtook their train of thoughts with a momentous announcement of her own.

"Guess what's happened? What I've been dreaming about…well it's going to come true. I'll soon be dancing an

Irish jig to a whole new audience. It's off to San Francisco I'll be going, would you believe it?

Mouths dropped open and looks of astonishment spread over both of their faces as the sisters looked at each other.

"But you haven't said a word about going west for quite a while. How…how did it come to you all so quickly, of a sudden now?" Rose stammered out.

"It seems that way, I know, but really I've just been waiting for the right moment. And now it's come. Everything just seems to have fallen into place."

She had recently received word from her relatives living among the significant Irish community in San Francisco and what they had said was favorable to her idea of moving on to California from New York. They not only had encouraged her to come but had even said they had sufficient space to put her up for the time it took until she could find a placement. According to them, a short job search was a very reasonable expectation because work opportunities were plentiful. And, San Francisco, much like, albeit smaller in population than Boston, had a strong Irish flavor to it, down to its famous foggy and breezy coastal climate. The damp could definitely penetrate whatever you were wearing at times, especially during the summer when you would least expect it! But, as they told it, the main difference was that there was plenty of sunshine as well and none of the harsh New England winters to contend with. And it wasn't crowded like Manhattan and some of the other New York boroughs—there was a feeling of space as opposed to the shoulder-to-shoulder crunch of the East Coast masses.

Siobhán needed nothing more than their firm invitation to come and stay, and actually she needed not even that to convince herself the time was ripe to go for she had long ago set her sights on going to San Francisco, before she had even sailed from the shores of Ireland. Their warm words of living support provided the necessary boost to her long-held conviction, serving to act sooner rather than later. So her own excitement had blinded her usual ability to be able to sense when others had something important to tell, to hold back and listen instead of talking, and she had launched right into it with her friends—as soon as they had exchanged their customary morning greetings.

"I've given in my notice. Sure, I couldn't wait a moment longer. Next week I'll be seeing the agent about booking a train ticket…all the way to the West Coast."

"When will it be for?" Rose asked.

"Normally, they would like two months. I told them I was hoping to make it one month's notice since I may not have a place to stay if I delayed too long in going. So we agreed on six weeks."

"Then you'll be leaving here before you know it, won't you now? It must cost a pretty penny to go all that way. How did you manage it in such a short time?" Mary wanted to know.

"It's not as much as you might think. I've looked into it already, of course. They have a low cost fare called the Union Pacific Emigrant. It's a kind of sleeping car, no less…with upper and lower berths so you don't have to sit-up the whole way…there's no extra charge like there is in first class."

"How many days does it take to get to San Francisco?" as Rose continued to pepper her with questions.

Siobhán had the information on the tip of her tongue: "Only about four and a half. There's an emigrant fare train leaving daily around six in the evening, so no lack of choice of day there. It goes through Omaha, Nebraska—over three thousand miles coast-to-coast for a total cost of about ninety dollars. It's a lot but not so much when you consider the distance and the number of days it takes."

"How do you eat? Do they sell food on the train?"

"You can bring your own and there is a cooking stove at the end of each car, although there's food at some of the stations along the way, they say. You bring your own blankets and wraps with you, too."

They continued the conversation, covering more of the details of Siobhán's forthcoming adventure, after they had sat down on a bench in the park. While the sisters' own news about their future plans was somewhat diminished by hers, they told her of their intentions as well. When they had finished, Siobhán was the first to put into words what they were all thinking.

"Isn't it something that we're all going to making changes so soon again? I knew it wouldn't be much longer before Mary would want to give Boston a try. She's like me. Once you get an idea into your head it stays put. But Rose, you too, having to find new work and move to another place in New York." And, then thinking of her friend's character and of the blow dealt to her marital plans, she chanced a suggestion.

"I couldn't entice you to look a wee bit further away. They say that the opportunities are there for the taking in San Francisco. And people on the West Coast are supposed to be so different than here in Manhattan. And wouldn't it be something if we could continue our travels, be shipmates of a sort again, this time aboard a train?"

Without seeming to give much attention to the actual

idea, a wry grin appeared on her face.

"That would really be changing employers, wouldn't it now!"

After the sisters had parted from Siobhán and as they walked back to the section of town where they lived, their thoughts about her grand news rattled through and swirled around in their heads. What struck the sisters first was that for the great distance it was, the price of the transcontinental fare was not all that unthinkable and unattainable. It made Mary's plans to move the relatively short distance to Boston seem much less like an ordeal in comparison. For Rose, what Siobhán had said suddenly started to sink in on a different level as well. And the more she mulled over in her mind the more a single question ran through her brain. Why not California for her, too? The very name "San Francisco" was in itself alluring. It was well-noted from others she knew how life really was very different, more open and less constraining there, on the opposite shore of this vast land. And her sister Mary would no longer be in New York to keep her company anyhow. She had enough savings to be able to afford the fare, and the opportunity to share the journey with a friend made a long trip so much more attractive. It would be like Siobhán had said; an extension of their voyage from Ireland onto New York.

Yes, as the idea to take the risk became anchored in her mind, it began to take precedence over other thoughts and concerns. It became almost as if it was meant to be. The timing was perfect. She still had had no word about John after the many months that had passed, more than a year in all, and it was time to shed all pretenses of waiting any longer for him from her mind and to get on with her own life. If somehow he should re-emerge someday, well then he would just have to come to San Francisco to find her! In letting herself come to this resolve, she was at once closing one chapter in her life while at the same time freeing herself for moving forward and opening up a new chapter—in an entirely new locale. It just felt like the right thing to do—now!

The hint of a frown and look of uncertainty framed her words: "Mary, I…an idea…just I've been thinking…" was enough for Mary to read Rose's struggling thoughts and to stop her in mid-stream.

"Say what you have to say—don't hold back speaking your mind, Rose. You don't have to worry about telling me. We are always family no matter what direction we decide to take."

From there the words came tumbling out. "What Siobhán said just seems right for me as well. I don't know why I hadn't thought before about something like this…like going to San Francisco myself. It's a chance I can't pass up. I know it might seem like I've just glommed on to the first thing that's come along, but actually I think something like this has been brewing there for awhile—it just took Siobhán to set it in motion and make me see the way ahead clearly. And there's no doubt that I've been unable to shake a feeling of restlessness I've known now for awhile, especially knowing yourself will be on to Boston soon."

Any fears she still may have harbored of what Mary would say were quickly put to rest. She understood, concurred and encouraged—a reaction that was most welcomed by Rose, and one that was worthy of the sister she looked up to for support for the future and who had been always so dependable in the past. Indeed, Mary was quick to recall that there were members of close Inishowen neighbors, the McDaid family, who were living in San Francisco—as well as some distant cousins—all the more reason to make Rose feel more confident and comfortable in her decision-making. And they could surely be counted on to lend a hand in seeing that she got settled despite the fact that it was their daughter, Nuala, who once played a trick on Rose when they were young girls, leading to her losing one of her shoes—and to the repercussions she had experienced when she had been asked to explain her partial shoelessness when she got home. They had fallen out as friends for a few months because of it. She wouldn't forget it, but she had long ago forgiven her.

Once broached by Rose and approved by Mary, the actions needed to put together the journey stole Rose's attention away from everything else. At the top of the list, she wanted to speak with Siobhán as soon as they had a moment to spare to see each other again. When they did, of course, Siobhán was ecstatic, having had no expectation her words had struck home with Rose and that she would actually take her up on the suggestion since Rose's reaction at the time had been minimal. Not long after, like Siobhán, she happily gave her notice in to her employers as well. Then she booked a train ticket for the same day, with a berth next to Siobhán's in the very same car. And so it was, within in a space of a few weeks, the three of them would be leaving their first American home, travelling once again to discover unknown corners of their newly adopted land.

Rose and Siobhán said their farewells to Mary first from the platform of the station early one September morning where they saw her off on a train bound for Boston, with promises of keeping in touch frequently. Then, two weeks later, it was their turn to climb aboard a long distance train at Manhattan's Grand Central Terminal. Fighting off goose bumps and shivers, despite being a typical summery hot and sultry evening, they leaned their heads out the window to watch the steam locomotive slowly drag the car they had boarded into motion. With billowy puffs and measured chugs, like a slow heartbeat responding to increasing exertion, the engine gained speed until it reached a rhythmically rapid pulse and its noisy strokes blurred into one steady background whir.

The emigrant sleeping car was comfortable enough although it could not compare to the Pullman Palace Cars with their plush horse hair mattresses and clean bedding, parlor furnishings by day and a bed chamber at night. Porters and conductors were on service duty at all times if you were one of those fortunate ones. Each day passed quickly in watching shapes and colors of the undulating landscape unfold, and in meeting and talking to fellow passengers. About midway in their journey the verdant landscape took on a notable change. The limitless shades of green and gold were swept away by hues of brown and tan, colors of a land thirsty for additional rainfall. And then from Omaha to Denver they passed from endless flat prairie into the highest mountains they had ever seen, passing through Grand Island, North Platte, Cheyenne, Laramie, Green River, Evanston and Ogden before transferring to the Central Pacific and moving on through Reno, Nevada. In between the larger cities, the route had taken them through the tiniest, dusty towns too numerous to remember, with names like Medicine Bow, Bovine, Pequod, Tulasco, Deeth, Raspberry Creek, Clipper Gap and Suisun. The final descent was made into Sacramento and from there it wasn't long before the train alighted at the Oakland Long

Wharf, western terminus of the transcontinental railroad, and where ferries were waiting and ready to provide transport onto San Francisco.

It was with much trepidation that they approached the Oakland wharf during their early morning arrival. In spite of it being over twenty years before, stories of a ferry boat accident that happened in 1871 still circulated about. Fifteen people had drowned during the tragedy, but their edgy nerves at the moment could be attributed as much to the reported sightings of ghosts in the ensuing weeks after the disaster, ghosts that were said to continue to haunt to this day the area near the harbor slip where the ferry sank. Their apprehension, which took the form of joking with nervous, self-conscious laughter, was not long-lasting, however, as they became lost in the crowd of disembarking passengers, all in haste to get their first look at the San Francisco Bay, and across it to the city of final destination itself.

As it was, they had plenty of opportunity for gazing for there still remained the tedious task of unloading the luggage of the more heavily laden passengers from the train and reloading the same onto the ferry. For their own possessions, they could well manage them without help, as they had done throughout their journeys so far, feeling much like the itinerant Irish tinkers they had often encountered at home. The ferry crossing was quickly over and done with, and when they set their feet down for the first time at the ferry terminal in San Francisco, it came with a sigh of relief. Their long passage was complete in more ways than one. No words were needed as they looked into each other's eyes then wrapped arms around one another in an embrace of shared understanding.

POSTCARDS

Central Coast, California, April-May 2007

Daniel had left for Ireland some days before. Each day following his departure, I looked for incoming messages for news on the elusive postcards reputedly in the hands of his brother in Donegal. Late in March the first indication the wait would finally be rewarded appeared in my inbox:

A brief note. I have been able to compare the other pictures you sent with my brother's collection. There are now three matches! Besides the one we already know about, there is the one of the sitting woman in a wicker chair and the other of the sitting and standing women mentioned before. My brother has about thirty postcards total addressed to different Cameron sisters. You will be receiving scans of them soon.

There are also some other pictures I have scanned. This message is from a Letterkenny cyber cafe and afterwards I will be returning to the house of my brother and will probably not be able to read your reply there. Tomorrow I will be going to Galway. I should be back in Donegal by Wednesday when I hope to meet someone who might have more information about the family of our great-grandmother, Mary. The attachment has a picture of someone who may be Rose, together with Anne, her sister, but not one hundred percent certain. There are others but they are too similar and the file size is more than two megabytes so they will not send from here.

More Later,
Daniel

He actually had seen them and they were all what we hoped they would be! To think that these old postcards had not succumbed to disintegration and had been kept safe all this time was astonishing to me. It was almost as if they were intended to survive in order to play an important role one hundred years later. And now we had three old picture matches. I didn't even hesitate a nanosecond before writing back although I knew he had said it might be days before he could write again:

You are really on the move. Just like us when we are travelling, always hitting the internet cafe or a public library to keep in touch. It's really incredible that after all of these years that we have three photos that are identical. I am envisioning your movements in my head and am sharing the astonishment as you uncover our links to the past. Not enough thanks do I have, Daniel, for your thoughtfulness in letting me know almost as it happens, and for taking the time to get Rose Anna's birth certificate in Letterkenny.

Can't wait to see the postcards. It's really surprising to hear that they were sent to sisters in Ireland with last names of Cameron instead of McMartin. In doing some research, I've located several items that indicate that both the **McMartin and Cameron names** have the same Gaelic root: **Cam-shron**.

I am fervently hoping that one of the many postcards that were kept has some kind of clue about Rose's sister Mary on it. With a little help, I think we will find her too. No exact matches of the photos you sent to mine but the oval one of a single woman at the bottom of the group of three you sent looks quite a bit like the woman in one I sent earlier entitled "Unknown photo San Francisco". Compare them when you have time. Also sending a scan of another one taken in San Francisco because it looks like it could be one of the sisters.

Ready to visit Ireland soon to see these places first hand. Looking forward with eagerness to the next installment.

It would take five long days before I was to receive further word from him again:

Returned to Glasgow early this morning and after a little sleep I am now doing errands around town for a few hours. Took time out to stop at a cyber cafe but will have to leave soon. I wanted to see if some cards are able to be sent, and also a possible picture of Rose Anna, according to what someone told my brother.

There is a good story well worth telling on how my brother obtained these pictures. Some years previously Cousin James McMartin, who now owns the house that once belonged to our great-grandparents, decided to use it for storing things but needed to empty it out first. He was able to have my brothers help him. When my brothers arrived James had started already and was about to put the cards and photos into a fire. They were rescued by my oldest brother. No one will know what had been destroyed before. The past was of no interest to Cousin James and he saw no importance in old items, but fortunately my brother did and he kept them.

With some time, my brother thought he might be able to figure out who a few of the people in these photos were. He acquired some help from the older folks in the area and together they were able to identify a handful of them. He did his best, and some of the photos look as if they might be of the person who could be either Rose Anna or her sister, Mary. It would be wise to treat this with caution as I am not the best at making these kinds of judgments, but taking everything into consideration maybe the information is fifty percent or better.

It was from Londonderry the cards were sent and it seems likely the people who sent them were working there at the time. I will try to send this group now.

Daniel

Out of the three image attachments, only one opened properly—the one labeled "annierightandrosie". But it was enough. It was the one I dreamed of seeing—the one that I needed to see. With a simple click, presto—before my eyes for the first time could be the spitting image of my grandmother. In the picture were two young women, both with hair worn up with a topknot in the pulled-back-and-up style of the era, the one on the left a few inches shorter in height than the other on the right and appearing a little younger, although difficult to tell for sure.

They were both wearing stylish tailored dresses with puffed out shoulders—and the one on the right was wearing a *polka dot scarf* that fanned out in the front. The woman on the left immediately looked familiar, and it wasn't but a minute or two that I found a photo in the old album that could well have been the same person. While still debating this in my mind, another message arrived from Daniel with three more attachments. Two of them were of postcards that wouldn't open in the previous mail, but the third one was a photograph of a single woman labeled simply Rosie. *Do you think this could be Rose?*

There seemed like a tinge of doubt in his mind, but to me it looked like the same person who was on the left in the earlier photo he had sent. And much more than that, it was an exact replica of the familiar photo in the album I had just picked out! There were a few more details to give him which might help in the process of identification:

The two postcards came through beautifully, as well as the picture. Have a look at the one I've sent you. Guess what, we now have four matches! And I do think it is very likely to be Rose.

From what I can tell, the sister you thought might be Rose in the picture you sent earlier of the two sisters, with Rose on the left and Annie on the right, looks very much like the same person to me in our two identical, single woman photos. Mine is mounted on photo board with a Morse, 916 Market St., San Francisco, California impression on it at the bottom. I'm thinking that Rose probably sent an unmounted duplicate home, it would be lighter and less expensive to post that way. Just a theory, though.

It's funny that I had already been comparing my picture of the single lady with the one you sent of the two sisters and thought that two of them looked pretty much alike, and that it could actually be my grandmother. That you, and others, should pick it out too as possibly being Rose reinforces my feeling. We really are operating via the same wavelength.

It looked like I could soon be on the receiving end of another picture thought to be of Rose Anna that could help me verify for sure which one among the old album pictures might be of her. To be able to put a real face on my grandmother with certainty would breathe new life into all of the information gathered to date. And maybe it could help me in sorting out who people were in some of the other uncaptioned photographs, particularly her sister Mary, whom I felt sure was sprinkled among those in the album as well.

As for the first two postcards that accompanied the photos, they were all that we hoped they would be. They were sent from Londonderry by cousins to the sisters of Rose Anna—each of them addressed to a sister's correct given name but using Cameron instead of their birth surname of McMartin. So an earlier deduction I had made was on the money—family members were working in Derry, the only city in reasonable proximity of their home. And with the next message came another batch of cards:

> Some more cards to go over are attached. That the surname Cameron was used by the McMartins is in much evidence so we definitely share a common ilk. I will try to go back over your mails to answer the questions you posed earlier as until now comparing and sending the postcards and pictures has taken up most of my interest.

> Daniel

From friends and cousins living in Derry and the United States, this group of cards brought written word from afar to all four of the remaining sisters in Donegal. Each of their forenames was prominent in the addresses on one or more cards. None, of course, were sent to either Rose Anna or Mary, who had sailed away before the early years of the twentieth century when these cards were posted. That a small number of these cards—all sent to the same address and the same persons in Donegal as the others—had McMartin as a surname instead of Cameron indicated the senders had either forgotten that the family was now using Cameron or they had never been informed of the change. Genealogically speaking, it was good it turned out this way for it gave another layer of primary source evidence to bear on what by now had become well-established fact.

Dear Cousin, began the next message from Daniel. The new salutation meant that there were no more doubts to dispel, and it also signified that we had now turned a corner and it was time to start fleshing out more of the family structure. This task was made easier from the years that Daniel had already spent in research, assembling an abundance of family history information on all sides:

It appears, for at least the present, that of the one son and six daughters Neil and Catherine had, only one son and one daughter got married. John, my grandfather, was the son. Eight children were born to him and his wife, Annie. They all survived until adulthood and children were born to four of them. Did Rose Anna have more than one child?

Two of my grandfather's children went to New York and New Jersey in America, but my mother who married Bernard McColgan stayed in Glasgow. A disk is in preparation which I will send to you and when done should help to clarify these relationships. My brother believes he remembers being told that Mary, sister to Rose Anna, never married and her will left some money to be sent home to Ireland, but this is not absolutely sure. There is speculation she lived in Boston in 1920, based on one of the postcards.

Daniel

It was a reflection of the times in Ireland—the late

nineteenth and early twentieth century—that so few of my grandmother's sisters were to marry. But it was still striking to hear that of my great-grandparent's children a son and one of six daughters, my grandmother Rose, were the only ones of these siblings to have children. Prospects for marriage were greatly diminished with famine-related deaths reaching over one million and another million Irish natives lost to emigration. This shortage of suitable mates was matched by a shortage of land to spread among the remaining inhabitants after so many generations of following the practice of subdividing and parceling it out in smaller pieces to male children—all in a milieu of subsistence living and impoverished circumstances for a sizeable proportion of the population.

All in all, a total of ten postcards were scanned and their image files emailed to me. Each one contained words of the writer, painting a better picture of the period. Two of them wrote about illness and death—that of my great-grandfather— others about a planned rendezvous or missing seeing someone. Brief words, but poignant in the way they were written—with an Irish lilt that could be felt in them. Not enough appreciation can be given to Daniel's older brother whose quick thinking and respect for the past saved them from the devouring flames. Like the destruction of so many other records, Irish and American both, fire would not be allowed to intercede to consume the tangible memory of our ancestors this time.

SAN FRANCISCO

San Francisco, California, September-December 1893

"Take a deep breath, Rose, and inhale this fine salty air. It's like tasting a potato of a whole new variety with a hint of the sea to it—one that's as good as or better than the best you've ever tasted. And it's almost as if it was boiled up fresh just for us."

With hands placed on their hips and their bodies arched backwards, they both inhaled as deeply as they could to fill themselves with this free-for-the-taking, welcome embrace to their new home. Siobhán wasn't exaggerating for Rose felt a new quality to the air as well, which was different from both Ireland and what they had experienced in New York. It was a positive sign for a good beginning to be buoyed up as they were with this first impression. They readied themselves for the next stage of their journey by looking for the next available coach to carry them and their possessions to their respective living addresses. They were both fortunate to be in the enviable position of having someone to stay with initially upon arrival. The scramble for the first vacant coaches they wisely left to the more eager and aggressive newcomers. More empty coaches and horsecars were slowly moving along the long line that stretched out down the wharf road, drawing closer to where they waited as soon as the full ones moved on, the horses shuffling forward automatically, without even needing prodding from the drivers, so accustomed as they were to doing their jobs.

When the crowd had thinned enough, they made their move towards a coach only to be greeted by a surly driver who must still have been in the throes of a late night out or of an earlier fare that had left him out of sorts. He seemed to have more than likely done without his morning meal as well. His sour demeanor left him reluctant to remove himself from his seat to lend a hand with their bags, much less doff his cap like the rest of the drivers did as a sign of respectful greeting when picking up a new fare. Not wanting to let this kind of attitude dampen their enthusiasm while only beginning to get acquainted with their new surroundings, the two of them, after a quick exchange of glances, told the driver they would take the next coach instead. This left him with an even deeper frown, surely generating fodder for further grumbling and an even darker mood for the next customer to endure.

The next coachman jumped down to assist them without asking or needing to be asked, as if it was the most natural and customary treatment for a person in his trade to perform for all passengers, restoring their faith that San Francisco was not the land of the uncivilized.

"The name is Patrick and where can I be setting you two young ladies down today?" were his first words after the loading was over and they were comfortably seated. Rose directed him to the address of the McDaid family living in the south of Market Street vicinity, not far from Saint Patrick's church.

Siobhán, staying at her friends not far away in the same area of the city, was dropped off first, since her address was the nearest.

"Don't forget in two days we're getting together to start looking for work. Shall we meet at the McDaids or do you want to come here, Rose?"

"Let's meet at your lodgings early in the morning. We'd be more likely to get a good start that way" was what Rose had in mind. And with that agreed upon and another warm hug, the coach was on its way again, heading for the second address.

"Have you come a far way to get here?" the coachman asked as they made their way down wide avenues dodging cable cars then winding through closed-in, narrow streets in-between.

"Very much so. We've just come by train from the East Coast."

"Quite a distance that is, I should say, especially as I would guess as you'd be coming from the old country not so long ago?"

"You're right there. A year in New York hasn't been enough to change my Donegal accent much. But I could say the same for your own."

"Roscommon is…was my home. Like you, though, I passed some time on the other side of this grand land before deciding to try my luck here in San Francisco. But that's a story long in the telling and we're pulling up to your destination now. Where would you like me to put your case?"

At least her first ride in the city by the bay had been a cordial one. Having paid the driver after he carried her luggage to the top of the stairs, Rose thanked him heartily for his help, making her best effort at emulating city sophistication.

"When I have the occasion to need the use of

transportation again, I hope all of the coachmen are as amiable and capable as you are." The smile that formed around his mouth and in the corners of his eyes told of the appreciation he had for her kind words. And with a second flourish of his cap, the amiable coachman was on his way again.

The welcome of the McDaids' did not belie the written invitation extended by them to Rose when she was in New York. Even though they had two children to look after and were already living in tight quarters, they rearranged things enough to make room for a fifth person as well. Not wanting them to worry about the inconvenience of providing space for her for a long term, she took the first opportunity to let them know that she and her friend Siobhán would be looking for work immediately and that they might even find a place to live together, depending on how working conditions and location worked out. John McDaid, the father, reassured her that they had been looking forward to her coming and she was to stay as long as she needed. At the same time, seeing the travel weariness written upon her face, he urged her to get some rest to restore herself before they listened to her adventures. Although they were eager to hear about the trip, the stories could well wait at least to the following the day.

After breakfast the next morning, Rose took a short walk around the neighborhood. By the sounds of the voices on the street and in the markets, it looked like half of Ireland and a good portion of several other countries had just immigrated to this section of town. She passed several buildings that gave the appearance of once being old hotels but had since become boarding houses instead, mostly for immigrants. She had already heard a little about the transformation of the neighborhood from wealthy to working class over the last few decades. There appeared little trace left of the legacy of the rich other than the size and number of large single family dwellings and the attention to detail in the architecture of these buildings now converted into boarding houses. Rose didn't stray too far from the McDaid's apartment, stopping just long enough to buy a few postcards at a corner shop before returning home.

Without delay upon arriving back, she sat down at a table and wrote her first message from her new, temporary California residence: *Well old dears I now write with pleasure hoping you are all well as I am myself. Give my best regards to all of our cousins at home. I will write more to you soon. I remain your Loving Daughter and Sister, Rose.* She smiled as she thought of their delight when they gathered in the cottage to read the few words that kept both them and her in mind.

The following day was one with no work for John, so in the morning they all went together to see a few of the nearby city landmarks. The Nob Hill cable car was what Rose wanted to go to first off. They all took the journey up to the top of the hill where they took in the views from near the Mark Hopkins mansion. From this vantage point, she could see the pockets of fog that had not yet cleared from various parts of the city and the glistening bay as she spun herself around in a three hundred and sixty degree rotation. She wondered in which area of this up-and-down, very hilly city she would find work and where she would eventually end up living. The day was enjoyably passed, but it would need getting down to just that with Siobhán when the new work week began the next morning.

When they met, both of them had already pulled together "help sought" advertisements from the Morning Call and the

San Francisco Chronicle and Examiner newspapers. They also had a few leads from the families they were staying with. From her experience in New York, Rose was skeptical of working in service in a household again but the majority of the jobs listed were exactly of that type. In the late afternoon, after taking turns visiting a good number of households, they made their way to an address listed on Octavia Street that had particularly stood out. Instead of the usual single opening, the advertisement was for "servants needed". It was a German family by the name of Roth, consisting of the head of the household—an elderly lady in her seventies—her two daughters, one a spinster and the other married to a husband by the name of Gerst, and their single child. The positions needed were for cook and server. Introductions were made and the specifics of the jobs talked over in detail. Afterwards they thought their interviews seemed to have gone favorably, however, one of the daughters would not be home until later. Both Rose and Siobhán had been asked if they could return to meet with her in the afternoon the following day.

The two young women agreed they had liked the family and the jobs seemed good. Rose's experience at home assisting her mother in preparing meals and in New York made her the best fit for the cook position and Siobhán was fine with server work. Sharing a workplace with a friend would make their jobs and life in general much more interesting not to mention amusing, if their past bouts of laughter when together were any indication. But now they both would have to anxiously wait to see how the meeting with other daughter went and what the rest of the family had really thought of them. It seemed like they were approving, but they were cautious enough to realize appearances were not always to be trusted.

"What would you be preferring, Rose, should we just go home, or maybe take a detour and walk through the Chinatown quarter of town we've heard so much about?"

"I think we should go to Chinatown. It's not too late and we've no other appointments to be at today."

"Let' go then. I think it will take our minds off all of the people we've met and questions we had to answer. We'll go home then with clearer heads on our shoulders."

Even though it was out of the way, it would be daylight for another hour or two at this time of the year so they decided to have a look at this much-heralded ethnic neighborhood on their way back home. They were not disappointed. The throngs of Chinese packing the streets in their distinctive fashion of dress, displaying different mannerisms even in the way they walked the streets, left no doubt this was a truly unique district in their newly adopted city. When the kind of foods that were being openly displayed and sold and the constant chatter in a most unusual sounding language, of which not one word was understandable to them, were also taken into account, they thought that they could easily have been in the country of China itself. But where were the women? Only occasionally could a female be spotted. Perhaps they were being kept unseen indoors for some cultural reason. More likely, as they had heard a little about, it was because mostly men had immigrated leaving women behind at home, which turned out to be the actual case as they learned for certain sometime afterwards. The lack of females in general and the few visible Chinese women there were on the streets who gave the appearance of looking somewhat timid and remaining as inconspicuous as possible in this male-dominated mini-society, contributed to their own feeling of uneasiness. They picked up their pace and left the quarter with a sense of relief. And both were thinking next time they would come with at least one male companion to accompany them.

"Did you ever see so many people dressed alike all in dark jackets and pants, and never without a cap?" They had kept their thoughts to themselves until they were well away from the area, however, Rose had been so enthralled by the sight of it all she couldn't wait any longer to let them out—talking and walking so fast Siobhán begged her to slow down on both accounts.

"The number of people smoking—I've never seen the like. And the practice of spitting on the streets, I can't get over it!" Siobhán was totally aghast.

"What a difference a few blocks make in this city. Gosh! Like a different world it was. We may have to learn a few words of their language before we go next time to get an idea of what's going on." Rose's fascination with a different culture already had her thinking of returning for another visit soon.

"I wonder how much English is understood or spoken there? Didn't hear a word of it myself."

They strolled down Stockton Street chatting the whole way, making a point to pass through Union Square before crossing Market Street towards home. The only stop they made the rest of the way was to post Rose's card off to Ireland.

It was late when Rose entered the house. The family had already eaten but Mrs. McDaid, hearing her footsteps, met her in the hall to tell her supper was waiting for her in the kitchen. The interviews and walking exercise had given her a hearty appetite and the meal was consumed in record time—followed soon after by drowsiness. She excused herself and was off to bed after only a very short recounting of the events of the day.

On top of the dresser drawer in her room she found a postcard that had come that day addressed to Rose Cameron. It was a separate story in itself that she no longer went by the name of her birth, Rose McMartin. Before her sister Mary emigrated from Ireland, Mary and other members of the family had, for assimilation and employment reasons both at home and abroad, decided to adopt a form of the family surname that had been used on-and-off again by past generations of the family. *Mary had swapped her birth name of McMartin for that of Cameron.* Rose had followed suit and most of their friends and other family relations, including the McDaids here in San Francisco, had by now grown accustomed to the change.

Noting at first glance that it was posted from Ireland, her eyes next narrowed in on the cramped signature of the sender at the bottom of the message. It was from her sister Bridget. A shiver rippled through her like the rolling wave from sea to shore, breaking hard on the back of her head. She sat down on the edge of the bed to steady her nerves. She knew it must contain news of John. But would it really after all the time gone by? In a few short sentences in tiny handwriting it concisely told of how Bridget had run into Casey who had told her the story of what had happened—the accident and how long it had taken for his double fracture to heal and to finally be able-bodied enough to get about again—and about how he had lost no more time in leaving for America, sailing only a few days before the card now in her hand was postmarked.

Dumbfounded and partially paralyzed by the news, Rose

reeled in confusion. She had tried to put John, her young Irishman, out of her mind for over year. And, for the majority of time, she had managed to do it fairly successfully. Finally she knew. He had had an accident! So that's why he wasn't there when their ship had weighed anchor. But the card's space limitation of a few words allowed for no details. She craved more information. He must be going to New York. Would he be looking for her there or did he really care any longer? If only Casey had seen Bridget in time before John left Donegal—Bridget could have told her that they had both moved away from New York City, and then John, too, would have known. As it was now, he could arrive looking for her and Mary only to find them gone. It seemed as if the god of mischief was again playing every last trick to prevent them from being together. In a way it would almost have been better to have never received the card, to have left old feelings and thoughts where they were, mostly dormant and only fluttering to the surface on rare occasions.

EIRE

Ireland, May-June 2007

Her origins had now been pinned down. There were no longer any doubts over the date and place my grandmother, Rose Anna, had been born and raised in County Donegal. The parish baptismal data obtained earlier from the website had proven to be spot-on, but without the contact with Daniel it would have remained nothing more than a remarkable coincidence of facts. The next order of business would be to try to obtain an official copy of her birth certificate from the General Register Office in Roscommon, Ireland, if one indeed existed, and if it did, whether it could provide any further details that were not on the baptismal record.

At the same time, the research report commissioned weeks earlier had arrived from Ireland. The researcher had done a fine job, especially since he had been provided with my grandmother's original birth surname only midstream into his research. He had already been on the right track and had closed in on the part of the Inishowen area of Donegal even without initially having the correct birth surname and he had been able to redirect his investigation to McMarin families without difficulty. It was the same area that I had started focusing on, the area in Donegal nearby to Derry City. Included in the report was information for the McMartin families extracted from the *Tithe Applotment Book* for the exact area in County Donegal that was described in *Griffith's Valuation*. More comprehensive parish information on the families concerned as well as a copy of Rose's baptism, taken from the actual church register, had also been included. Photos of the church cemetery and relevant headstones along with pictures and color maps of the area completed the report. The only thing obviously lacking was a copy of her civil birth certificate.

When her civil birth certificate did arrive from Ireland, unsurprisingly because of what I had learned previously from the Derry genealogy center, the birth date did not match the baptismal record—nearly two weeks difference separated them. Why should there be such a discrepancy between the two dates when normal practice dictated baptisms occurring within two or three days of birth? Daniel soon provided an explanation as he had also picked up a copy of her certificate while visiting the Civil Registration Office in Letterkenny:

Keep the questions coming, no problems. I will try to help as much as I can. When I was at the Registrar Office in Letterkenny I asked about the problem of the date of birth of Rose Anna. At the time she was born, the clerk explained, births had to be registered within twelve weeks from the date of birth. The parents would be fined if they failed to do so. When it was closing in on that limit, to be safe, parents would change the date of birth, as was the case for Rose Anna if you look at the time of registration. Often a father may not be able to easily go to the office for whatever reason—possibly due to distance or maybe it was seasonal harvest time. She said this was a very common occurrence. She added that the record she found was the only one matching the criteria, based on the information I provided such as name, date including date of birth you provided, and the church baptismal records. No other records met the requirements after she had checked all of the other Rose Anna and Rose entries. She also said that the church records for date of birth and baptismal date should be believed as they were more likely to be the correct ones.

Another one of the lynchpins of my grandmother's origins had now fallen into place, but there were still a raft of details that continued to torment me. What had happened to the other members of her immediate family? Did her brother and sisters outlive their parents and stay for the rest of their lives in the small hillside village overlooking Lough Foyle? When did they pass away, and what did the land look like now where they had once farmed. And what about the cottage in which they had lived? When did they cross over from being tenant farmers to owning their own land, or did they ever? When exactly did Rose emigrate from Ireland? What had happened to her sister Mary who had gone to America before her? And, of course, the ultimate question: when and where did she finish her life in San Francisco? There was only one way really to tackle some of them—a trip to Ireland was in order. To answer the last questions, discovery of new information would be needed from somewhere within the confines of California or elsewhere in America.

I had been to Ireland only once before. It was a long time ago, during my early twenties, when my recently wedded wife and I went on an extended trip to Europe together. Hitchhiking around the United Kingdom first, we had toured the cities of Edinburgh, Inverness, Glasgow and points in-between, standing on the roadside in the freezing winds—which even the thickest fleece-lined cowhide coat could not stop from penetrating. Near St. Andrews we caught a ride to the Scottish port of Stranraer before ferrying across the Irish Sea to the port of Larne in Northern Ireland. From there a lift drove us to Belfast for a short visit to that city at the beginning of period known as "The Troubles". Crossing the border we headed southwards through the Republic of Ireland, stopping only briefly for the day in Dublin on the way. We managed to squeeze in Cork and Blarney Castle and its gift-of-the-gab stone in wet and slippery weather, an abbey ruins, a small section of the Ring of Kerry and the city of Waterford along with a few other stops in the week we had. One of the most memorable rides came from a local priest who picked us up somewhere in the vicinity of Cork. Not only did he regale us with stories and songs while he drove, he possessed the prodigious mathematical ability to be able to add the numbers on the rear license plate of the car in front of the car we were in then do the square root of that number in his head! At least that's what he said he could do. But who was capable of checking to see if he was right or not!

Looking back, it was such a short trip that it could not even be considered a decent overview of the province of Munster, much less the diversity of other parts of the country. But we hardly knew better at the time. We were just thankful to get a sense of what turned out to be an old-fashioned, more traditional perhaps, and definitely more impoverished looking Ireland, which preceded the boom era of the Celtic Tiger by more than a couple of decades. The fact that my grandparents were Irish played a negligible role, especially since I had no knowledge of where in Ireland they had come from nor had any interest in my own family history at the time. So we returned to England via the ferry from Rosslare to Fishguard in Wales without an inkling that one day there would be revealed a true affinity and significance to Ireland which would serve as a springboard to inspire a much deeper look into its myriad nooks and crannies.

But for this momentous journey about to be undertaken several decades later, tickets to Ireland were booked from Switzerland where we were staying for the summer. Along with flights, a car was reserved for two weeks—our hitchhiking days being definitely a thing of the past. Our first two nights in a bed and breakfast northeast of Dublin in the town of Trim were also booked in advance. After Trim we would find places to stay each day while en route, often not the most efficient way to allocate time but giving maximum flexibility, which was fitting to our style of travel. The single essential destination was the place of birth of Rose Anna. Daniel had alerted his two brothers who lived near each other and only a mile or so away from the old cottage where my grandmother had been born and raised to expect us, sending us their addresses, a phone number and a map on how to find the small road leading to their houses. Natives of Scotland like Daniel, they had chosen to return to the land of their ancestral roots to live out their retirement days.

Trim itself was chosen as a launching pad because of its proximity to several of the most important Irish historical monuments and sites. Our first full day in the country was devoted to a visit to Newgrange, the fabulous Neolithic mound that even predates Stonehenge by some one thousand years. Earliest dating of its building harkens back some five thousand years. Like its English counterpart in concept and probable connection to ceremonial events such as burials, Newgrange, in County Meath, was constructed so that on the day of the winter solstice in December a beam of sunlight would be aligned to pierce the opening in the stone facing and illuminate the floor of a small internal chamber at the end of a narrow, low ceilinged, passageway. Both the entrance stone to the passage and passageway itself are adorned with quintessential megalithic spiral art engravings.

Our bed and breakfast also put us within easy striking distance of the center point of ancient Irish civilization—the Hill of Tara. Situated in County Meath as well, this Hill of Kings was the reputed but disputed seat of the High King of Ireland. More certain is that it was a prehistoric and early historical meeting place for the kings of Ireland representing the four quarters: Ulster to the north, Leinster to the east, Munster to the south and Connaught to the west. And it was the place where new kings were crowned at the stone pillar known as the Stone of Destiny. Views from the frequently wind swept Hill of Tara extend outwards for miles and the place is definitely imbued with a magical feeling about it for those open to receiving it.

The Boyne Valley and the River Boyne where these ancient sites are to be found are also the setting for another major event, one that had the consequence of framing long spans of Irish and English history. The Battle of the Boyne of 1690 in Ireland saw Protestant King William defeat Catholic King James, ending James' aspirations to regain the English crown. The victory by William of Orange and the loss by the Jacobites also locked the fate of Irish Catholics into a Protestant domination for years to come. The battlefield, so bucolic looking now as we strolled through the rises and falls of the windswept, rolling countryside, was hard to imagine scattered with sixty thousand soldiers from the two warring sides engaged in a ferocious battle.

For our last evening in Trim it was high time to have a look at the town's own famous attraction of Trim Castle. Likewise situated on the River Boyne and in Meath, this imposing castle cannot be overlooked. One of the largest and most intact in all of Ireland, the massive edifice with its extraordinarily high walls demonstrates the seriousness of the security required by those within, and stands apart in fortress-like strength and scale from the many other ruined castles we visited later.

After these first introductions to Irish history and culture we were ready to begin our drive northwards towards County Donegal. The first stop we made on the way was at the town of Kells. A walk around the Abbey of Kells with its round tower and the church cemetery nearby was a must-see. The round tower could have been the place where the Book of Kells, now kept at Trinity College in Dublin, was completed and remained for a period of time. A debate still stirs as to where most of it was actually made. And in the cemetery, excellent and huge examples of High crosses, also known as Celtic crosses, were interspersed among the other tombstones.

From Kells we passed through counties Louth, Monaghan, Armagh, Tyrone and Derry on our way before reaching Donegal. The city of Derry, or Londonderry, was surprisingly vibrant after the small-scale, subdued character of towns such as Armagh, Cookstown and Dungiven that we had paused at along the way when driving to it. Derry's old Guildhall and St. Columb's Cathedral were among the important landmarks to be seen in this historic town, but the Diamond, the central square, was where much of the bustling activity thrived. Intact and walkable, thick and substantial walls surrounded and enclosed the old part of the town. Shops were busy and people on the move up and down hilly streets. Higher up on the hill the Church of Ireland and the Catholic Church coexisted in a city with a long history of religious divide. From the walkway on top of the Derry Walls, strategically overlooking the Catholic majority enclave of Bogside, the last remnants of British military installations could be seen below. These super sensitive listening posts were in the process of being dismantled before our eyes. The close proximity of Derry city to the border of County Donegal and to where Rose and her family had lived—less than ten miles away and slightly inland from the shore of Lough Foyle—made it central to their lives. It was the only urban-like conglomeration with associated amenities within the broad district of East Inishowen.

At last in Derry City we were in easy striking distance of Rose Anna's home. A phone call was made to Daniel's brother from a booth in a mall in the center of town to arrange a time to visit. In short order we were on our way out of Derry and motoring along the shore of the sparkling waters of Lough Foyle northwards. Denis and his wife Margaret were waiting to welcome us to their beautiful home. Within minutes we were joined by their daughter Moira returning from a shift at her job in Derry. A second brother and his wife lived only a stone's throw away. Whether it was their particular personalities or typical Donegal hospitality, we were conversing like we had known each other for ages within ten minutes after arriving. Second cousins we all were, just as with Daniel in Glasgow. Part of the afternoon flew by examining old photographs and the actual postcards that Daniel had scanned proving our relationship. The evening ended with a great meal together and a promise to be taken on the following day to the quarterland where the McMartin ancestors had lived to see their old house.

The next day broke bright and we met again after breakfast. After a five minute drive down a couple of small country roads in the lush Donegal hills we were there. We were met by another McMartin descendant, James, a nephew, who now owned the land and the old buildings that were once inhabited by our ancestors. The cottage from the outside was easily recognizable from the old photos I had seen, which had been taken over a hundred years before. It sat next to two other houses one unpainted and the other white like theirs, both abandoned as well. It was common for a small number of families in the heyday of the rundale system prior to 1900 to have their houses clustered together with the surrounding land apportioned out among them in an equitable manner with regards to the best crop growing and the less fertile, pasture-suitable fields. Rundale, a cooperative farming and living practice, lingered on in some places well into the first half of the twentieth century. The track from the road that led to the small houses and the areas around the buildings were wildly overgrown with thick greenery, indicating the lack of habitation for a long time. Indeed this was the case for my grandmother's house now was used for sheltering sheep when they were not in the pasture. While they were not presently inside, the scent of their recent presence was undeniable with straw scattered throughout the premises.

As we looked around the interior in the dim light, unbelievably, traces of ancestors still remained. Most prominent were the cooking utensils hanging in front of the hearth and the mismatched set of dishes stacked on a shelf in a small, recessed alcove in the next, and really only other, room.

The living space, of course, seemed altogether insufficient for a family of nine in any era, especially since there was only a partial second floor, more like a loft, suitable for sleeping only. But in comparison to today's standards in Ireland, even two people would have found it cozy. And it was a wonder that the unrobust looking, modest interior framing had lasted, more-or-less, intact in spite of the pounding that the shuffling sheep had given to it in recent years. As for the current whereabouts of the flock of woolies, we were soon to be treated to an exhibition of the prowess of the nephew's sheepdog in one of the fields behind the houses. Obeying whistles and other commands, the clever dog, with head held low in a no-nonsense-I-mean-business position, first herded them together at the far end of the pasture, then moved them closer to where we were watching and finally brought the herd to a complete standstill only a few feet from where we stood.

Before we left the cottage, nephew James, who had noted our keen interest in everything about the place, kindly offered to let us help ourselves to any of the old dishes in the nook said to be left over from the times of my great-grandparents. We chose only one plate, *a plainish, small-sized creamy white one with a thin band of silver just below the rim and with a worn four-leaf clover in the center.* A keepsake that would serve as a tangible link to the past in the future.

The rest of the morning was passed visiting with the second brother and his wife at their house, again in the most welcoming and hospitable atmosphere. Then, before leaving the vicinity, an essential trip to the local church and its graveyards was made. St. Brendan's had been rebuilt more than once so it was not exactly as it had been during Rose Anna's time. Still, quaint, small and decorated with rich, warm colors, it too radiated an aura of welcome to those who entered through its doors. Its two cemeteries were divided by the church building itself. On one side of the church, to the east, lay the newer one while on the other side, the old graveyard overlooked Lough Foyle on the west. There were only a couple of markers with the family name inscribed on them, but it was said that many more family members rested in unmarked plots, a testament to what economic conditions dictated at the time.

Next on the agenda was a driving tour of the rest of the Inishowen Peninsula. So it was onto Moville then Gleneely, Culdaff and the town of Malin on Trawbreaga Bay with its harbor and parade of fishing boats, and from there to the northernmost point in Ireland—Malin Head, where the wind was fiercely blowing as it does much of the time. Returning south, a stop in Carndonagh was mandatory. Carn, as it is locally called, was the town nearest to the village where my great-grandmother was believed to have been born and raised before marrying and moving away to her husband's village overlooking the coast. The Inishowen circuit was completed after passing through Buncrana and Burnfoot.

But our Irish sojourn certainly did not culminate there. The gorgeous weather continued and the diverse countryside offered surprising new contours and ground coverings every few miles as we continued our journey south westwards. From forested national parks to barren, golden brown mountains jutting almost straight up from the flatlands with a minimum of foothills, to small lakes and ancient stone circles, the landscape was ever-changing, ever-enchanting as we proceeded from Donegal south through Counties Leitrim and Sligo, the latter known as Yeat's country since the poet

William Butler Yeats spent a good deal of his time there. Next, Mayo and Galway counties, including the rock strewn but scenic Connemara, left us with dual images of beauty and of the often unforgiving nature of this harsh land in the province of Connaught. The forbidding shadows of treeless mountains, lacking any hint of topsoil or chance of growing a successful crop, loomed as if to say to the prospective migrant, Beware, a hard life lies ahead if you should attempt to tame this land. Wandering sheep scouring the countryside for something on which to graze seemed to be all that the land could possibly support, and even that must be doubtful at times. To think that so many displaced Irish forced out of more fertile counties during the times following the siege of Cromwell had to eke out a living of subsistence farming in these far western counties is unconscionable. It is no wonder that famines and other miseries were accentuated within their borders.

Even without the same kind of precise information we had in hand as was the case for my grandmother, Rose Anna, our tour of various parts of Ireland could not be concluded without visiting the place in County Roscommon where Grandfather Patrick very likely came from. Some data collection and the heavy concentration of Cavanagh families, in addition to the conclusion drawn by the Roscommon genealogy center, suggested that the triangle formed by the towns of Tulsk, Strokestown and Elphin was the most likely section of the county for his home. Consequently, on a day starting with rain in Galway City we found ourselves a couple of hours later in Roscommon Town on a much sunnier late afternoon, close by the intended destination. After walking through the town, the hour being what it was, a comfortable bed and breakfast was found down a small road a few minutes beyond the outskirts. Flat or gently rolling, County Roscommon could be considered as nearly the center of all of Ireland, although officially it is part of the western province of Connaught. Many small lakes and farmland interspersed with peat bogs made up this local section of the county's dominant low-lying scenery, but in other parts larger rivers and forests could be found as well.

Next morning, a climb among the ruins of Roscommon Castle on the edge of the town itself was greeted by more sunshine, which intensified the color of the green grass of the castle grounds and adjoining park. Then it was off to visit the small village center of Tulsk where a handy Heritage Centre housed well-done displays and archaeological artifacts from the many ancient ring forts and burial mounds scattered throughout the local area. This museum and its friendly staff were well worth the stop in presenting an overview in short order of the natural surroundings of my grandfather's possible birthplace.

From Tulsk we set our sights for Strokestown and its Famine Museum at Strokestown Park. The story of the Great Famine, An Gorta Mór, housed in the old stable across from the former manor house of a once huge estate, was told through the enlargement of primary documents into poster size display copies accompanied by pictorial representations, to form a series of telling exhibits within the rather fittingly stark walls and dim lighting conditions that the building afforded. A tour of the manor house itself filled with its original furnishings and embellished by a good dose of humorous Irish banter from our tour guide followed the museum visit. The Strokestown experience taken as a whole gave a vivid graphic impression of a country locked into a pattern of ever shrinking farm sizes in an ever increasing population scenario. Overdependence on the potato for sustenance, the potato blight and famine brought death and even greater poverty compounded an incongruous situation. It stimulated economic incentives to emigrate, changes in the traditional rundale land management system, and a trend which saw many family members passing through life never to marry. The population of Ireland, now around six million when the North is included, still has not attained the number that it was before the beginning of the famine years in 1845. In excess of eight million inhabitants had lived there then.

It was tough to leave County Roscommon, and in particular the town of Strokestown, because I feel certain that it is this town that embodies both the story of Ireland at one of its lowest points and its hope for the future. And somewhere in the vicinity the answer to the home of Rose's husband, my grandfather Patrick Cavanagh, could be waiting to be uncovered. But there were several other places calling out to us before we headed to Dublin City to finish our Irish sojourn. The compass pointed to the southeast and it was off towards County Wicklow that we were bound. After crossing the River Shannon, we travelled through the counties of Longford, Westmeath and Kildare, the last in which a stop was made in the town of Maynooth home of Ireland's famous university and prominent Catholic seminary. Finally we entered Wicklow and visited the Valley of Glendalough, at the top of our list of intended destinations for this part of the trip. It did not disappoint. With numerous monastic ruins to explore, the setting was a perfect choice of the early monks. A steep walk up to the top and along the valley ridge provided outstanding views of the lakes below and the long expanse of the valley itself. The inspiration the monks of the past inhaled from the air of such a place must have truly lifted their thoughts to new heights of enlightened consciousness.

There was one last great site on the list: Powerscourt. The large mansion was only matched by the magnificent gardens and ponds, laid out to emphasize grandeur of scale while extending an invitation to explore various surprises in walking the paths leading in all directions. Again, the site for the estate was chosen with care, high on a hill with views of the gorgeous encompassing countryside. It was a real gem not to be missed.

Dublin was the final stop of our visit, a bustling city with plenty of well-known sites to take in. But this trip was not about cities rather it was the little places off the beaten track, the small villages tucked away in a landscape that had farming as its backbone—it was about discovering the rural roots of Rose and Patrick before they left to seek a new life. And that is exactly what we did.

JOHN

The South, January-March 1894

Walking the streets of New York City during the few days leading up to Christmas without a proper winter coat to deal with below zero, frigid air temperatures and icy remnants of the first major snow storm of the season was grueling. But what was much more of a hardship to John Harte was his failure to make any headway in finding Rose, or her sister Mary, based on the old and now obviously out-dated information he had brought with him from Ireland. All of his leads had failed to pan out. He had addresses of where they worked and lived and at each place he went the answer was the same—they had moved on without leaving any forwarding addresses at which they could be contacted. All he could ascertain was that the likelihood they had left New York altogether was strong, and the city of Boston and even the far-and-away one of San Francisco were mentioned in passing as having been talked about. Either of these places was well within the realm of reason. There were others from their corner of Inishowen who had gone to stay in both of them. However, there were many other destinations people he knew from home had gone to as well: Pennsylvania, New Jersey, even Tennessee.

When all was said and done, John was left grasping at straws and really had nothing to go on that could take him in one direction over another with any conviction it was the right one, one that would warrant the effort and expense. Where would he start if he went to Boston? He could randomly make inquiries at boarding houses and elsewhere but the chances of success were minute in such a large city, especially since there were no assurances that either of them were even there. And San Francisco was like being an ocean away in distance. It presented even a bigger gamble not to mention the fact that he had insufficient funds remaining to take him all the way even if he had been fairly certain Rose had gone in that direction.

Christmas day came and he found himself alone and lonely in rooming quarters of the shabby kind making matters even worse. Sinking into a depression under these dingy and gloomy conditions only one thought was prominent— spending the winter in this bleak city was not an option. He needed warmth for his body and distance to clear his mind from a place apparently devoid of the presence of Rose.

Earlier, when he had registered at the hotel, with numbed fingers of a bluish hue which could barely grasp a pen, he had noted the accent of the clerk and a rhythm of spoken English he had never encountered before. The peculiar way of addressing him with the expression *y'all* multiple times when he had checked in had piqued his curiosity. And now, after returning from a brief walk, he could not stop himself from asking the clerk about his origins even if there was a risk it could be taken as a smidgen rude.

"Are you, like myself, from another land, if you don't mind me asking? Couldn't help but hear the difference in the sound of your words and the way you string them together."

The clerk gave a friendly chuckle, seeming not in the least offended. "Expect y'all haven't come across my way of talking much yet as being recently arrived, and anyways there aren't many other folk in this city that sounds like me, I'll be bound. I'm from the South…from the mighty state of Alabama to be exact. Everyone talks like me down in my neck of the woods."

"Alabama—sure, the name has passed my way somewhere before. There's no forgetting the musical ring it has once you've heard it. Near to the other southern states of Mississippi and Louisiana, if I'm not mistaken? What's it like there in that part of this country?"

The eyes of the clerk lit up. "Well first folks take their time there in what they do compared to the rush-rush of life hereabouts. And folks take pleasure in each others' company with a cold drink in their hand, in the shade, for there's no shortage of sunshine, heat and humidity in Alabama. And there's such an abundance and variety of greenery it'd make your head spin…the types of trees, bushes, flowers that don't grow anywhere else but down south. But don't get me talking too much or else I'd be wanting awful much to see it again."

"It sounds like an interesting area to see, so. Thanks for the description. But I'll be saying goodnight to you now."

Still shivering from his walk as he entered his room, what he would do next with his life suddenly became crystal clear. His failure to find the sisters in New York had momentarily left him at loose ends and downcast. But what the clerk had said had struck a nerve and stuck with him, and now it seemed like an answer to his predicament. He'd make his way from the North to the South, perhaps even all the way to Alabama, where the warmth of the sun would thaw his frozen bones and restore his equally addled brain. He'd use the small amount of money he had to start the journey. Then he would try to find work along the way when he needed to. And once there he would write home to Donegal to see if anyone there had heard anything more recent about where Rose and Mary had taken themselves off to. If he received news that pinned down her present whereabouts, well then he would reset his compass towards whichever direction was required as soon as he could.

John did not need to waste any time in further reflection. His decision was made. He went back out again and bought and studied maps covering the East Coast and Southern states enough to see it wasn't beyond reason to aim for Tennessee as an initial destination. Relatives had settled there some years before. He remembered the name of the town, Knoxville he believed, where they had gone. He hoped they were still there and would be willing to take him in, at least for a few days, before he carried on towards the Deep South, on towards Alabama. He packed his bags that night and checked out leaving early the next morning.

Each day as he travelled further southwards by hook or by crook—taking trains, coaches, wagons, along with plain old foot power—brought a sense of accomplishment and a modicum of contentment by keeping his mind occupied with the planning of each day's journey and by forcing him to keep his wits about him as a man of the road. His faith in what the future would hold grew as the temperatures increased and his body and spirit thawed and thrived. On passing through Pennsylvania, his thoughts shifted to the recollection of the stories he had heard of Donegal kinsmen who had gone to lay track for a new railroad line a short distance from Philadelphia in the 1830s. They had been employed by a fellow Irish contractor named Philip Duffy, a surname not uncommon to Inishowen and to his own ears. These newly arrived immigrants just off the ship—some from the adjacent Irish counties of Tyrone and Derry as well—had completely vanished shortly after they began work on the railway stretch now known as Duffy's Cut, none of them ever to be seen or heard from again. Cholera was rumored to be the cause of their demise. But since none of them survived and the exact whereabouts of the gravesite lay shrouded in mystery, the possibility of solving their disappearance seemed remote. This in itself was strange because as deadly as cholera can be, it would be rare that every last man would succumb to it.

Other theories abounded as well, including those anchored in the strong anti-Irish Catholic sentiment and prejudice that was prevalent at the time. He was certain that his fate would not take him down the same path, but just the same remained wary of the people he met and the nature of the surroundings he passed through as he moved from place to place.

It was well into January by the time he reached Maryland. Although he felt he should stop soon to find work for a few weeks since his funds were becoming critically low, his urge to make greater progress before stopping won out, so he tightened his belt a few notches and continued on until crossing into the state of Virginia. Despite being the dead of winter—albeit a much kinder winter than the one he had said goodbye to in New York—the tobacco industry offered the kind of work that John knew he could do. This was the season when a portion of the tobacco leaves that had been grown during the spring and summer months two years before were removed from storage and made ready to export abroad. Able hands were needed to prepare the tobacco cargos for transport to the port for shipment in the coming spring. Although much of the crop was consumed at home there was still ample supply to send overseas. He was grateful for the opportunity to spend the remainder of January and the whole of February doing tough physical labor, living in company-provided housing. And he was equally as grateful to be able to put enough extra money in his pocket to carry on to Tennessee, the next state entered in his southwards route, with financial worries much less of a concern.

It didn't take long after the border was crossed in early March before he found himself in the town of Knoxville. After making a few inquiries, the location of Cousin Anne's address was determined. Anne had met and married a man named Carter Findley when he was on a business trip in Philadelphia many years before. Ironically, as John was to later learn, the Findley's belonging to Carter's family line had been well-ensconced in Alabama for generations, and it was Carter who was the first member of his generation to leave the Alabama homeland to move to the Volunteer State of Tennessee.

When John approached the gate to their modest-sized home it was with some trepidation, for he came unannounced and unexpected. The first looks received and words spoken to him were of a quizzical nature, perhaps with a tinge of suspicion thrown in. But as soon as it sank in who he actually was, who his relations were, Anne threw her arms around him in a great big bear hug. Almost engulfing him, she was a woman built of substantial proportions, unique in size in comparison to John's own family and most of his other relatives as well.

"Last time I set eyes on you there was only a wee lad to be seen as I recollect. It's no wonder it took me a time to recognize the man standing before me, strong as an ox by the looks of you. There's the dark good looks of the rest of the Harte's now as I can see in you. That's what finally tipped me off for sure. We're just about to sit down at the table for a bite to eat and now you'll make us happy in setting a place for one more."

Their conversation continued at the supper table, after John was shown where he could leave his few possessions. "How did you come to pass our way? Not many folks from the old country make it here."

"It's a long tale in the telling. You'll no doubt be soon guessing it could be something to do with a lass, and you'd be thinking right for that's at the start of it all. And the slight hitch to my stride you may have already noticed, that has something to do with it as well. It's not as pronounced as it was not so long ago. Every day it loosens up a bit more. It was much stiffer in the weather I left behind me up north than here. I was so worried coming through customs in New York, that they'd not let me stay and put me on the next ship back, but no one seemed to pay much attention. I guess I must have covered it up pretty well."

"Saw right off that you were a bit gimpy. What's caused it? Carter has a hitch in his gait too."

"It came about when I took a fall working on the landowner's house. Broke it in two places. That's what turned everything upside down back home—with Rose. We were going to immigrate together on the same ship and marry after we arrived. She sailed off alone, without knowing what happened to me, I guess."

"Hold on, hold on now and back up a pace. Who's Rose? Was she a lass from a local family that we should know too? Have you come here to find her?" were the next questions to come into Cousin Anne's head.

Not wanting to go too deep into particulars of the relationship, he limited his explanation to a few brief remarks. "No, she was from another area, not so far away, there were family differences…I couldn't get word to her in time even though…before the ship sailed. By the time my leg was healed enough and I made it to New York she and her sister Mary had already moved on. I was too late and who knows where she is now. Then, with the cold numbing my bones and nowhere else to turn, all I could think of was getting off to somewhere warmer. My plans are to make my way further south, on to Alabama. When I get there and get settled I'll try to get in touch with someone back home who can help me find exactly where she's gone off to."

But there was no pulling the wool over their eyes and they easily read between the lines. Intending to marry after leaving Ireland rather than marrying there and afterwards departing because of "differences" could probably mean only one thing in this instance—the Catholic-Protestant problem. But the look in Anne and Carter's eyes also gave them away to John. They had understood the underlying situation but neither of them wanted to spell it out any further either so it was silently put to rest under the table.

"Well there's an extra bed in our home to lay your head, that is, if it suits you, till y'all get started. You'll find Tennessee a lot warmer place than New York in more ways than one", Carter promised with the typical southern hospitality the Findley's shared.

"That's good of you to offer. But before I settle in anywhere, I've got to have a look around your neighbor, Alabama. It's what I had mind when I set out southwards and I guess it won't let me alone until I crossover the next borderline. And it's so close now, I can almost see it."

"You're dead right there, son and there's a packet of Findleys that can put you up in places scattered about the state. If you have a mind to, go to my sister Emma first. She lives with her daughter, Mollie, in Scottsboro, not far across the state line. Just tell them that Carter and Anne sent you by, and be sure to say that we asked after them."

Anne added "Emma will make you at home just as if you're back in Donegal. She and Mollie will treat you as if you're their own. Her husband passed on a couple of years back."

After two weeks, John was ready to move on. The Findley's had put no pressure on him, in fact to the contrary, they were sad to see him leave. He had pitched in with the work to be done while bringing them up to date on all of the happenings in Ireland since they had left. However, they understood and appreciated the wanderlust of the young and independent-spirited. So it was with tears in all of their eyes that John said goodbye.

"It's been grand to be with you. I won't forget the way you both took me in." And with wave of his arm he was down the lane Alabama bound.

LANDBOOKS, DUBLIN AND AUSTRALIA

San Francisco, California, May-December 2007

The final resting place of Rose Anna somewhere in California and the townland in County Roscommon in which Grandfather Patrick was born were the two major pieces of the puzzle still missing. But without any new ideas on where to turn next, it was time to set aside these questions and let what I had learned thus far remain in the background for awhile. Perhaps something would fit together if I stopped thinking so hard about it. In the meantime a fresh approach was sought, one which focused on garnering more information from Irish resources about the McMartins of Donegal, in general, and on when and where Rose Anna's siblings ended their lives in particular.

Upon our visit with Cousin Daniel in Glasgow, he had showed us a copy of an old survey map of the village in which our ancestors had lived in Inishowen. Each parcel of land that was occupied was laid out on the map and each had a letter-number combination attached to it. The map also included tiny rectangles representing buildings on the property at the time. Although the survey maps were actually drawn earlier than *Griffith's Valuation*, the alpha-numeric symbols on the map were still valid for indentifying parcels in the GV 1857 recording of land assessment in Donegal. But in order to make a correspondence between a map and the valuation sheets I already possessed, I needed to get my own copy of this very detailed map. Somewhere along the way, either during our visit to Ireland or through rummaging on the internet, I had identified the Valuation Office in Dublin as a source for historical maps. This office was now duly contacted with success; they could indeed provide the map I desired. It was a six-inch scale map—six inches to one mile—first published in 1833 and revised in the 1840s, based on individual holdings which included the boundary lines of fields. In passing, I asked if there were any other historical sources available from their office that might be of use for establishing land occupants at different points of time. There was one more resource I had not yet heard of, another land tax valuation known as *Cancelled Landbooks* in Ireland while called *General Valuation Revision Lists* in America. After some research, it was found that the LDS library held microfilmed *Revision Lists* but these reels only covered occupant changes up to the time when the filming took place many years ago, whereas the Valuation Office in Dublin held the complete set of the original paper *Landbooks* almost up to the present day.

Their office was requested to trace all of the McMartin land listings over the years when the family name was associated with the land as well as for all the years afterwards for their specific parcel and townland in Donegal. The *Cancelled Landbooks* were intended to follow on the *Griffith's Valuation* of 1857 in Donegal, periodically surveying and updating land and building values for taxation purposes over the succeeding decades, noting changes in names of occupants or owners, number of acres held and current land value as well as any buildings and their respective value. The death of the original tenant of the land—described as the occupant—often led to a wife, brother, son or even possibly a neighbor, assuming occupation of the parcel. Even what appeared to be a totally new occupier's name might provide additional clues because he or she could have a connection such as a distant relative bearing a heretofore unknown surname or a male marrying into a family. Thus these entries could often trace and substantiate lines of descent, unravel relationships, and even show when a given parcel of land became the true property of the occupants as opposed to a tenancy arrangement. Each change in land occupancy is recorded with the new name of the principal occupant placed beside that of the crossed out previous tenant's name. The year the transition took place is also specified. Different color inks were used to correlate name changes with the dates in which they occurred, noted in the far right column. When several occupier changes happened during a given date span, ink colors were indispensable for telling who took over occupancy when.

There were nine of these books that covering entries for McMartins, each book spanning a specific subset of the overall date range years of 1858 to 2002. The entries showed how the land changed hands from Rose's grandfather to her father's brother Edward, then to a shared arrangement—acrimonious, as I would learn later—between Edward's son and Rose's father. And how finally in 1942 the land, still held in a form of rundale long after the practice had ended almost everywhere else in Ireland, was subdivided with other McMartins, who all became part owners of the entirety under the Land Purchase Acts administered by the Irish Land Commission. These acts saw the eventual transfer of hundreds of thousands of acres from freehold tenancy to actual ownership. For most estates in Ireland land had passed out of the hands of the estate owners and their middlemen and into the hands of former occupants many years prior to 1942. Perhaps their particular situation, involving a rather long-lasting, complex rundale system of land sharing and working, contributed to this rather late timing. And most landlords had discontinued land held in joint tenancy by family members and others in the open field rundale system long before they relinquished ownership to the land itself, opting for enclosed, individual farms as a more economically productive and viable method of farming to support their estates.

Landbooks added to learning more about the chronological sequence of the McMartins but did not do much in the way of identifying the role of Rose's sisters and brother during the time they were alive until the last of them passed away in the 1950s—except for the fact that none of them appeared in them, which in itself was telling. Cousin Daniel was able to gain some insight from one of his brothers in Donegal on why at one point the land was transferred the way it was because of the aftermath of a dispute:

> The story passed down has it that another McMartin, cousin to my Uncle William, outbid him when he tried to buy the land. It seems that whatever amount William bid the cousin would raise the bid even more. That side of the McMartins bought the land for £650 and from then on owned the land apart from the plot on which the house stood and the small field which appears on the old map sent earlier.

As for the objective of filling in some of the blanks about Rose and her family during our visit to Ireland earlier in the year, not much was successfully achieved to this end. The single weekday we were in Dublin unexpectedly turned out to be a bank holiday and the National Library of Ireland and all of the rest of the public offices were closed. So a few months later, in the autumn, a second short two day trip to Dublin was booked from Switzerland, this time travelling alone, with the sole mission of focusing squarely on research. At the National Library on Kildare Street a microfilm reel of images taken from the actual parish baptismal registers for the McMartin sisters and single brother was consulted. More extensive research was also done on the possible parents of Grandfather Patrick in County Roscommon by using their online subscription to *Griffith's Valuation* hosted by *Irishorigins*. A visit also was made to the National Archives on Bishop Street in an attempt to pin down whether school records might exist. During this visit an effort was made as well to determine if there was any information relating to the conversion of the land from tenancy to ownership in the Land Commission records also housed in the same building. This was based on entries in the *Cancelled Landbooks* I had obtained earlier as a guide to the most likely date that it occurred for the family. These two endeavors led to nowhere as the records for the school in which they attended were not among the collection and because the Land Commission records were now part of the Department of Agriculture, an entity with more restrictive access policies.

Taking by far the longest amount of time—nearly an entire day—were the hours spent at the General Register Office on Lombard Street East which holds the paper indexes to birth, marriage and death records researchers can access for a fee. Once a client finds index entries of interest, the staff of the office searches for and supplies a photocopy of the relevant portion of the page of the corresponding full civil registration vital record. Here, the effort focused on finding death records of any related McMartins, and particularly any that preceded my great-grandfather. Even in a day, not all of the possible years could be checked, but luck was with me and another generation of McMartin's appeared to be found, later gaining confirmation from my Glasgow cousin as indeed belonging to our great-great-grandfather.

The short trip was worthwhile in that new avenues were explored and my curiosity about different resources satisfied even if it did not provide any significant discoveries save for moving the McMartin ancestry back one more generation. But now it was back to the drawing board. While contemplating my next move, Cousin Daniel provided a tantalizing diversion when he plugged in one of Rose's sister's names in a wide open internet search. Quite unexpectedly, a posting surfaced that caught his eye. It looked promising on the one hand but was quite dated on the other, having been posted several years before. When I tried to retrieve the same posting by searching in what I thought would be a similar manner, a second posting containing identical information hosted by a different genealogy site turned up. This site had a different name for the poster, Anne, and gave her email address. As Daniel's discovered posting led to no further information after he wrote to the author, the discovery of the second site which I passed onto him proved to be important. He contacted Anne and was rewarded with a reply that opened up a whole new and unanticipated vein of possibilities:

A descendant who organized a family reunion quite a few years ago put together the O'Neill Book. The information I have on the McMartin family was taken from this book.

Bridget was the daughter of Denis McMartin born about 1805 and Mary Herald born about 1812. It was in the Donegal/Derry district of Ireland this family lived. The known siblings of Bridget were Patrick, Mary, Edward and Neil. I can tell you about Bridget's life in Australia, if this family is yours. This is all I have on the McMartin family.

Australia now! Could this be a Bridget of ours? The birth dates of her parents were close to what we had surmised they might be for the parents of our great-great-grandfather and grandmother, the townland and quarterland were a match, and, from the initial posting, Bridget's birth date was close to that of our great-grandfather Neil McMartin. Could Bridget have been his sister? If this were so, then we could very well now have the knowledge of the maiden name of our great-great-grandmother, a feat that took us back into Irish family history much further than most seekers ever dreamed of going.

Up until to now Anne had been summarizing relevant parts of the extensive O'Neill Book. But once Daniel reported back that the likelihood was good of a family relationship here, she must have agreed with him because attached to her next email was a copy of a multi-paged account of her own family's history, both detailing what she had written before and providing the Australian context in which not only extensive vital facts were described but also the story of how the family had come to settle there. She also provided Australian death certificates of Bridget and her husband who had married in Donegal before they emigrated. Even the name of the ship and the date and place of its arrival, first docking in Sydney then in Moreton Bay, Queensland, the state where they were destined to live. And from the passenger list their ages could be verified.

As much excitement as these new discoveries caused on all of our parts, there was an equal need for us to remain level-headed with a shade of skepticism in taking it all in. A substantive link proving the parents of Irish-born Australian Bridget McMartin and our great-grandfather were one-in-the-same needed to be found. Frustratingly, another message confirmed that no other definitive documents were in the possession of our Down Under counterpart. But the chance there could still be salvation existed if the author of the O'Neill Book who had done all of the Irish-side research could be located and contacted. The catch was that while Anne remembered having the address of this researcher at one time, it had slipped away and was now lost from her files despite her best effort to find it.

Several attempts were made using different approaches to find the Irish researcher but all of them left wanting. Our only recourse seemed to be a needle-in-a-haystack search for death certificates for all of the people who had matching married names of McMartin in the unlikely event that in one them a detail would be dropped that would support that the maiden name of Herald for our great-great-grandmother provided by Anne was the correct one. This shotgun approach, using as a starting point a much-valued pilot website of the LDS which included an index to Irish civil births, marriages and deaths, ended in another futile effort when none of the likely possibilities gleaned from the website that Daniel ran by a clerk at the records office in Letterkenny turned out to be right. So without the knowledge of where to turn to next for another means of proof, regrettably, the Australian connection had to be put on the back burner for the time being. And as time went by, the case to be made for an Australian arm to the family grew dimmer and finally petered out almost altogether as not even the smallest piece of evidence came forward confirming this supposition.

PATRICK

San Francisco, California, January 1894-January 1901

Her shock followed by renewed excitement at having unexpected news of John Harte in the postcard from her sister Bridget ebbed as the days following turned into weeks and months with no further communication about him. At first, with her memories reinvigorated, Rose could picture their happy reunion and the start of a long-delayed beginning of life together in America. She could imagine his strong body in front of her, with determination behind his eyes and etched in the contours of his jaw that said nothing would have stopped him from making his way to her. Little did she contemplate that his lack of precise knowledge of where she had gone could be a major impediment in a country the size of America. Guilty of still thinking in the small-scale framework of Ireland, she simplistically envisioned him suddenly crossing her threshold then falling into his arms with her face leaning against his chest. But with the passage of time and the routine of work and daily life in San Francisco, these vivid reawakened fantasies once again faded, and thoughts of John were tucked back away in a remote place where they were seldom allowed to escape.

The second interview with Mrs. Roth's other daughter had gone as well as the first. Both Rose and Siobhán had been hired. They started together on the same day in the household with Rose quickly adapting her cooking skills to the tastes of a family with German origins. In truth, that Germany and Ireland both shared the potato as a food staple made her new position much easier. Her friend Siobhán slipped comfortably into the role of server and wash-up person. Both young women did most of the shopping for the food they prepared and served. They worked a six day schedule with either Saturday or Sunday off each week. While their wages were not significant, they paid nothing for rent and ate most of their meals in the kitchen, leaving them both able to put a little away in savings each month while still being able to spend a token amount in the city on recreation and clothing. Contentment with their situation was shared by all, openly expressed by the family with regards to the high quality of their work and acknowledged by Siobhán and Rose in the life they were allowed to lead. They appreciated the freedoms afforded to them in a city where most people were too absorbed with their own concerns to pay much attention to the likes of their doings. You could say that they had adapted well to their West Coast surroundings and had settled in nicely at the Roth household.

Over the next couple of years either Rose alone, or together with Siobhán, had the occasion to run into the man who had driven them to their destinations when they had first arrived. Once, while they were walking, a coach passed them by, the driver giving them a small salute as if he recognized them, and twice, afterwards, Rose had encountered the coachman called Patrick on the street while she was running errands. And there were a few other times that they ran into each other on her day off when they could stop and talk a bit longer. When they met he always remembered to inquire of her relatives in Donegal and she asked of his in Roscommon. In these brief, random meetings, Patrick began to take on more than the guise of a mere acquaintance to Rose, and a true friendship began to form between them. It was one of the few friendships she had made beyond the household members where she was employed and, of course, the McDaids', Siobhán, and a few other distant relatives sprinkled around the city.

Rose was at the produce market on a cool September afternoon when another chance encounter with him took place.

"Well, hello Rose. I haven't caught sight of yourself for a while now. It must be at least three months since we last bumped into each other. This town is growing too fast—more and more unusual to see a friendly face you recognize nowadays amongst all the strangers."

"Isn't that the truth, Patrick. The three years before the century turns will whisk past us before we know it. And the place will be swarming with even more newcomers, just like us not so long ago. I think everyone has discovered that San Francisco is a good place to live. But it's nice to see you again. I've never asked before but what was it that brought you here in the first place?" she was bold enough to ask.

"Guess I was just taken by what I heard and read about the place. And it was time to move on from where I was living in Massachusetts. It had sort of worn out its welcome for me."

"Would it be Boston that you were staying in?" Rose wondered, a tad bit taken back and left wondering by his last remark.

"That it was, when I decided to go out west. But before Boston, I worked in a town called Fall River. You might have heard of it. It's only about fifty miles to the south of Boston.

It's another place where a lot of Irish flocked to for work when they first came over. Mills upon mills everywhere. They dominate the town and cotton is king there, just like linen rules in Ireland. There's no dearth of work in that town—for those who are willing, that is. I went there in the year of 1867 when I was just a young lad. Left New York almost straightaway after our ship docked. We knew all about the town of Fall River well before I left the old country though."

Rose too had heard of the town before but in a wholly different context. "Isn't that the famous place—the one where the lady was accused of killing her parents with an axe? I remember reading something about it because it was the year I first set foot in America and it seemed so peculiar."

"It is that, Rose. Lizzie Borden was her name. She was found not guilty by the jury but many have said that justice was not served. That was all back in '92 and '93. Long after I arrived here and long after I left Fall River."

"You've been here in San Francisco for a long time then?"

Patrick nodded. "It seems that way, so…since about the end of 1880. In Boston I met the woman I was to marry later but she thought she was too young and not ready at the time when I first asked her. She and her twin sister had recently immigrated to Boston from Canada. They came down from the province of Nova Scotia to be exact, and it was true that they had not been long in the states when I first saw them. So, like a bloody fool, when she said not now to my proposal, I took it as a no, a forever no, felt rejected, and soon after took my leave for this coast. Too much of a dolt to think it over first, try to put myself in her shoes, and stay a bit before fleeing away—mostly out of hurt self-pride, I guess. But it all turned out in the end, for she was the one who did the real thinking and followed me out to San Francisco not so many months afterwards.”

“Well, it all worked out for you. So it must have been the right way to handle things after all, wouldn’t you say?” In the few times they had chatted, this was the first time that Rose had heard him mention a wife. And not admitting to herself the reason for why she reacted the way she did, she suddenly felt a bit deflated. But it wasn’t to be for long.

For some reason when they met on this occasion, Patrick felt like this listener would be one that he could take a risk with to open up to about his personal life without danger of leaving himself exposed and vulnerable. He had learned the hard way this was a city that could sometimes be harsh and unforgiving when it came to gossip—but it just felt different with Rose. Her words and demeanor had somehow made him feel he could trust her.

“She was laid to rest in 1888 after…only thirty-three years of age. Ellen, Ellen Kavanaugh, was her name before we married. You’re right. It sounds just like my name and it’s easy to get confused. Her name was spelled with “K” instead of a “C” like my own Cavanagh. They’re both pronounced the same. And she became Mrs. Patrick K-a-v-a-n-a-u-g-h in the year of 1880. Yes, you’re right again. I took to her spelling of the name since back in Ireland there were both spellings down the generations in my family, so why not keep hers and mine both.

“She was what you’d expect of a…energetic and full of life, before the sickness came upon her. We both were so happy in tackling everything together at the same time in a city brand new to us both. We only had eight short years together before she was taken away. Almost ten years ago now."

At first Rose was at a loss as to what to say back to him. No wonder she had had no previous hint of a wife. Any fleeting thoughts about why he had not been more forthcoming, why he had held back about this part of his life, were silenced in an instant. Even though a good deal of time had passed, she could tell that it still hurt this man now called Patrick Kavanaugh with a "K" to bring it to the surface again.

"Way too young, she was. Were you working as a coachman then like now?" she attempted to swing the conversation around in a new direction, "or was it some other trade you were after?"

But Patrick was not so easily deflected. "It's time I should be getting back to my job. I promise to tell you more about myself next time we meet, Rose, and hope you'll return the favor." And realizing that he still never had gotten her last name, "What is the rest of how you call yourself, if you don't mind me asking?"

"I don't, and it's Rose Cameron."

"Well Rose Cameron, is it often that you make your purchases at this market?"

"That it is. Nearly every week, so."

"Then I hope to see you soon again here as I will make it my usual place as well. Now I must be on my way to work. So it's goodbye but only for now." And with that Patrick was on his way.

Several months elapsed before the pair of them met again. For her part, Rose fully expected to—and wished to—see him much sooner than the length of time it eventually took. Nearly every week she visited the market at least once, often lingering as long as she could but not so long as to cause alarm about why she hadn't yet returned to her household in a timely manner. She couldn't quite grasp exactly what it was about Patrick that made her desire to see him again. That he was affable and not aggressive in character were definitely in his favor. She didn't think it was out of any feeling of pity or sympathy for the sorrowful end to his marriage. In the end she gave up trying to put her finger on what she felt and simply put it down to the look in his eyes. They were alive with vitality and spoke to her in a way that said that this was an honest and kind man—essential traits without which she knew that she could never be so interested and attracted to him. And when she looked at him eye to eye she believed this was an honorable man, too, one who could truly care about a person—who could maybe even truly care about her.

As for Patrick, his growing interest in Rose was only tempered by his previous loss of Ellen. In short, he felt conflicted. He wanted to continue to get to know her better and was conscious that her friendly turn of the phrase and ease at letting laughter spill out naturally when they had their occasions together were things he needed to still troubling memories of the past where his thoughts all too often tended to dwell. On the other hand there was a fear that this petit creature, slim and shortish of stature, could be as delicate as Ellen—as susceptible to being brought low by an insidious disease and taken away as she had been—and this he could not tolerate a second time. So urges pulling him towards seeing her again were countered by even stronger impulses telling him to be cautious. Maybe it just wasn't worth the risk. For a while these combative voices prevented him from deepening a new relationship that seemed rushed. That by the furthest stretch of imagination could anyone think their drawn out and infrequent encounters could be perceived of as hurried by someone else did not occur to him for a long while. But finally these confusing thoughts tipped the balance scale in the other direction and he began to dream of seeing her again, then to actively seek her out.

When they did meet again they were both hesitant to start up a conversation after so much time had gone by, even if this is what they both longed to do. But slowly, the awkward feeling of distance from such a long interval between meetings disappeared, overcome by their mutual attraction to each other. As talk stretched from minutes into hours a point was reached that seemed right for adding a new dimension to their growing relationship. Since it was nearly noon, a bite to eat was suggested by Patrick at a nearby café, to which Rose readily agreed. It was here that she learned Patrick Kavanaugh's work experience went beyond dealing with horses as a coachman in San Francisco. Indeed his childhood in Ireland had involved daily exposure to a horse-centered environment because of his father's occupation in the business of horse equipment. He had at first watched him at work. Then, when he was old enough, he was taught by his father everything he knew about working with leather and practicing the craft of saddlery and harness-making. By the time he left his native land he was as proficient in the required skills of the trade of horse tack as his father was. He only lacked in years of experience because of his young age.

For the few years he had lived in Boston after leaving Fall River he had worked both as a laborer and in horse-related occupations, piecing together small jobs to cover basic needs. He described to Rose where he had lived in the thickly Irish populated district of the city—on Salem Street in the North End. He was working as a hostler when he had met Ellen, who worked as a used clothing seamstress and lived near her place of work only a few doors down on the very same Salem Street. Then, after moving across the nation to the West Coast and finding work as a laborer in his early years in San Francisco, he had returned to his family's occupational roots in 1886, performing an assortment of work that combined driving carriages with making saddles and harnesses for J.C. Johnson Co. at their yard location on Howard Street. It was touch-and-go at first, since he was almost immediately faced with the threat of an impending strike by the harness and saddlery-workers union. The union was demanding a twenty-five percent increase in wages and review of the grades of work. Of course, the bosses maintained that their employees were already fairly and comparatively well-paid, and if they chose to take the action of not showing up for work, well then they could just stay away for good. They claimed they had plenty of stock of leather goods from East Coast makers and could get more if needed at a lower price than the workers were being paid in California. Adding insult to threats of financial injury, in essence throwing salt into the wounds, they said California-born workers, in any event, were not as good workers as those born on the other side of the country, neither of which applied to him.

A good deal of the workers' unhappiness, and a major part of their grievances, stemmed from the accusation that their employers were hiring too many lower paid apprentices in comparison to journeyman. One claim saw the ratio as being five apprentices for every one journeyman worker. It was an obvious way of using cheaper labor to lower labor costs on the backs of experienced journeymen who were expected to cope with training and overseeing the quality of work under nearly impossible conditions. Somehow Patrick managed to navigate his way through these initial treacherous waters, along with most of the other dozens of co-workers at J.C. Johnson, weathering each storm when it hit to carry on for several years to come.

Indeed, if that was not enough, he filled in as hostler—a stableman tending to the horses at the livery and stables run by Patrick Sullivan on the same street, when time permitted. Small living accommodations were provided nearby. He had done one or more of these jobs at Sullivan's, and later at another company named T. G. Morgan, right up until the year of 1898.

As the turn of the century drew closer, there was already in the air the feeling things were changing for the worse in view of Patrick's stock-in-trade centering on horse-drawn transportation. In San Francisco, both cable car and electric street car contended for supremacy among the new mechanical conveyances making inroads on traditional modes of moving people, with the latter gaining ground and spreading more rapidly because of its lower cost. Several of the smaller companies based on horse-drawn vehicles had already disappeared. And on the horizon loomed the introduction of mass-produced automobiles. So far these motorized contraptions, particularly the American made Duryea, were more or less considered to be a novelty toy for the wealthy. However, those in the know, and especially those in a conveyance-related business, could see the writing on the wall. Plans were already in the works for expansion and improvement of the existing road and street systems and there were a growing number of places where one could take on fuel to keep motorized vehicles running.

When Patrick expressed concern for the future of his livelihood, Rose took on his worries as well.

"Then what can be done with the type of work you know—what will you be able do?"

"Well maybe I'll just start making leather saddles to fit into these new-fangled automobiles…they still have to sit on something, don't they?" he quipped with a twinkle in his eye.

She knew him well enough by now to know when he was joking: "Give over. You'll not be pulling my leg so easily, Mr. Patrick Kavanaugh."

"Aye, so right. Never could. Many of us are wondering where we'll end up. I've already had hints from the boss man. He's starting to feel the pinch too. Future orders are trailing off quickly, he says."

It wasn't but a few months after their conversation that the business was, in fact, trimmed back by a half, and Patrick found himself seeking new work along with most of the other of his co-workers. Fortunately, there were still plenty of manual labor jobs to be had and a new hat was soon placed on his head. For the next three years he continued in this general line of work. Employers and jobs changed several times during these years with some periods of no work at all, and while the amount of time he and Rose spent together continued to grow, the uncertainty of the future weighed heavily on his mind; he felt he didn't have sufficient economic stability to offer to her for starting a married life together.

So, in thinking what he could do to better his position, he listened attentively to, and was taken in by, the suggestion from a friend on how he might substantially build up his wealth in relatively short order. A mining company in Shasta County was looking for additional labor to work the Midas mine, a significant gold lode in the Klamath Mountains which had been discovered not long before, in 1894. In only two short years, by 1896, operations had grown to a major scale and there was a need for many more miners. He told Rose of his plan to go to the area for a very limited time to try his luck. It wasn't far away from San Francisco, only about forty miles south of the town of Redding, California. The money was supposed to be good digging gold, but no matter how good it was, he swore that he would not be overpowered by the smell of wealth and would be back as soon as the cold weather set in. And lodging would not be a problem. He would be staying in shelter where the mine was—in Harrison Gulch.

It wasn't easy for Rose to see him go. Although it was so long ago now, the memory of her first loss returned in a haunting vision. In her heart of hearts she believed the distance that had divided her from John might recur with Patrick, and he too might never be seen again. But she also was wise enough to know it would stifle his ambition to better his position to say anything to prevent him from leaving; she knew he had made the decision because he wanted to provide for her. So she resigned herself to having to wait to see what happened while praying for the best of all outcomes. Her approach proved to be the right one. After spending the better part of 1900 away, he returned to San Francisco, even before the cold claimed its grip. He came back neither a great deal richer, nor poorer, thankfully. His gold miner phase had been a short-lived one, a brief interlude that taught him his destiny did not lay in that direction.

Then, as the official year ending the nineteenth century

neared its completion, an opportunity allowed him to apply his horse equipment skills one more time. W. Davis & Son, another company located on Howard St. which had somehow survived the threat of the automobile up until this point, required someone immediately. One of their key craftsman had suddenly passed away leaving a number of orders on the books needing to be filled.

Feeling more satisfied and worthwhile than he had in a long time, Patrick decided now was the time to retake his own horse by the reins when next he saw Rose.

"Would it be much of a bother to you if I asked you to consider a change from your present location?"

At first at loose ends of what he meant by this question, after a moment of reflection a quizzical look was replaced by a smile and eyes that lit up her face.

"But whatever do you mean, sir?"

"Sure, I think it's about time that we stop meeting each other to walk in the park or to have a meal now-and-then and start seeing each other more often—say on a regular daily basis. So I'm wondering if you'd consider giving me a chance…if you…marrying me…in your own good time, of course."

"Let's see. Ah, would you be giving me a little time to think on it. There now, that's enough. The answer's yes. Will it be this afternoon then that we'll be calling on Father Flynn to make the arrangements?"

Now it was his turn for a yard wide smile for her swift answer was all that was needed to seal their future happiness together.

And they did see Father Flynn that very day and a date was set for their wedding. The day they chose was the very first day of the very first month of year number one of the new century—January 1, 1901.

SCHOOL REGISTERS AND NATURALIZATION

Central Coast, California, April 2008

Around the same time as the Australian information came to light a letter was written to the priest of the local church in Ireland at which Rose Anna and her family had attended and were baptized. Contacting the parish priest directly was suggested by the office of the Derry Diocese after I had written them concerning their publication of a book on the history of this local church. In this book that I had picked up on the trip to Ireland were transcriptions of the names and ages of students who had attended local national schools during the second half of the 1800s, as well as the names of their villages in which they had lived. While Rose and several of her siblings appeared to be listed at one of these schools, the ages denoted in the entries varied by a sizable margin from what they should have been for each of them, casting doubt on the veracity of the transcriptions themselves. If someone could be found who knew how this information was obtained then possibly this could lead to getting at the original school registers, or at least accurate copies of them, with the objective of rechecking ages and school levels to assure that the entries were truly valid and actually for ancestors. From the original records learning more about the duration of education of the McMartin family members might be an additional benefit.

By a stroke of good fortune a message was received back

from a woman named Hanora who had actually worked on putting the church history book together. The parish priest had thoughtfully passed my request on to her as the person who would best be able to answer questions about the old school registers. This new contact turned out to be definitely the right person. From her came a windfall of information. Hanora was presently living in Donegal only a few miles from where my relations had lived, but had actually been raised even closer, almost within a stone's throw of their home. Because of her interest in family histories of the area, her own foremost, of course, she had contributed her effort in producing the church history book and while doing so had gained the confidence of the parish priest who had then also graciously granted her access to the original baptismal registers. Having had prior experience with deciphering the names and dates in the registers and having the names and dates of the ancestors I gave her in hand, she immediately and correctly identified their entries in the church registers then proceeded from there to finding the corresponding individuals in the old national school registers to which she also had open access.

What she found confirmed my hunch that somehow between the transcribing from the original school registers and the printing of the church history book, portions of the entries had gotten crossed with other entries and the information had become corrupted. The result was incorrect ages and grades for the pupils while parents' names and place of habitat were correct. Besides disproving the accuracy of the church history book data, the actual school registers contained much more information, showing the date when students first enrolled in the infant school, when they transferred to the upper level school and the last year they attended, plus all the years in between, including gaps, which usually meant children had been needed at home to help out on the farms.

Ultimately, what the school registers showed was the McMartin children were well-educated for the time period. Remarkably, Rose Anna herself attended school until 1889, when she was seventeen years of age, less than three years before she was to emigrate from Ireland. Also, for one of Rose's sisters, Bridget, who had not been listed in the online baptismal list for the parish that had included all of Rose's other siblings, the age school data gave a huge clue to the year in which she was most likely born. Hanora also took it upon herself to meticulously make and send photocopies—taken directly from the original documents and not from secondary microfilm copies—of the church baptismal register entries for all of the family members, except for the same sister Bridget whose name continued to be missing from these as well.

But there was one further surprise yet to come from Hanora. Earlier, I had asked her if there might be an official burial register for St. Brendan's. Now, almost as if it was of passing interest, she presented in a new message a short list of death or burial dates for a number of people who matched the forenames of my McMartin ancestors. How did she acquire this information? At the beginning of the message she had mentioned while a burial register did exist, it was very incomplete and none of my McMartins were in it. But Hanora had something else to offer to offset this absence. When she was a young girl she had seized an occasion that had come upon her to copy a notebook kept by a family friend. In it the man had kept track of all of the deaths or burials in the local area starting from 1933 and lasting until 1961. And it covered the very same area where my relatives had dwelled! My own interest in family history developing so late, I was astonished that at such an early age anyone would have enough life perspective, subject interest and foresight to think of the importance of this kind of information. Dates for five of Rose's siblings were given, including even the elusive Bridget, precise enough to probably permit death certificates to be obtained on the basis of them. Only Mary, who had immigrated to America before Rose did, and Rose herself, were lacking from the list.

Thus, the life circle for all of Rose Anna's siblings who had stayed in Ireland was completed, including knowledge of their final resting place in the local church cemetery. As for Bridget, the ages at time of death jotted down in the notebook allowed Cousin Daniel on his next annual visit to Ireland to confirm that her birth had been unusually registered in the district of Letterkenny as opposed to that of Kilderry, which had been the district of registration in common with all of the other siblings. It was question of overlapping jurisdictions. But still lacking was the fate of the two remaining Irish immigrants to America—my grandmother Rose Anna and her sister Mary.

As noted earlier, previous attempts to uncover naturalization records for Grandfather Patrick among the collections of the National Archives in both San Francisco and New York, the latter being his probable port of entry, had not produced a solid match. The possibility of learning more about his place of origin, and perhaps something more about Rose as well, through naturalization records had been at a standstill for many long months. But the door was reopened a smidgen by a last minute, chance question that was posed to a staff member in the California History Room on yet another visit to the San

Francisco Public Library to tap into their extensive collections and knowledge.

Halfway out the door, in a last ditch effort to leave no stone uncovered, I turned and asked a nearby librarian who had been helping me earlier with historical voter registration research if there was any other source that I was overlooking that she knew about and could recommend. Wracking her brain with a bowed head for a few moments something else suddenly clicked. She looked up and said yes, there was one more actually, a quite rare source. She proceeded to retrieve a single, very worn and tatty volume that no longer even had a clearly written title on the cover. It was not another listing of all voter registrations names for a specific year like the Great Register of California or the Great Register of San Francisco for 1890 I had come that day to peruse. Instead, it was an alphabetical index compiled in 1920 of *San Francisco registered naturalized voters*, no matter in which state they were officially naturalized, plus a 1923 supplement of voters naturalized since 1920, covering citizen newcomers who had moved to the city in those three intervening years. Whatever the length of residence, the significant fact was this was a list of people who had become American citizens through naturalization. I had done plenty of research in the library catalogs of SFPL and of the California State Library as well as in different bibliographies of voting resources and had never come across a reference for this very special book.

Unlike other voter registration lists that I had comprehensively searched online for Patrick and Rose in San Francisco that had helped to fill in gaps as to where they lived, there was no age, party affiliation or specific election year mentioned. What was given was address, country of birth, and *date and place of naturalization* for each person included. From the research that was done previously in tracking the various and sundry joint addresses of residence of my grandfather and my grandmother Rose, I was able to positively identify and separate the correct Patrick Cavanagh instantly from those other entries with exactly the same name. Sure enough, it cited Ireland as his birth place, but totally unexpectedly, the place he was naturalized was neither San Francisco nor New York—it was *Boston*! The door to finding his naturalization papers had been thrown wide open again!

A return to a leading online source for genealogical databases was a necessary next step and then to a specific database entitled *Index to New England Naturalization Petitions, 1791-1906*, covering Massachusetts, among other states, and the Boston area therein. With a bit of patience, the enigma of the Soundex codes, codes under which were grouped like sounding surnames with variant spellings, was unlocked and there, before my eyes, the Soundex Index card for Patrick appeared. On the card there was further proof of the Irish county of my grandfather's birth: County Roscommon, Ireland was plainly marked. And the date of his naturalization, 1876, correlated exactly with the information found in the San Francisco index. Most importantly, the certificate number and the title and location of the court necessary to locate and obtain the actual naturalization papers were included on the index card.

While Naturalization Service staff created the index cards, it was due to someone's foresight in the department in which Works Projects Administration workers were employed in the 1930s to make photostatic copies, known as *dexigraphs,* of naturalization proceedings in all courts—local, county, state, and federal—in the New England states of Massachusetts, New Hampshire, Maine, Vermont and Rhode Island. And these dexigraph images were now housed as part of the collection of the National Archives Northeast Region of the United States.

It didn't take but a long portion of an afternoon and night before a telephone call was made to the NARA regional facility early next morning. In possession of the exact file number and credit card, an order was submitted for the complete naturalization documents on file for Grandfather Patrick, whether they were just the naturalization petition itself or possibly the added bonus of a declaration of intention as well.

Strangely, and weirdly quite appropriately, at the top of the first of the two pages sent from NARA Boston the handwritten given name of Patrick appeared followed by a scratched out *Kavanaugh* version of his surname with the *Cavanagh* version entered right above it as the corrected spelling. Even in the year 1875 when he began the citizenship process at the Boston Circuit Court surname spelling confusion had been an issue! There had been no declaration of intent papers filed because according to his court statement on his citizenship form, his age at the time of his arrival in the United States was only fourteen and he was, therefore by law, considered to be a minor and excused from having to go through the extra step required of those immigrating at the adult age of eighteen or older. The earlier date of birth noted on the papers he did file was in stark contrast by some ten to a dozen years to those dates found on later census sheets and most voter registration lists. It seemed as if he had knocked years off his real birth date, aging more slowly, for each successive census taking year when living in San Francisco. The net result, though, in stating he was minor upon arrival in America, was that instead of the normal minimum five years of waiting between filing a declaration of intent for naturalization and a petition form for citizenship, only three months were necessary for him to become a citizen of the United States because of only having to file petition papers. These papers were filed at the court in late 1875 and he took the oath in early 1876.

The court papers did not divulge a townland in addition to County Roscommon; this was once again a frustration to be endured even though naming a specific village was not normally done and could not be expected. Since Patrick became a naturalized citizen in Boston, there was little likelihood any of the facts gleaned from the documents would have any connection to Rose's early history in America, to where she spent the unknown amount of time after arriving in New York before going on to San Francisco. However, the dates on the papers did coincide to when Ellen, his first wife, was thought to have lived in Boston. So when an opportunity presented itself to visit the Boston Public Library on a stopover on the way back from a trip to Europe, the city directories were consulted for both Ellen and Patrick. The entries for Ellen began in 1878 and ended in 1881; a short span of years indeed. This made eminent sense in terms of looking for her presence in San Francisco only in the years after 1881, and in tracing her emigration from Nova Scotia, Canada to Boston sometime before 1880, according to the census of the same year, the year in which she was only twenty-five years of age. As for Patrick, although it could not be an absolute certainty as yet, it appeared that he was living quite near her on the very same street in 1878, two years after the completion of his naturalization. So through these papers a bit more of the history of the persons of interest was able to be reconstructed with a fair degree of certainty that it was accurate.

The ultimate discovery of my grandfather's naturalization papers was by no means insignificant and rounded out the collection of traditional genealogical resources normally sought after. But the fact of the matter was that I was still in the dark about his exact place of birth and still stymied in making a family connection across the great Atlantic divide to Ireland. For Rose, also, nothing new had come to the forefront to help in filling in the still existing gaps in her personal journey.

ROSE AND PATRICK

San Francisco, California, December 1901-April 1917

The beginning of a new era was well on its way in 1901 when Rose and Patrick married. Further gravitation towards a motorized world at the street level was unavoidable, and the swift movement to the acceptance of the automobile in particular was greeted with enthusiasm from the well-to-do. Patrick and Rose both knew that a change in the type of work for him would not be long coming. Horse transportation was definitely on its way out and there were fewer and fewer who could hang on to the old ways. But Patrick was content because, at least for their first year together as a married couple, he would still be able to ply the trade that was most comfortable and satisfying to him—crafting leather into saddles and harnesses at the factory on Howard Street—while continuing as a coachman on the side. Who could tell what the future would bring as far as work went afterwards. Only a few short months after saying their church vows the pair of them were sent over the moon by the news that Rose was pregnant.

When Patrick ran into Denny Kelleher, a cousin of Rose's, early one morning not long after learning the news himself from his expectant wife he tried to hush his emotions and wipe away any hint of a broader smile than usual that would give him away. Although both Patrick's and Rose's natures were to keep things to themselves, especially until her pregnancy was further along and more obvious, their bright eyes and perpetual lighthearted demeanor had already spoken too loudly on more than one occasion, and it would not take long now, they knew, before word spread and all of their friends and distant relations became aware as well.

"It's a fine spring morning it is, Denny—one that you could stow away the turf for the day at home."

"It is that, it is. What brings you out and about at this hour, Patrick? We don't usually see the likes of yourself behind the reins of the horse and carriage at this time of the morning. Before the work day begins in earnest."

With a contrived yawn to mask his impulse to grin and a tilt of his head to show he agreed with Denny about being an out of ordinary time for him to be at work, Patrick intoned, "The horses were feeling their oats and I guess it caught on with me too. Rose said it's off with you—out of the house— go out and take advantage of the day and let me get at the housework. So here I am at the crack of dawn looking for the first fare of the day."

If it had only been the minor difference in the cadence of Patrick's voice Denny might not have grown suspicious. But when he also sensed an attitude seeming more upbeat and cavalier than normal, he thought something had happened and there was news of some sort that he was not telling. And Denny had his own way of nudging it out of someone when he was fairly certain he was right.

"And how is married life treating you so far? Are the two of you thinking of any other changes now that Rose has given up the job she was at with the German family?

In spite of all his efforts at self-control, his mannerisms in the end betrayed his vague reply. "No, nothing in the way of work. Just have to wait and see what's in store for us in…what else comes down the pipe when it does."

That was enough for Denny. "Out with it, man. What's going on? My fingers and toes are crossed that whatever it is, it's meant to be for the good."

"Well, I see it's much too hard keep anything quiet in this city. Especially from another Irishman like yourself, Denny. Although there's a good deal of time before us until the expecting day, but yes, we're going to have a baby. She's not due till January next. So we decided there was no use for her to look for work again just now. There's plenty to do in getting our place ready for a new family. As for me, I want to work my fingers to the bone. Not let anything pass me by so we'll be off to a good start. It's not an easy state of mind for us leather workers these days with already so many layoffs. And changes are coming so rapidly, although business at W. Davis & Sons seems to be busy enough right now."

"That's the kind of news I was waiting to hear, man. Here's my hand in congratulations to you. If it's alright, we'll be stepping over later to give the same to Rose as soon as I've had a chance to tell the wife." And Denny lifted his arm with his hand holding a non-existent drink: "Slàinte, my lad— here's to you and Rose. And to the future Kavanaugh!"

For the next few months Rose and Patrick spared no effort in preparing for the baby's arrival. Ever-growing rumors and evidence indicated that even for the largest of the harness and saddle-making businesses things were growing increasingly dire as each day passed. In November the axe finally fell on all but a dozen of the most senior workers at Davis, and Patrick joined the ranks of the jobless alongside many of the co-workers who were laid off with him. This meant the Kavanaugh's must also move from their present residence as their housing was subsidized by, and partially attached to, Patrick's work place. As Rose's time was now fast approaching, they moved into action immediately and within the week they had managed to locate new living quarters on Garden Avenue, quarters in which they were much more cramped then the ones they had just left. What was more of a handicap, though, was that they must start all over again to make the place ready for a baby. Rose tried to do as much as she was able but it was up to Patrick to do the bulk of the heavier work, juggling his search for another job with painting, some carpentry, and shifting their things from one place to the other.

By the end of November Patrick still had been unable to secure employment. He had given up on finding another leather industry job, given the state of affairs, and was open to taking almost any kind of work that might come his way. Patrick's situation combined with the stress of the move seemed to have taken its toll and wearied Rose; she often felt unwell as she approached her eighth month of pregnancy. As much as he coaxed her to take it easy and rest in bed as long as she could, he often found her moving about their apartment, busying herself with whatever she could even if it was just dusting the furnishings one more time. It was too ingrained in her nature not to continue doing things right up until it was time to sleep. She simply couldn't stop herself even if she knew his advice was for the best.

On an afternoon during the first week of December he returned home to find her nearly doubled over and as pale as ghost. Her feeble words blasted like dynamite into his consciousness. "Could you be getting the doctor…I need him now!"

He took a hold of one arm and guided her to a chair.

"What's wrong? Try to sit down and don't move."

Rose could only wave a hand to motion him to go.

"I'm on my way."

While it took him only a short time, less than an hour to bring the doctor there, to Patrick the sixty or so minutes seemed forever. Rose gave birth within minutes after their arrival to a baby a month short of full term. The frailness of the tiny boy and his struggling to breathe were pitifully apparent from his first weak cry. The doctor was candid in forewarning them of the seriousness and possible consequences of such a premature birth.

Four days later the tiny one died of convulsions in their small Garden Avenue flat.

Patrick was floored. His only salvation was Rose had survived; he had not lost the two of them. She had also been left in a precarious state of health from the ordeal. For this he would remain eternally grateful and from this he was able to pull himself together to cope with their loss. It was a different story for Rose. As could be expected, she was devastated so profoundly she could not speak of it, or nearly anything else for weeks to come. Starting almost from the moment the doctor said there was no hope, her husband's attempts to talk to her were met with hardly any response save for wide-eyed stares from her impossibly large brown eyes, eyes which seemed to have grown even bigger in size while losing their usual luster, becoming little more than a hollow stare at nothing. What was going on behind these blank looks would not be drawn out for the time being. When Patrick mentioned her state to others, their advice was that it was too soon for her to regain any semblance of normalcy and to give her as much time as she needed to come to terms with it. Pushing her could just make things worse. He could not disagree. It was just that her behavior was so far from what he had ever experienced in their relationship. It was a side to her character that he would have never guessed she had in her. No obstacle before had ever been too big not to be met with strong dose of optimism, with a positive let's-get-it-done attitude from her.

Weeks turned into months and while Rose made small signs of returning to her old self—going out to do the shopping, and talking to Patrick on occasion about his new job as a janitor—she was different. It was not the same lass he had married. There was a distance entwined in her remarks and demeanor that had never been present before. As she moved about their apartment, glancing here and there as if hunting for something she had misplaced, the sense of emptiness she was feeling was almost tangible. He felt it, too, to some extent, but the daily routine of his job, a job that was only meagerly supporting them, and the firm belief there would be other opportunities to begin a family had conquered much of his own tendency towards moroseness as days passed by. He could not allow both of them to be depressed, downtrodden by fate, at the same time. If that happened there would be no chance that their ship would right itself to stay afloat. So he saw it as his mission to lessen her despondency as much as he could and by whatever means available to him.

Its time had passed. Any thoughts of being able to return to a horse-related trade were removed completely from his mind as the next few years rolled by. The automobile and auto makers continued to proliferate, moving relentlessly ever forward to a position of prominence then to one of dominance.

So it was with a sigh of resignation that he stayed on with his janitorial job. At least they were able to move from the flat filled with negative memories to a new apartment in the Noe Valley neighborhood, closer to where Patrick worked. Settled in a new place in a different part of the city, Rose noticeably showed rapid improvement in her attitude, and her relationship to her husband took on once again many of the marital aspects they were accustomed to before the tragedy. Rose's positive, tough spirit had never been broken in all of life's trials and tribulations she had undergone in the past, but once her strength had finally snapped, it had been equally difficult to rebuild. It had taken five long years. But in the end they had overcome them, even the worst of all, by staying together.

***

There was no warning. The force of it was like nothing felt by any of them before. People were flattened like they had been hit by heavyweight boxer's left hook, they were tossed out of their beds, bounced off their chairs, and some were crushed by the collapse of structures that surrounded them. What didn't topple or crumble swayed and shook for the longest minute of violent upheaval that anyone had ever experienced. On this eighteenth day of April 1906 the earthquake that no one will ever forget changed the face of San Francisco and the lives of those who lived there forever. As bad as it was, the resulting fires that were fueled by "earthquake weather"—abnormally high temperatures and strong winds—brought even greater ruin to the city over the next few days.

Anxiety stayed frozen on the faces of the survivors for

weeks and months on end afterwards as the fear of another earthquake remained a constant worry. But finally, as days wore on, even for the most distraught fear lessened and was recast into joining the collective effort to create a new, better San Francisco out of the rubble and ashes. It was the final elixir needed for Rose, strangely enough, to complete the process of restoration to her former self. While their own apartment had on the surface seemingly survived the disaster—neither having collapsed like a pancake nor succumbed to raging fires—its foundation had been damaged and dislocated enough to require all of the tenants to move out. With much regret this time, Rose and Patrick found themselves once again on the lookout for a new place to live. They had come to love the Noe Valley neighborhood, finding renewed happiness in their cozy quarters within its boundaries, so they confined their search to the streets they now considered old familiar friends.

It took them nearly to the end of year to secure another apartment, this time on Sanchez Street, close to and with views on the beautiful Saint Paul's Church. And the old axiom that out of every catastrophe an opportunity is born held true for the Kavanaughs. In a city with its infrastructure in tatters from the devastation, a work force of hitherto unheard of proportions would be needed to replace and improve upon water systems, electricity and lighting, growing telephone communications, streets and street cars, and sewers and drainage, among those services of the greatest importance. The citizens and the city leaders were of one voice—the restoration of San Francisco could abide no delay in getting started. And the doors of the Board of Public Works were flung wide open in solicitation of a small army of laborers to complete these tasks as soon as humanly possible. Hired on at a steady job at a wage nearing four dollars a day was like a dream come true for Patrick. His assignment saw him working on the rebuilding of the city's sewer system. Hard work—backbreaking work—work that he could channel his energy and enthusiasm into wholeheartedly for the betterment of their situation and for the sake of the city itself. He was proud to call himself a San Francisco sewerman, to play his part in rebuilding the essential foundation necessary to underpin the more visible infrastructure soon to follow. It was a city taking on a new shape and substance on the backs of workers like him and so many others.

The change in their financial circumstances coupled with their move to a new flat marked a post-earthquake transition that seemed to Patrick, at least, to call for further renewal—a turning of the page. He had never spoken of the idea before to Rose and he now wanted to see what she would think about a change, a change to something she had automatically taken on when she married him.

"There's something I think it might be a good time to put right now. It's been in the back of my mind to talk about for a long time. You remember the spelling of my last name—mine and yours for a good while now—was not the one I was born with? It was Ellen's variation of Kavnaugh that we used. Would you be against making a change back to the original spelling? The one with which I was christened. It would be sort of like giving us a fresh start …Cavanagh is a letter shorter than our "K" version.

"And it's the spelling that seems first to come to mind to folks most of the time after they hear it spoken. What do you think? If you're against it, well, then we'll just leave it alone then."

Rose paused for a moment to think. "You know, I've always had a liking for the name Cavanagh with a "C" when I've seen it down on paper. And it would be good to get back to your native name. So you'll be getting no argument from me, husband. But is there anything special that we need to do? Officially, I mean, to make the changeover and start using it?"

"There may well be but we won't let that bother us. For us it's Cavanagh with a "C" from this day on. And that's the end of the story!" And so it was. The old spelling that had been used for some twenty-six years, since the time when Patrick had married Ellen, was tucked away for good now for both Rose and Patrick *Cavanagh*.

The next two years flew by with ever improving economic circumstances for them personally and for many others who supplied their labor in creating a new city of a splendor much greater than it had ever known before. Early in the year of 1909 on a workday evening, Rose offered a novel suggestion to her husband.

"Would you be thinking it's a good idea to be making our home a bit more lively?"

Raised eyebrows and crinkled forehead framed Patrick's wondering eyes. What could she be up to now?

"Should I be afraid to try to answer that, m'dear?"

"What I'm getting at is…well, you know…we still haven't been able to add to our family. And there are so many displaced people. Especially youngsters without parents from the disaster. And we both know about the conditions in the orphanages. Some of them have been made to turn over children to other agencies with better care. I've seen notices of homes needed and there's a monthly supplement provided to fostering parents for each child who is taken in. It's meant to be a temporary placement situation until permanent homes are found with parents who adopt them. So I was thinking what better way to help out now that we can. I would like to do…and it would be good for us too."

"But we're happy now the…" he caught himself in midstream, "…no it's a fine idea. It's a grand idea, in fact. Didn't I always say now you were the smarter one of the family? But our place is hardly large enough the way it is now. How can we manage it?"

"I was talking to Emily at the flats next door yesterday. She told me that a family is moving out of her building. The folks living in it now told her they wouldn't mind at all if she showed it to me. It's much more spacious than ours. With a really nice kitchen. The price is not above what we could afford. And the placement agency will contribute to the upkeep of the fostered children until they leave."

"Then we ought to go after it before it gets away to someone else. When can we see it? This evening, maybe?"

"I'll check with her to see if will be all right, so."

As it often seems to happen in life when you are least thinking about it, within months after making the move and of taking their first two boarders in—a youth of eleven and an elderly man who needed short time housing until a broken arm mended—Rose found herself with child for a second time in her life. They had already committed to take in two more children, a promise which they kept. This time, in spite of the responsibility of taking care of so many mouths to feed and a constant state of semi-chaos, the first and last months of Rose's pregnancy passed without consequence. The amount of energy she expended left her normally and happily fatigued by the end of the day, and it was with peace of mind she could feel things were going differently with this baby. But when the birth of their own healthy and beautiful daughter made them a true family, they decided to take in no additional children after the last one had found a permanent home. Their little Mary Cavanagh with her twinkling hazel eyes was their dream come true and she was all they needed.

Rose rebounded quickly from the birth and soon Mary had passed her first birthday. All of the foster children were gone and taking care of just one child rather than several left her feeling much less fatigued. "Now that we are smaller in number again, I think we could do with living in a bit smaller place. One's that more practical for a family of three. I almost hate to mention it since we've made so many moves. But I think now would be a good time to look into it."

"If you are willing to go through it again, I don't see why we shouldn't, Rose. I'd not be minding. And Mary certainly wouldn't, either", Patrick joked.

So once again they changed apartments, scaling down this time to a smaller more affordable one on 29th Street. The rebuilding of the city continued to progress at a rapid pace and Patrick continued with his Public Works job in spite of beginning to feel his age and the rigors of the manual labor in his joints, especially on damp days. Rose could tell in the way he walked stiffly around the flat after rising in the morning, taking him longer and longer to loosen up and get ready, that something was happening. Both of them just hoped it was a passing phase, or at least that it would not grow any worse.

It was 1911 and a momentous event was on tip of everyone's tongue. For several years prior, the women's suffrage movement, begun in earnest in 1893 and defeated in a statewide referendum in 1896, as well as the issue of equal pay for equal work, had been gaining support in California. Wage earning, working class women were by now prominent, especially in positions of teachers, factory and laundry workers, servants and waitresses, and also as agricultural laborers. On October 11, 1911 men only cast their votes in San Francisco County overwhelmingly in favor of enfranchisement of women. It had taken the importance of the role women played in contributing to the workplace and to overall economic well-being to finally establish a clear cut reason for equality and for their right to vote to finally occur. Rose and Patrick went for the first time together, arm-in-arm, to their polling place in 1913 with a swelling of pride in their hearts.

By the time Mary turned five it was clear that the creeping ailment afflicting Patrick that had been steadily worsening had changed pace. Lifting her as he did on occasion had become a painful effort as were the heavier, more onerous tasks he faced at work. The doctor's diagnosis was an acute form of arthritis and his prognosis was not a favorable one. And now the disease had begun to rapidly progress and there seemed to be no remedy he could propose that could abate its course, much less reverse or cure him. The one positive factor was the currently quick progression generally did not last. If he were fortunate, he should see a slowing at some point in time soon and perhaps even stabilization. In 1916 they decided to move again from their upstairs flat to a first floor apartment on Noe Street to lessen the stress of going up and down stairs. But the debilitating disease overtook all efforts to make life easier for him and by early 1917 Patrick could no longer work and became, for all intents and purposes, incapacitated and mostly bedridden.

***

It was unimaginable that it had gotten to this point for them. Without the resources to bring in home care, Rose was simply physically incapable of lifting him in and out of bed. And now having the sole responsibility of fending for a young girl while at the same time needing to find work herself to feed, clothe and house them, there seemed no other option open to her. The day that Patrick was taken away to the nursing home, with the help of Rose's cousin, Denny, was a pivotal day in the life of all of them. Financially and physically strapped as he was, Patrick Cavanagh was admitted to the Laguna Honda Relief Home with few questions asked.

CIRCLE UNBROKEN

Central Coast, California, May 2008

It just didn't add up. With the wealth of information accumulated on the life of my grandmother, Rose Anna, my grandfather Patrick, and their daughter, my mother Mary, the only logical conclusion that could be envisioned was that Rose must have wound up her life in San Francisco. It didn't stand to reason that she would have pulled up stakes and moved somewhere else just at the end of her life. I had census sheets, voter registration records, city directory addresses, school records and church register information all indicating the chances were extremely slim she had ever left the city. As for my mother, she had never mentioned living anywhere else until she married my father and moved across the bay to Oakland in 1940. The records show Rose did not move with them, besides it was very likely she was no longer living by then. I already knew that Patrick had died in San Francisco. But what had happened to Rose Anna and why I was unable to find any trace of where her life had ended remained a burning question?

Letting things linger while I followed other areas of interest eventually paid off in freeing my brain from the pressure of over-thinking. And gradually my mind pushed back to earlier times, quietly going about its business in the background. Then one day the semi-recollected single instance of when my father had mentioned the word *stepfather* when briefly referring to my mother's parents resurfaced to slip back into the forefront of my thoughts. If my memory was not playing tricks on me after nearly thirty-five years, leading me astray with faulty wishful thinking, then there could be something worth pursuing there. Why not? This could be the key needed to finally unlocking the answer. Just supposing Rose had married a second time after Patrick had died and had assumed a new, and heretofore, unknown surname she had then carried with her to the grave. So far the content of the collected documents—spanning the period from 1900 to 1930—had revealed no mention or clues of the existence of a second husband. I had enough knowledge by now of habitat changes of the Cavanaghs over time to effectively rule out any possibility of a second marriage for most of those years. Barring any unforeseen events, such as divorce, it seemed then it must have taken place after Patrick's death in 1930, if she had remarried at all, which would have put Rose into her late fifties. Divorce itself was very unlikely since she and her husband were Catholics during more religiously strict times.

There was one gap in core information gathering still needing to be filled in. Inexplicably, neither Rose's nor my mother's name had showed up together or separately in the 1930 census. My mother would have finished high school by then and would have been about twenty years of age and she could well have been living and working on her own. If they had indeed been caught in the census net under a different last name and there were some way to find one or both of them, separately or together, by linking their first names, or some other backdoor method, the 1930 census could still be instrumental in getting to the answer.

It had been ages since I reviewed the San Francisco city directory data so painstakingly compiled for a long span of years. I had paid most attention to tracing my grandparents but had also jotted down the various addresses for my mother before she was married as well as after her marriage for the year or two she and my father had lived together in the city before moving across the bay from San Francisco to Oakland. Her address and occupational information had consistently appeared in the directories for most of the years after she left home, all under the surname of Cavanagh as I recalled, the one with which she was baptized. So up until now, because the possibility of the existence of a stepfather had nearly been forgotten, there would have been no real reason to revisit her addresses for the purpose of uncovering if there had been indeed somebody else. Still, there was something about these entries that was nagging at me, and it was worth another look to see if there was a detail to which I had given only scant attention or, perhaps, inadvertently skipped over entirely.

What I hadn't remembered was that the first appearance of an address and occupation for my mother's name alone, without any connection to either or both of her parents, appeared in the 1928 directory. She was about eighteen then and was gainfully employed, which apparently met the criteria needed to be independently listed in the city directory. And since it seemed to be a policy that wives and children living with a male head of household, all under the same family name, were not given separate listings even if they were employed during this era of directory publishing, she appeared to have been already living on her own at a quite young age. For both 1928 and 1929, the years of the beginning of the Great Depression, she was listed at the same address. Her entry under Mary Cavanagh for 1930 indicated that she had moved and was residing at a new address on Grove Street. She continued to live there during 1931, afterwards changing residences at least two more times before marrying my father in 1939. What stood out, though, and what I had neglected to realize the importance of earlier, now came to mind: there was a city directory address for her in 1930, the same year as the census! So why had the 1930 census failed to provide an entry for Mary Cavanagh while the city directory did?

The next question that plagued me was—if, in the 1930 census, my mother was not listed at the address or at any other address by the name that she had reported for 1930 city directory purposes, then who was listed at that exact Grove Street address provided in the census? The temptation was to start plowing through the online version of the census page by page until the street and address turned up but with a San Francisco population of over six hundred thousand inhabitants in 1930, the project seemed too daunting even for the most stalwart of researchers to undertake. Perhaps there was an easier way? Could it have been overlooked that there was a "search by address" option in the census database from the well-known online genealogy vendor? It seemed definitely worth taking another look. For the 1930 United States Federal Census, and for other census years as well, there was no street address search index per se but what did exist, located beneath the data entry template and below the information about the database section, was a browsing feature which allowed census page images to be sorted through in smaller packages of geographically grouped entries. Covering the entire United States, a specific state was first selected, then a county within that state, followed by a town within the county. Then the town was broken down into census *enumeration districts*, each district covering a geographical area that had been assigned to a census taker. And for each separate district, the four streets that formed its boundaries were given, drawing a box, so to speak, within which all residents were counted.

By comparing a map of San Francisco to the named street boundaries of the enumeration districts provided by the census database, it could be determined that the district Grove Street fell into could be narrowed down to three likely enumeration district possibilities. This would be a far cry from having to face browsing through all of the four hundred and nine ED districts the population of the city was split into for census purposes. The pages for each of the three districts had to be looked at one by one until the portion of Grove Street that contained the exact address was found, still a somewhat tedious and time consuming process.

It was learned sometime afterwards, that for major U.S. cities, a nifty address locating utility on an internet website provided a much quicker, more precise way of finding the correct enumeration district into which a specific street address fell. It took the guess work out of matching map street coordinates with the closest street boundary names on the list of districts in the census database. After using a mapping website to pinpoint the exact street address and nearby streets, all that was required for the ED finder to do its work instead was to choose the census year of interest then plug in the desired state, select a city, select a street from a drop down list of all the streets in the city, and finally choose the nearest cross streets on either side and, *voila*, the number presented after the hyphen was the enumeration district associated with that address. Instead of three districts, the ED finder narrowed it down to just one to browse through.

When my eyes finally closed in on the page of the census that looked like it held the street address numbers I was looking for, I was prepared for another disappointment, fully expecting to see unknown names that I would be unable to associate with my family. And, at first glance at the last name of the group of family members listed at the Grove address, this seemed to be the case. The surname was one that I had never come across before. Then, when my eyes moved over to the first names listed for each of the family members a ripple shot through my body: there they were, Rose and Mary, my grandmother and my mother, together with someone named John, both subsumed under his surname of *Harte*! When writing my cousin in Glasgow later the first words at the top of the message were *She's found!*

How fortunate it was that a confluence of circumstances had taken place back in April of 1930, the year of the decennial census, that had found my mother, already a working woman, but still living at home with her mother Rose, and with someone who could now be considered definitively to be the missing link—her stepfather. Whoever provided the information to the census taker provided sufficient details on all three of them to prove beyond any doubt that Rose and Mary Cavanagh had now become known as Rose and Mary Harte, at least for this survey purposes. That the 1930 city directory had given my mother, Mary, a separate listing because she had stated her name as Mary Cavanagh, not Harte, even though she and Rose and John Harte were all living together at the same Grove Street address, and even though she was not in reality a head of household, had been the necessary entry ticket to cross referencing the two sources and to ultimately solving the mystery. The following year, according to the 1931 city directory, my mother was living at another residence with a unique address to herself only, under the surname of Cavanagh. Apparently she had been mistakenly enumerated under the surname of Harte in the census!

Next, with breath held and fingers crossed, Holy Cross Cemetery, the Catholic cemetery where Grandfather Patrick was buried, was called to see if she was buried there as well. Their computerized system spat back her name, death and burial dates instantaneously. She was there—alone in a plot with no others. Her supposed date of death in 1936 now in hand, but still hoping the cemetery record was truly for the right person, another visit to the San Francisco Health Department was made to seek out a copy of Rose's death certificate. This time it was found. Though replete with inaccurate information, the singular fact that my mother's signature, Mary Cavanagh, appeared under Informant was more than sufficient proof this was the Rose in question that had been so long sought after. The date of her birth was off by a year and the first name of her father was incorrect, but clearly noted down as the birthplace of Rose and her parents was Donegal, Ireland.

There was only one last thing do—a trip to the cemetery to see Rose's final resting place would complete my search of her life's journey. On another beautiful day with sunlight and shadows sweeping across the rolling green expanse of the magnificent Holy Cross Cemetery we stood beside her simple slightly inclined grave marker. Now this person whom I had never met seemed whole again. From birth and baptism in a small hamlet on the Inishowen Peninsula of Donegal, to her passage across the Atlantic to America, to her marriages in San Francisco, to the places she lived in the city, to where she died and where she lay in repose, the fundamentals of her story were complete. After two years of research in finding Rose—now calling her *my grandmother* had real meaning behind it.

REUNITED

The South and San Francisco, California, 1898-1945

Life in the South had done wonders of good for John. Climate—especially the restorative power of the sun—when coupled with his youth, had combined to heal his injuries as completely as possible. Although the scars of his wounds would be borne forever, he no longer showed any signs of a limp and his energy and stamina seemed to be abundant. Deciding not to rush to Scottsboro where Emma and her daughter lived, he headed south through the Smoky Mountains into the massively forested area stretching across the western part of North Carolina and the North Georgia mountains, stopping to offer his labor to earn wages to sustain himself at various timber harvesting jobs along the way. It took him six months before he carried on towards the East again, eventually returning to Tennessee and reaching Chattanooga, the first town of any size since he had departed from Knoxville. It certainly was not the most direct path he could have taken, but day-to-day living during this extended trip through wilderness and woods had given him pause enough to come to terms with his failure to succeed in finding Rose. The vastness and variation of this corner of the country of America had humbled the belief he had once held of someone being found without having fairly precise information on their whereabouts. He now saw how foolish it had been in thinking it would be an easy affair to accomplish when he had stepped aboard that ship in Ireland and off it again in New York.

Chattanooga was a place John knew from the moment he set foot in it was not meant for him. With the burgeoning iron industry, textile mills and railroads there was plenty of work no doubt to be had there. But the smoke-laden skies and blackened buildings arising from the combination of iron smelting and roaring locomotives made for a living environment he could not long endure. Indeed, the few days that he lasted in the city only served to remind him how much he missed the country sights and smells of his native Donegal, or even the kind of open space he had just travelled through. It was with some haste that he took himself off again, leaving the noise and filth of this factory town behind, moving on towards Scottsboro where he would be able to see for himself if it was truly the kind of area his cousins had described—a primarily rural place where farm life predominated, and one in which he could feel welcome staying with Emma, the sister of Cousin Anne's husband, until he settled on somewhere of his own.

He knew it was going to be all right as soon as he saw them on their land. The Findley's had not exaggerated. The two and half story, white wood-sided frame house stood by itself, alone in the middle of fields radiating out on all four sides from it. This was what he was looking for. Compared to Chattanooga it looked like paradise. And then Emma and Molly welcomed him almost as if he was already a member of the family. After Emma's brother Carter had written to her that John was already on his way just after he had left, they had expected him shortly in Alabama. They had worried for weeks, lengthened into months, over the possible reasons of why he had not yet arrived. All their worries and fears of something untoward happening to him along the way were now laid to rest, and they lost little time in doting on him. It had been such a long time since Emma's husband had died and they now had a young man in the house.

While at home in Ireland he never felt working the land to be his calling, but now John took up the life of a farmer with no reservations. Every day that he spent in the crop fields with the hired hands was a day spent with joy in his heart. From early morning to dusk he labored by the sweat of his brow, thanking each droplet as it rolled from his forehead to the corner of his eyes and fell to the ground. It was done with a deep gratitude to the washing away of any concern about where the next meal would come from no matter how hard you worked, as had been the case for so many at home in Ireland. It did not escape him as well how special it was to be accepted so fully, to be able to so quickly share in the warmth of the small household. And it was a good thing he came when he did for two farmhands left within weeks to join the Unite States Army to fight against Spain in Cuba. The skirmish, later coming to be known as the Spanish-American War, had been predicted to last only for a few months duration in 1898. His understanding of this conflict was limited by his newness to the country and a lack of understanding of American history and politics in general. For him, it was the working of the land that captured his full attention and that was enough for the present. Sure enough, as predicted, even though the war had spread to the Spanish held Philippines as well, the Treaty of Paris signed at the end of year appeared to mark the end of conflict.

But it turned out not to be the case. In 1899 war erupted

again—this time between the United States and the Philippines. The people of the Philippines, finally rid of Spain, were in no mood to willingly accept submitting again to the presence of yet another foreign ruler. To them, the United States was simply another oppressor with the objective of forcing them into a non-independent, territorial status, and they were most reluctant to let this happen. As the fighting wore on over the next year and a half in what was often termed The Philippine Insurrection, a growing desire to become more involved in, to serve his new country like others around him were seen to be doing, meshed with the adventurous nature of the young man. His life in Alabama had been nothing but good to him and maybe this was a part of it too. In a sense it had been too good and a nearly perfect situation had come to him too early in his years. There was still more that he wanted to do before settling down permanently. He had only met one woman to whom he would have devoted his early manhood, and she was now long gone from his life.

So in February 1901, at the tender age of twenty-two, John Harte enlisted as a private in the United States Army and was paid passage to present himself for duty at the Presidio in San Francisco, California. The Presidio served as the training base, having sufficient housing for large numbers of recruits. It was also perfectly situated as a staging embarkation point for the shipment of troops across the Pacific Ocean to the Philippines theatre of battle. It all happened so rapidly. He barely realized he was on the West Coast, in a totally new part of the country once again, before he was on board ship and bound for points even further to the west from California, points known as the Far East, towards where the sun is said to rise. The Pacific voyage was anything but calm and peaceful and John and many of his fellow soldiers were ill much of the time. There was little time to recover once on the islands, for while they found the outbreak of battles sporadic and unpredictable, they were quite fiercely fought when and where they did occur. By the official ending of the conflict on July 4th, 1902, he had proved his mettle as a good soldier many times over. Unofficially, fighting continued on a lesser scale for rest of the year and on into the next. John requested to stay on until it ended, when he finally shipped out, returning back to the Presidio in 1903.

Honorably discharged and no longer in uniform, he was free to return to Alabama or to choose a different path altogether. Unfettered by family obligations and set down in a place looking to hold considerable interest, he felt free to take the time to stay where he was for awhile to explore the great city of the West. Change and adventure had been a remedy serving him well until now in preventing the dredging up of past memories and dreams. Why not continue along the same path? He kept his thoughts fixed on the future—most of the time. And being in a city that was not freezing in the winter like New York and where sweat did not pour off you like it did for most of the year in the South and the Philippines was actually not a bad thing at all at this stage of his life. San Francisco was a magnet for immigration and a tourist destination of repute making it all the more interesting. Each day he walked to a different quarter of town with his eyes wide open and without the compulsion to find work as long as his service discharge pay lasted. And each day he felt more at ease in it, becoming a part of the hustle and bustle rhythm of vibrant city life.

But as the months passed and his funds finally dwindled to a dangerously low level, a decision on what to do next had to be made, and made soon. And a solution was found swiftly in the end. A large rooming house next door to where he was staying had an immediate opening for a servant. It was a job he had never done before, but it was an easy way to get started. He took the job working alongside the large staff it took to tend to the needs of the mostly aged or very young residents. Asked to assist on several occasions to lend a hand in fixing inevitable problems in an older building, John soon proved his value and was acknowledged as a quick learner who had an aptitude for understanding intricacies of building mechanical systems. So within two years his job had evolved into more of a handyman dealing with heating, plumbing and electrical problems than with duties as a servant, which was much to his liking. The building manager never regretted the shift, as John had established himself as their prized mechanical engineer by 1910. As the years passed his life was consumed by his work, punctuated only by brief involvements with the fairer sex, romances none of which lasted more than a few months. It wasn't that he was prone to dalliance in his relationships. He had simply found it difficult to meet the right person. Then in 1911 he met a woman he felt closer to than any he had met so far since his ill-fated relationship with Rose. They married shortly thereafter but the marriage proved to be a short-lived one. Within three years she passed away leaving John bereft and once again on his own.

The outbreak of the First World War in 1914, albeit remote from the shores of America, caught the attention of most Americans since it seemed only a matter of time before United States involvement would be required, despite the country's reluctance to break with a policy of isolationism. Affected emotionally by the reminder of his earlier military participation and the early loss of his wife, John decided that a change was once again needed. He gave up his job at the hotel and left the city to take a job in the town of Suisun, in Solano County, about fifty miles away. There, he worked as a laundryman, another new experience, for barely a year and a half before hearing about a job more suited to his skills back again in San Francisco, working as a repairman engineer at the Mint Hotel. And as expected, in 1917 President Wilson officially entered America into the war and by 1918 the push was on to draft a much larger army. John registered in September at the Local Board in San Francisco but because of his age he was never called up to duty. The war drew to a close by the end of the year in any event.

At thirty-nine years of age John's life consisted totally of his work and other daily routines. His memories of Ireland and his years in Alabama had all but evaporated like the morning fogs often did in his coastal home. The only memory which awakened quite vividly, if something should provoke it, was the loss of his first love—the Irish lass from Donegal. That would never completely leave him until he was dead and buried.

On a typical day carrying well-used work clothes down to his usual local laundry off of Fifth Street he received the shock of his life. He had seen on several occasions over the years women who had similar looks to his long lost Rose, and it was particularly at those times he reflected back to their old days in Ireland. But this time the woman behind the counter bore such an uncanny resemblance to her it caused him to do a double take; then, unthinkingly rude under any circumstances, he stared intently at her for a third time. He simply couldn't take his eyes off of her. When he had spotted others looking like her in the past there were always distinct differences upon further scrutiny of the details of their features. He saw none of these in this person. She looked exactly like what a somewhat older Rose would look like in his mind. Could the many years that had elapsed and a powerful subconscious yearning to see her again be leading his mind astray like a desert mirage?

Engaging her attention away from the other customers, he said "You look very much like someone who I knew a long time ago, someone…in Ireland." And when he was allowed to gaze directly into the big brown eyes that were so unforgettable and unmistakable, he started to believe the unbelievable. "You couldn't be the girl from Donegal that I once knew so long ago, could you now?"

Struck dumb by seeing a glint in his eyes that could only belong to him, the clothes she had taken in from the previous customer fell from her arms to the floor. She remained speechless for what must have been an eternity. Waves of chills and tingles rolled up and down her body from head to foot and from side to side. Then, catching her breath, she willed her jaw to unclench. "John can...John Harte, is it really you I'm seeing standing here before me or am I just dreaming?"

"That it is, Rose—the very person I am." And just like that, in a flash, long contained recollections of a relationship formed in their youth well before either of them had emigrated from Ireland, distances of miles and miles they both had travelled, and a separation lasting twenty-six years came to an abrupt end in a small laundry on a side street in San Francisco.

And after a long embrace and then a few additional

minutes more of work before Rose was allowed to take a break, they sat together on a bench around the corner and down the block to talk. They didn't have long together until duty called her back, but it was enough time for the two of them to arrange to meet again after work the same day. The afternoon found them both counting down the minutes until they would see each other, both wondering if what was happening was really true.

Only portions of the stories of the paths they had taken leading them both to eventually come to San Francisco could be exchanged during the first evening of nervous reunion. But when the conversation turned to recounting more recent events, it seemed more difficult for Rose to speak freely. In measured and sometimes broken phrases, she related to John the circumstances surrounding her marriage to Patrick Cavanagh. But when it came to explaining how she had gone from homemaker to laundry worker because of his incapacitation and confinement to a nursing home, words were squeezed out even more hesitantly.

"Our daughter now is almost nine years old now. She needs to have a good education, needs to do better for herself then we did. I don't want to see her working in a laundry ten years from now. Mary's enrolled in a good Catholic school where standards are set high. It's worth the cost, no matter how many extra hours I have to work. There's no telling how it will go with her father who... he barely could move at all when he was admitted to the home about six years ago. And there's been no improvement since then. Just the opposite. A bad situation for everybody. But we're not giving up hope as there are promises of new treatments coming about soon. Any day now, they say."

A daughter! Why hadn't he thought to ask? And a sick husband to worry over to boot.

"Sorry to hear about him, so. But to have a daughter to share your life with must be something else, something at least to be happy about." It was all he could think of saying for the moment.

What Rose couldn't bear to tell him in their early days of getting to know each other again was that her husband's growing debilitation over the years had been a challenge to their marriage. In fact, before Patrick was about to placed into the home to face the bleakest of futures he had convinced her it would be for the best for all of them if they considered themselves in a state of marital separation. He had been insistent the chance of happiness for Rose and Mary should not be sacrificed for the sake of someone whose long-term outlook was four walls and group of attendants to see to the servicing of his basic needs. At first Rose had refused to agree. How could she further isolate herself from someone who was suffering with pain and feeling as if he was down and out, from someone who had stuck by her through thick and thin, from someone whose patience had nursed her back into a healthy state of mind at her lowest point? But eventually she recognized and accepted their marriage had been under a heavy burden and strained for some years because of his illness and, in a way, his release of her would be a freedom from responsibility and worry for him as well.

John and Rose continued to talk until Rose realized the time. She must get home to prepare dinner for Mary but they planned to meet again soon. Both of them were possessed by a flood of reminiscences that evening, images of the past that carried over into their dreams after lights and eyes were shut tight that night. Good—and bad times—they hadn't thought of them for so long. Most especially the day they were supposed to have gone off to America together swirled through their heads. It could not be swept away despite all efforts to think of something else. And they both awoke the next morning with heads dazed by the poor night's troubled rest.

***

The renewal of their relationship began cautiously with brief encounters near the laundry and occasionally sitting down together at a café. John continued his work as mechanical engineer at the Mint Hotel. Gradually over the next year they began taking regular walks together along the city front and in the parks. John became better acquainted with Rose's daughter, Mary, and they sometimes all shared a meal together. At first, there had been a fairly thick wall between them, but time and patience worked their ways and Mary's acceptance of John as someone important in her mother's life, past and present, became less grudging. She began to see John as someone of significance not only to her mother's life but to her own life as well.

Patrick's condition progressively worsened as the number of years of his stay in the Laguna Honda care facility mounted. His decline became as much mental as physical. Day-after-day of the same faces and surroundings had reduced the scope of his attention from family, friends and news of world happenings to a set of strictly controlled routines revolving around his own basic needs. It was a landscape of limited variety, lacking stimulation and, like so many nursing home patients, his memory appeared to be reduced proportionally. Only some of the primary sensations such as the taste and texture of food and, of course, pain seemed to exist for him now. And much of his life was spent in various states of drowsiness, if not outright sleep.

In 1925, eight years after Patrick's admission to the nursing care home a decision which would have been rarely entertained in the old country was taken by Rose and John.

"Mary, would you come over to the chair here and sit beside John and me. John and I have been talking over something that would make life a lot easier to us. Better for all of us, really. I think you know how we feel about each other. We wondered what you would say if we were to all take to living together under one roof? It wouldn't be much different than what we've been doing now. There just wouldn't be the need to waste money on rent for two places, which could be put towards other things. Not so much back and forth all the time, either."

They knew that her reaction could have gone either way to the suggestion and had prepared themselves accordingly. However, Mary had rather expected it. She blinked a few times quickly then lowered her head for a moment. When she raised it up again she gave them the answer they were wishing for.

"It's alright by me. You know, it won't be long now before I'm off living on my own. I think it would be fine while I'm still here if we all shared a home. So don't worry about me. It will all work out the best."

After carefully explaining to Mary their present feelings for each other and what had occurred in their past lives in Ireland once again, she too seemed to understand and agree with them that it was personal and financial folly to continue maintaining two separate households when her mother and John felt they were a couple. There was no question of divorce from Patrick and a marriage to John while Patrick still lived, but the care Rose and John shared for each other which had never completely ceased was quite evident even to their teenage only child. There was no reason then in their remaining years they should deny themselves the happiness of being together and, with Mary's consent, they chose a modest apartment in the Mission District. In a city the size of San Francisco, with a population nearing six hundred thousand inhabitants, there would be no recriminations to fear.

***

In 1928 Mary graduated after earlier transferring for her final year from Catholic school to a commercially-oriented, public high school which prepared students with the requisite skills for entry into the job market. She found immediate employment as a bookkeeper where she was able to put her newly-acquired short hand, stenography and typing abilities to good use. As soon as she arrived home from work on an April evening, her mother called to her to come to the living room. When she entered the room and immediately saw pain written all over her mother's face, she had already guessed the news.

"It's father, isn't it?" Nothing changed except for the lowering of her mother's eyes. She knew instantly she had guessed right. The silence between them was almost palpable.

Patrick Cavanagh, the once good-natured coachman and maker of harnesses and saddles, from County Roscommon in the Irish heartland, after a struggle of thirteen years, had succumbed to an age-weakened heart and body ravaged by arthritis. He was laid to rest on the lower slopes of Holy Cross Cemetery in the year of 1930, alongside his first wife, Ellen, in the plot he had purchased at the time of her death in 1888, shared also with his and Rose's short-lived baby.

***

Marriage vows were exchanged between Rose and John the following year with Rose taking on the new last name of Harte. Their voyage had a been a long one, but finally culminated in what they had set out to do so many years ago on the misty, northern peninsula of Inishowen, one which had been fraught with many twists and turns of fate. But they considered themselves as among the blessed ones whose destinies had been guided by a power making it a certainty they should be together again someday. They had no regrets for the lives they had led and were thankful for the love they had experienced with others. But they could only view their partnership for the few years remaining to them as something that was intended to be.

Mary continued to live at home with her mother and newly acquired stepfather. They changed residences twice, to flats near the panhandle of Golden Gate Park in an area called the North Park neighborhood. Mary changed jobs as well, working as a stenographer for J. H. Miller, a lawyer's office. Approaching the end of 1935, Mary moved to her own apartment, leaving the Harte household much the poorer by the lack of her presence. It was high time for her to spread her wings everyone knew. But the bond between mother and daughter, a single parent of an only child for the majority of the years of Mary's upbringing, many of them spent on the verge of poverty, was not an easy one to break, even by the tiniest of fractures. Fortunately, the redeeming factor was the small geographical size of the city which would lessen worries of a separation caused by distance, making it easy for them to visit each other often. Public transportation was readily available and walking was Mary's forte. She was famous among her friends for long distance marches throughout the city and from shore line to shore line!

***

Perhaps it was Mary's absence from the family table or perhaps the years of work in the laundry had finally worn her down, whatever the cause, Rose had not been feeling herself for the past few weeks. Fatigue was now in constant battle with her normal level of mental and physical activity and she often had to sit down to take a short break while doing housework. On a weekend day, while sweeping the floor in their apartment, the toll of the years collected its ultimate price. Dizzy, with visions of patterns of lines spinning, overlapping one another, and swirling like the spiral Celtic art of her childhood, Rose fell to the floor.

John found her lying there when he returned from downtown. Mary came soon afterwards. In an individual plot, in a different section of the same magnificent cemetery, Rose Anna joined the others on a fine spring day in the year of 1936.

***

With the death of Rose, John's own existence became

meaningless to him. He could not come to terms with losing her again and with each day it became more of a burden to carry on alone. Hours were passed staring at the top of the dresser where the *polka dot scarf* Rose had never been without had been neatly placed. The bottle became his best friend, the only one in which he could achieve a modicum of solace. He lived, if you can call it that, for another nine years before it was his turn. He never held a full time job again, and in 1945 he fell into his final sleep. Some say he died from the effects of chronic alcoholism, others knew differently. He left this world with the image of Rose at the market in Derry with the polka dot scarf wrapped around her neck as his final one.

EPILOGUE

Central Coast, California, October 2010

It cannot go without telling. A full four years after beginning the quest to seek out the family history of my mother, the second, even more entrenched "brick wall", the exact location in Ireland of my grandfather's origins, was finally broken down. The names of the parents of both Rose and Patrick had been determined earlier from their 1901 church marriage record in San Francisco. His parents were Michael Cavanagh and Mary Flaherty. These names appeared a second time on Patrick's San Francisco death certificate almost thirty years later, lending further weight to their legitimacy. Since these great-grandparents were born, and later married, well before civil or church recording took place in Ireland, any hope of finding further proof in the records there of a Cavanagh/Flaherty pairing beyond the naming of his parents in the church marriage register of my maternal grandparents was miniscule. The same vital record barrier would most likely hold true for any siblings my grandfather may have had. The Heritage Centre at Strokestown had searched their comprehensive database of births and marriages covering all of County Roscommon to no avail and the online, public version of their data collection yielded the same negative results. Nothing appeared in the civil records index for all of Ireland in the LDS database either.

Still, even in the face of this, these very same websites were revisited again and again over time, using different and enhanced search strategies as their databases became more sophisticated, knowing full well it was with only the slimmest of chances anything new would surface. But then in a recently added LDS database of Irish marriage records covering the years 1619 to 1898, a search was executed by names of the father and mother of either a bride or groom, omitting altogether a name for either the bride or groom themselves. No county or narrower location was specified in order to make the search as broad as possible. Thus, the names of Michael Cavanagh and Mary Flaherty as parents were entered and County Roscommon was omitted, opening the search to any couples in the entire country who married with parents of those names. While their names had never been specifically associated in Roscommon, it seemed there must have been a Cavanagh who married a Flaherty somewhere in all of the millions of entries for the totality of Ireland. Probably there would be several. There were not—but there was a single hit—in County Galway!

The details of this church marriage extract listed Mary Flaherty and Michael Cavanagh as parents of the groom whose name was John Cavanagh. The bride's name was Catherine Hayes. It gave the names of her parents as well, the date of the marriage in 1865 and the name of the parish in which it took place, but several of the spaces for entering other important information were left blank on the form. But Galway? It didn't take long to realize that County Galway was one of the counties bordering on County Roscommon, along with quite a number of others: Sligo, Mayo, Leitrim, Longford, Westmeath and Offaly. But Galway by far shared the longest stretch of border, while also being part of the West, in the province of Connaught, like Roscommon. The civil parish was listed as Killian and Killeroran and, after some effort, it was found to be located on the east side of the county and not at all far from County Roscommon. It was also in the Diocese of Elphin whose scope encompassed a major part of Roscommon while extending across the border into this part of East Galway as well. Suddenly, an all Ireland search had grown much more relevant.

Two of the pieces of key information missing on the record transcript were the groom's and bride's birthplaces. Now that I knew as much as I did about resources, if I was lucky, the Ireland roots database might have a civil record for the same marriage since it occurred just after the cut-off date of 1864. If one existed, it could provide these missing crucial facts. One record in the index seemed to fit best the search criteria entered, and in order to see its complete details, credit card information was keyed in. The pay off was immediate— the names, marriage date and place matched up perfectly with the church record, and residences were given for both the bride and the groom. The bride's address was traced to a Galway townland in the same parish where the marriage ceremony had been held. But under the name John Cavanagh there was a parish address that seemed halfway familiar, one I felt I may have come across in reviewing the half dozen or so Cavanagh farming families listed in Griffith's Valuation of the 1850s for Roscommon. Within computer research seconds it was determined this parish was indeed in County Roscommon so now there was no doubt John Cavanaugh had crossed county borderlines to marry a Galway girl! What the civil marriage record did omit, standard practice for these documents, was the all-important name of the groom's mother, the one given on the San Francisco church record transcript.

Revisiting the Michael Cavanagh listings in Griffith's in County Roscommon to see if the parish given for John in the civil record was associated with any of their land holdings was the make-or-break next step necessary to connect the circuit. Previously, I had focused on the triangle formed by the towns of Elphin, Tulsk and Strokestown where, along with the parish of Creeve, the highest concentration of Cavanagh families lived, and where I had expected my grandfather's home would be among them. But now I learned this belief had been wrong. *There was a Michael Cavanagh who had evaded my attention who was listed as a tenant in the same parish named in John's Galway marriage record as his residence! The single instance in all of Ireland of a Flaherty/Cavanagh couple, the parents of the husband of newlyweds, had been enough. Following this "missing link" marriage record to Griffith's had now provided the name of the exact townland, and the known whereabouts of the home of Patrick had finally joined that of Rose by virtue of a brother named John.*

A flurry of investigation followed on. Recent and historic maps were captured online pinpointing the actual land plot and house on the property. Cancelled landbooks were obtained from the Valuation Office in Dublin which provided details on the changes in the name of the lead occupant of the farm property from the 1850s into the 1980s, indicating the Cavanaghs interest in the land had ceased in 1894 when their name had disappeared for good. What had happened to those family members who may have remained in Ireland?

Over the past six months I had taken the lengthy

methodical approach of looking through rolls of microfilm of civil births of Cavanaghs in County Roscommon to see if any clues might be present to help in identifying my grandfather's home. For this low chance of success measure, a scan of the Cavanagh entry on each film had been made and was saved on a flash drive with date of birth, maiden name of mother and place of birth noted in the file name. There were over thirty pre-stored birth record files on my computer now waiting to be checked for possible children of John Cavanagh based on the maiden name of his wife and their place of residence in Roscommon. This earlier labor paid dividends as one civil parish record correlated—a Michael Cavanagh was born in 1869 in the same townland as John Cavanagh and Catherine Hayes. And with this record a closer generation of my grandfather's brother had been revealed. Once again the Ireland roots website was reverted to in order to look for a church baptismal record for Michael, and to see if any other offspring of John and Catherine could be determined by entering only the names of mother and father. Success!—in both instances, although there appeared to be only one additional sibling to Michael—the earlier birth of an older sister named Anne near the end of 1865.

With this new line established through John Cavanagh, my great uncle, and his two children, the prospect for learning of other descendants was reopened. If the circumstances of Michael and Anne and their parents could be further delineated, there was even the potential that descendants may still be alive somewhere. There was only one death record for a person named John Cavanagh in Roscommon around the date his last entry in the cancelled landbooks was lined out. It wasn't his. And for Michael and Anne neither marriage nor death records could be found in Roscommon, which would lead one to surmise they could have emigrated or migrated to somewhere else in Ireland, or something altogether untoward happened to the family. In filtering through the LDS family history database for marriages without narrowing by country, an extracted entry appeared matching Michaels's name and those of his father and mother (although her name was a variant spelling but sounded out the same). The marriage took place in 1899, in Boston, Massachusetts, and was to a woman by the name of Bridget Quincy. An image of the actual marriage document was next located the at the New England Historic Genealogical Society website which verified the accuracy of the details contained in the extract.

The hunt was then on again to gather more information about this couple who had married in Boston, which led to the discovery of a census sheet for a family living in Hillsborough, New Hampshire, not far from Massachusetts, in 1910. I was sure I had the right family, since this family's name and date characteristics matched almost exactly those of Michael and Bridget, until two weeks later when I saw in an earlier census record what appeared to be a totally different last name for Bridget from the one known to be correct. A call to vital records in New Hampshire confirmed that this couple was not the same one who had married in Boston. Deflation. But it didn't last long before another family, a family living in Boston in a different census year, also looked promising. This time there was no being led down the garden path. Both the Michael and his wife Bridget were indeed the same people who had married in 1899. On the 1920 census sheet seven children were listed, the youngest born in 1917. There was a slim chance one of them could still be alive and even a greater chance, almost a certainty, there would be children of these seven siblings living still. A long look was taken at the Cavanagh forum on the *genforum* website, sifting through numerous postings which mentioned Boston and people who had ancestors from Roscommon. Two were found with potential and replies were sent to both of them. Neither of them answered within the next few weeks. A second email was sent to the more likely of the two, just in case something had gone awry. An answer came back the next day—it was from a granddaughter of Michael and Bridget! However, it was with great regret that she knew less than I did about her forebears, but at least she was able to substantiate Michael's home county of Roscommon, Ireland. And more significantly, she was able to clarify what had happened to his sister Anne. Anne had immigrated to America too, before Michael, and was remembered as having been seen on her sick bed in Boston by my newly discovered distant cousin when she was a small child. As no other siblings were known to her, it now appeared fairly certain that my earlier conclusion that Michael and Anne were the only two children of my grandfather's brother was correct. Michael and Bridget's seven offspring had remained and multiplied in Boston.

It was a good feeling to now be aware of the many other cousins currently living in Boston despite never having met any of them. But there was still a question of the ancestors in Ireland. Not only what happened to John and Catherine, the parent's of Michael and Anne who went to Boston, but also the deaths of the father and mother of John and my grandfather Patrick; Michael Cavanagh and Mary Flaherty had still not been accounted for. In the case of the elder of the two, Michael, the outlook was dim that his date and place of death would ever be known because he was noted as already deceased on the 1865 civil marriage certificate of his son John in County Galway. But because Mary Cavanagh had been noted as present at birth on the 1865 birth form of her grandson, it was evident that she was still alive at this juncture and her death should be among the civil death records. Efforts to locate a death record in the various databases had not gone well as nothing could be definitely identified as belonging to her. The result was the same for both John and Catherine. Then a different approach came to mind, one which would involve a systematic database search done by the heritage center in Strokestown, and one that could not be duplicated using their public access website. Since the townland, registration district, place of registration and superintendant's register's district were on the birth documents of both John and Anne, a search was requested for all the variants of Cavanagh and Kavanaugh deaths which occurred in those geographical areas between 1864 and 1901. Surprisingly, even though death records for John and Catherine were not among those in the public IFHF database, nor were they among those in the LDS database, they did appear in the search conducted at the center, which is the main reason all three sources must be searched since each one has records the others don't have. John and Catherine both died in the townland of the family patriarch Michael Cavanagh and both died close to the beginning of the twentieth century. Two more question marks were erased from the curiosity slate. As for the patriarch's wife, Mary, the search still goes on.

Roscommon, Ireland, November 2010

Ireland was calling again. With digitized records having finally resolved the issue of where my grandfather came from, including a map of the plots of land tilled by his parents, I was eager to go and see for myself before the winter set in. The second and third week of November is not the most popular time to visit the country, but having spent parts of several autumns in England in the past, with generally favorable weather, we didn't let it discourage us. Shannon airport was our point of entry on this trip where we rented a car and immediately set out for Roscommon Town, to a bed and breakfast that had been booked in advance. On the way there we stopped in the town of Ballygar in County Galway to meet by prior arrangement with the parish priest who had brought the parish marriage register from nearby Newbridge to his house next to the church. In the back of my mind there was still a worry the transcribed database information was not accurate. I needed to see for myself the "missing link" entry in the original parish register to make sure the names were correct, and that it matched the facts laid out in the LDS database church extract. If Mary Flaherty and Michael Cavanagh were actually in the register as parents of John, a small cloud of doubt would be lifted from my mind.

The parish priest was most accommodating, inviting us in to sit down at the kitchen table while he brought the register over. He opened the book to the entry and soon all fears disappeared. Not only had the transcription been accurate, but, amazingly, the entry had much more information, more even than what I had from both the church extract and civil records combined. The names of the townlands where the groom, bride and their parents lived were precisely given as well as the names of the sponsors. The extract had been correct as far as it went, but it had been incomplete. Perhaps this was due to using an image of poor quality from the microfilmed original record for deciphering and transferring the relevant data into a digital template. But since I had previously looked at the microfilm supposedly containing the entry and had found it so faint that it was entirely illegible, it is hard to believe this was the reason. The data must have been extracted from another source altogether. Although the parish priest promised to send an official certificate of the entry plus a photocopy of the register, I took, as a precaution, several photos of the entry spread across two pages with a digital camera. Later I would find that the photos did capture the pages fairly well and while the priest kept his word about sending a certificate, he failed to do so with regard to a photocopy. But the complete "missing link" record proof was finally in my hands, which was what all that really mattered.

A light rain had begun to fall and as we said goodbye to the priest at Ballygar and drove off in darkness towards our bed and breakfast in Roscommon Town. We had telephoned the proprietors in advance to say that we were on our way, not to worry, and to expect us within a half hour. Driving in Ireland takes concentration for the uninitiated, and on a pitch black night in the rain, it was even more challenging, so we were happy to safely arrive and be welcomed into the warm and pleasant accommodation. Next morning, after a hardy Irish breakfast including boxty, an Irish potato pancake, and armed with a load of maps, we drove off to search for the land once occupied by my ancestors. The weather was chilly but with blue skies so we had that going in our favor. On the way we stopped to visit the old churchyard of the Catholic parish. Once a monastery and afterwards a protestant church for a period of time, the building, now in ruins, was surrounded by a graveyard which has been the burial place of the locals for hundreds of years and was the place where my relatives would be surely found as well. Unmarked graves far outnumbered the sites with markers and those with markers had weathered writing that was hard to decipher although, as we were to learn later, transcriptions had been painstakingly done through the diligent work of one of the local residents.

From the church we carried on down the road until we reached the village where we made a brief attempt to locate the Castlecoote House, once residence of the estate owner who had been landlord to tenants in my great-grandfather's time. After failing to actually find the house and the ruins of the castle that were said to surround it, we inquired at the nearby local all-purpose shop about its actual locale and how to exactly get to it. Following the directions, we proceeded through a nearby gate open to the public and up a dirt road for about a quarter of a mile until we found the house and castle remains on a hillock facing the River Suck. The house was closed for tours for the season but we took advantage of another unlocked gate to take a closer look at what was left of the castle towers and an enormous hearth so large that a person could stand upright in it. From there we continued down the same road we had driven on from Roscommon Town until we reached what we determined from our maps was the land once occupied by the Cavanaghs. The primary plot, the one on which their house had been situated according to the most detailed map, was now half forested, planted with a dense expanse of evergreens as a timber crop. The building itself would have been located within the wooded section making it unlikely any remnants of the structure still existed. We took pictures from a small dirt road running alongside the fields and viewed the lay of the land in all directions from it. With the other two plots of land, one of which that was a long thin slice adjoining other long thin slices of turbary—bog lands where peat can be dug—and the other a shared plot divided in half and possibly used for grazing, the total amount of land comprised only seven acres. Under ten acres, it definitely met the standards for small farm appellation.

After leaving the ancestral land, there were only a couple of hours left before dark and they were given over to taking a more thorough look at Roscommon Town. The landlady of the bed and breakfast greeted us when we returned by holding out a sheet of paper containing a message from a local person I had been in contact with by email. He had also telephoned after we had left in the morning before hand delivering the note with a map of where he lived, inviting us to join him so he could show us around the area on the following day, if we had time. I rang him immediately and we arranged to drive to his house early the next afternoon following Sunday morning mass.

Emails had formed the basis of our communication up until then. But it took only a few moments after meeting Allen and his wife Bernice before it was evident that the friendliness and willingness to share local knowledge which had been evident in his written words were completely indicative of his in-person personality as well. After getting acquainted, we started a day that would be one of most significant in my life. In two cars, ours following his, we began our journey with the first stop at a nearby ancient site in Castlestrange. The round La Tène Stone of the Iron Age, estimated to be over two thousand years old, one of two in all of Ireland with similar features, carved with the intricate Celtic swirling art of this early period, lay before us in bright sunlight and blue skies. It was a fitting start to the rest of the day for a slight wind shook and rattled the remaining colorful leaves in the large beech tree that stood close-by while Allen related the story of the first female veterinarian in Ireland who rode on her white stallion past the manor house, now laying in ruins nearby, to make her rounds down the small road we had come on to reach the site of the stone. From Castlestrange, we revisited the old graveyard where we had been the day before. The origin and significance of the remarkable religious slabs mounted on the remains of the old church wall were explained and a gravestone bearing the Cavanagh name and engravings common to the occupation of a shepherd was pointed out for the first time; our walk around the graveyard the previous day had missed this corner. Afterwards we continued on to the land of my great-grandparents for a second visit, this time for a much more in-depth exploration. Now, with Allen's guidance, we were able to delineate the exact boundaries of the property and even climbed over a gate to experience the thrill of treading in the footsteps of my grandfather over the length of the open grass-covered field until it abutted the thick and impenetrable planted forest.

Before leaving this area, our new friend and guide had one more stop to make. We climbed back in our cars and followed him up the road which passed in front of the Cavanagh's field. In front of a house on the hill, we were motioned to park. Suddenly we were in the middle of an abundance of activity, tractors and several people moving about. Our guide went up to one of them whom he recognized and brought him over to us to be introduced. His name was one that immediately rang a bell, one that I had encountered on the cancelled landbooks from the 1850s. Astonishingly, his family had continued to occupy land neighboring the Cavanaghs' right up to the present day. His ancestors had occupied many more acres than my great-grandfather's holding which had given them a greater chance to survive during difficult times. And over the years since then they had increased their holdings to form a large farm of over two hundred acres, affording pasture for some two hundred head of cattle. Tommy's apparent love and knowledge of the land was only matched by his abiding interest in the local families that once lived in the townland. He had been the one who devoted days and weeks to deciphering, stooped over on hands and knees, the inscriptions on the weathered tombstones in the graveyard. He showed us his original handwritten notebook of all the entries, among which there were two belonging to the Cavanagh family. He also had much more detailed maps of the townland and with these, along with his personal knowledge, he was able to show us a second house in which, according to stories of the past, the Cavanagh family had lived after moving from the house in the center of the plot to be closer to the access road on the edge of the property. While we stood in front of it in the dwindling light, fog began to swirl around us and raindrops made sputtering attempts to be included, Tommy, who seemed the gentlest of souls, provided the icing on the cake. He said in its time this small house had been known as "Cavanagh Corner". What a story to add to a most incredible day and what a pleasure it was to be able to take back with us a photo of a neighbor whose ancestors had lived beside mine, standing near it.

But the day wasn't over yet. Even though darkness was upon us by then, the moonlight provided enough illumination to be able to make one more stop. The building of the old National School still stood in the village; this would have been the school at which my grandfather attended. And close to it was the old church of his day now replaced by a newer, larger structure next door. In seeing these sites, some of the most important parts of my grandfather's village life were accounted for. It was with immense debt of gratitude we finally parted from our wonderful guide amid the growing cold that had by now worked its way well into our bones. The drive back to Roscommon Town was met with now seriously dense fog and heavier rain. Having checked out of our bed and breakfast in the morning with the plan of staying somewhere else, given the hour of day and conditions, the best option was to try to find another accommodation in or very near the town. Fortunately, we weren't left driving for long because my wife, remembering how comfortable and inviting the old and central Abbey Hotel was when we had stepped in for a quick look and a cider the previous day, and how easy-to-find again it was behind the ruins of the Roscommon Dominican Abbey itself, suggested we try there. They had plenty of rooms at a favorable winter's rate so a perfect end of the day was spent dining on country cooked fish and chips in front of a cozy fire in the lounge area. In fact it was much more than a perfect end of day—the whole experience had been a perfect awakening to a new beginning of my past and present.

***

During the following years there were three other unusual documents uncovered of interest. They confirmed and extended the history of the Cavanagh and Flaherty families in the same townland. The first was a large book held at the National Archives of Ireland in Dublin. In it were townland maps and names of primary tenants of lands held by Sir Charles Henry Coote in County Roscommon. The earliest Coote family had gained lands in several Irish counties at the time of Cromwell. While the first Coote has gone down in most historical accounts as cruel and murderous, Sir Charles of the nineteenth century was said to have been a decent landlord. Whatever the case this atlas-like book, dated 1818 on its leather cover, included the townland of my ancestors, and listed as one of its occupying tenants the name of the person who was most likely great-great-grandfather, Michael Flaherty.

The second document was said to have been recently discovered in the shed on the property next to where the Cavanaghs lived. It was a survey of the townland in 1845, some twelve years prior to *Griffith's Valuation*. And on it the name of great-grandfather Michael Cavanagh was written within the boundary lines of his property on this extremely detailed map as well as a second time on the Detail of the Several Holdings list. There is a strong likelihood this special document may be found nowhere else either in duplicate form or as a copy.

School registers for the national school Rose had attended in County Donegal during the 1870s had existed for her and there was wishful thinking that they should have been kept somewhere for Patrick as well in County Roscommon. It would seem to be against human nature if they had been simply tossed away. During the time of the discovery of John Cavanagh's marriage record in neighboring County Galway, a parish priest in Roscommon was asked if he was aware of the existence of the local school's old registers. Similar to Donegal and the rest of Ireland, the Catholic parish priests held much control over national schools, even though they were religiously diversified. He said the registers no longer existed, unfortunately, for the school my grandfather would have attended. A thought occurred to me that before they disappeared, they may have been filmed and be part of the school register collection held at the National Archives. But they were not there, either, so there was nowhere else to go.

However, during the preparation for a special event in 2013, in the old school house now used for storage, another mini-miracle happened. The parish priest had been mistaken. In a quite worn, but completely legible condition, a set of registers was discovered. And while they didn't go back in time as far as my grandfather's schooling, they did have recorded information for the next generation, the two children of my grandfather's brother, showing name, age at entry date, place of residence, examination results and years of attendance and absences for each of them. Thank goodness for a collective archival conscience!